The Perfect Shot

Camden Grove Series: Book One

Tessa Kinkade

88 Plumes Press

The Perfect Shot

Copyright © 2023 by Tessa Kinkade

88 Plumes Press

All rights reserved.

ISBN Paperback: 978-1-958994-00-9

ISBN E-Book: 978-1-958994-03-0

Editor: Jennia D'Lima

Cover Design: Pretty Indie Book Covers

THE PERFECT SHOT

For the man who recreates my true-life romance every day.
You are my favorite human.

Chapter One

Jex

New York City—Early December

After trudging through a fresh layer of snow to his upper west-side apartment, Jex Radcliffe would ordinarily have been looking forward to a quiet Friday evening alone. Half a decade beyond most peoples' prime marrying years found him happy enough living solo, and the extra hours alone had given him time for some much-needed work.

Nothing since September—when his relationship with Marla had come to a salty end—brought him more joy than thinking about his prospects as an up-and-coming entrepreneur. Focusing on that part of his life seemed much more productive nowadays than dating, despite an occasional nudge from good-intentioned, married, or otherwise committed friends that he should get back on the proverbial dating horse and find that kind of happiness for himself. No one, according to their logic, should be alone for the Christmas season.

His quick stop at Ming's Corner Teahouse to pick up take-out for two would have excited most of those well-meaning friends, but their enthusiasm would just as quickly have faded after finding out his date for the weekend was his younger sister.

With the brown, Hanzi-stamped paper bag in one hand, he hefted his camera case's strap higher onto his shoulder, unlocked the apartment door, and shook off his coat in the foyer.

"You're so lucky I'm here." Natalie's voice rounded the corner from inside the living room.

He set the case on the floor and glanced in a hall mirror. Brushing a hand through his hair to comb out the melted snow, he slicked back the longer brown strands crowning an otherwise military style cut.

"I'm sure you're here to tell me exactly why. And, by the way, don't be shy about letting yourself in." Hanging his coat on the foyer rack, he draped his scarf across another peg to dry.

When he stepped into the living room, he spotted his sister lounging on the couch with a laptop propped on a throw pillow in front of her.

"Being shy has never been on my list of things to try. And you're predictable. Key under the flowerpot? C'mon. Besides, I've come to solve all your problems, so why on earth would I wait for you to get home before letting myself in?"

"You assume I have problems to solve."

"Of course you do." She nearly snorted. "You're a man without a woman. Yin without yang. Mac without cheese."

"I'll take my yang-and-cheese-free chances."

"After your tryst with Monster Marla I can see why." She jumped up from the couch and bounded across the room for what most would think was an overdue hug from her brother. After all, they hadn't seen each other in person for a solid three months. He suspected Natalie's trip from Chicago to the Big Apple was as much a self-care trip as a need to visit her big brother. SoHo Christmas shopping was always a draw. Instead of offering a hug, she stopped short, popped her hip against his, and grabbed the take-out.

"Mmm, my favorite." Looking him over as she sniffed the savory bag, she cocked her head. "Man, those luscious locks of yours are getting longer. Do me a favor and don't go back to a total crew cut anytime soon. We'd have to redo your branding, and I'm not in the business of working my magic *all* the time."

"Whaddaya mean 'all the time'?"

"I, my dear brother, have performed yet another astonishing feat. I've found the answer to the Marla problem. Thank me now. Then thank me again later. My ego will approve."

"Are you still hung up on my using that girl you were telling me about for the photo spread?"

"Uh, yeah." She plopped back onto the couch. "Doppelgangers are a thing. And believe me," she said, "this one's a dead ringer for Marla. I wouldn't be so willing to arrange this if she weren't."

"How'd you find her anyway?" Jex sat down across from Natalie in an overstuffed chair. As she pulled take-out boxes from the bag, he scooped one up and peeled the paper wrapping from a set of chopsticks.

"Coincidence, really. Remember about six months ago when you asked me to jump onto your account in the Digital Review Forum to get up to speed on the photography scene?" She began unwrapping her chopsticks. "It was just after I agreed to become your virtual assistant."

"You mean after you begged me for a job." He smirked.

"What. Ever." She wadded up the wrapper and tossed it at him. "Anyway, that's when I met this girl, Honeybee, online. Too cutesy a username for my tastes, but she's got some talent. She was asking for some guidance—maybe some one-on-ones—on the forum. Says she's a hands-on learner. I think she's a little unsure of herself."

"I like it—the name." He opened a box of Kung Pao chicken, and steam escaped from the container.

"Anyway, you remember when you brought 'Marla the model' home?" Natalie air-quoted her description and further punctuated it with a subtle eye roll. "Well, that was shortly after I met this girl on the forum. Remember, I even asked Miss Prissy Pants then if she had a sister? She looked *that much* like Honeybee's profile picture."

"Yeah." He remembered some of it alright. It was when the Marla problem all started. Her coming home with him was the reason he was in this mess in the first place. He thought she was flying with him from New York to Chicago to meet his parents, but she had another motive altogether.

Weeks before their trip, he'd told her about scheduling his first meeting with Hughley Photographics to present his new camera prototype. After she'd sufficiently pumped him for details, she stepped in with a request. Maybe "demand" was the more accurate word. She badgered him, until he finally relented, to let her pose as his assistant-slash-model while he presented the prototype.

Getting in front of the CEO of a company specializing in all-things photography, she said, would give her some networking clout on the modeling scene. Jex just wanted to present his concept.

The biggest problem? When they went for the meeting, Hughley liked Marla. Called Jex back and said she had the right look to represent the product, and he wanted them both. Unfortunately, that came a few days after Jex had pulled the plug on his relationship with Marla.

"If I'd only realized then the trouble she'd cause coming to Chicago. I could kick myself."

"I'd line up for that." Natalie grinned over her take-out box. "But all is said and done. No sense in moaning over it now. From what you've told me about Hughley's demands, I *would* be tempted to tell him and his people to kiss off, though." She poked at the box of rice with her chopsticks.

"And ruin my chances of landing the contract of the decade? We've had our silver spoon, Nat, but I'd like to make my own name in the world—something besides being Langston Radcliffe's son. That's why I moved to New York in the first place. And I'm still a little wounded about having to go back to Chicago to get my sea legs under Hughley."

"I'm just saying, if they hinge your genius on your fiancée's looks?"

"*Ex*-fiancée."

Natalie huffed. "Anyway, I see no merit in their judgment, that's all." She stabbed the air with her chopsticks. "Pretty face?" —she lifted the Kung Pao chicken box— "or genius? Put those two on a scale, and genius tips it every time in my book. I don't understand why another model wouldn't do."

Jex shrugged.

In the follow-up call that came two weeks after the breakup, Mr. Hughley's assistant had requested for Jex to come back with the prototype flaws corrected and a montage of shots with Marla as the model, showing it off. That would still leave plenty of time, he said, for fine-tuning before the unveiling of the new design at the Digital Imagists Association's spring awards ceremony.

For added measure, he also expected Jex to have the model in tow on ceremony night, if he cleared all the other hurdles. According to the assistant, Hughley fully expected Marla to play a part in the public unveiling.

"And you said Hughley wanted her at the ceremony too? Why?" Natalie frowned. "Even if you did have her for the montage, her job would be done once the pictures were complete, right?"

"If only." Jex sighed. "You want to know what I think?" He didn't wait for an answer. "He likes his women tall, tawny, and tethered."

"Tethered? You know I have no warm fuzzies for Marla, but she's not a goat. So, what's that supposed to mean?"

Jex smirked. "I've got my theory."

"Which is?"

"If she's in a relationship, he sees it as more than a business conquest. I made the mistake of introducing her as my fiancée when we had that first meeting."

"Your species can be so obscene!" She rolled her eyes again as she set the half-emptied box on the table.

"The problem is Hughley's the top dog for pushing this project. I deliver to them, or I don't deliver at all. And my chances of catapulting my career will take a nose-dive if word makes the circuit that Hughley tossed Jex Radcliff out with yesterday's junk mail."

"Look, I want you to get this deal, but as your top aide, not to mention your exceptionally astute sibling, I'm attaching some strings. If I do set up the mentorship with this girl from the forum and you can get her to fill in for Marla in those photos, you can't let Hughley make moves on her if it goes all the way to awards night. She's not some piece of meat. What's this guy? Probably twice her age?"

"Assuming she's close in age to Marla, yeah, at least. How'd you guess?"

"He's old enough to have a multi-million-dollar company, it must have taken some time to build his empire, and ninety-nine-point-nine-two percent of the time it's always the middle-aged man with a Don Juan complex . . . or is it Don Quixote?" she asked, mostly to herself. "I always get those two mixed up."

"Yeah, well, *if* I do this, I wouldn't plan on her sticking around once I have the spread and she signs the release. If I could just get my pictures, surely I could sell Hughley on the prototype without having to feed his ego with the model."

"Don't get too cocky. You might have to run this little charade all the way from beginning to end."

"Nah." Jex shook his head. "He's likely to have his sights on someone else by then. He strikes me as too impatient to wait around for one solitary girl."

"Either way, if anyone sees potential of any kind in Honeybee—specifically of the professional variety—it should probably be you, since you'll be lined up to help her with her own photography business."

"She obviously has some potential, or she wouldn't be on the forum. That group's admins are selective."

Natalie dabbed the corner of her mouth with a brown paper napkin. "Yeah, and who knows. You could meet up with her in Chicago and find out that she's more than just your ticket out of this mess."

When he caught his sister's gaze over a box of rice, he shook his head. "You're not suggesting—"

"Yeah, I'm suggesting. Listen, I get why you were attracted to Marla. She's drop-dead gorgeous, but she had the personality of a dummy in a window display. Painted lips and a disposition as stiff as a board. I don't get that vibe from Honeybee. I figure if you two meet and you ease her into what you're doing, you may hit it off, and then you'll owe me for the rest of your life. I wouldn't mind that—claiming my brother's eternal indebtedness." She grinned over her chopsticks.

"Remind me again why we aren't just being up front with her."

"Are you kidding? Do you know how fast you'd scare off any girl with an IQ above your bicep measurement if you went to her and said, 'So I'll teach you a few things about business if you pretend to be my girl for a couple of weekends this year?' She'd tell you to flash a Benjamin Franklin at the nearest shady street corner and draw in a catch that way. Sheesh!"

He put up his hands in surrender. "Alright. Point noted."

"So, is that your go-ahead to put plans into play?"

He let out a long sigh, agitation creeping into his thoughts. Setting the now empty take-out box on the coffee table, he stood and walked to the window. The tapering flurries falling on the streets of Manhattan left a covering like a tufted quilt, pleated around the corners and tucked over curbs and parked cars.

He studied the dips and drifts in the deepening snow, trying to convince himself that this was a good idea—a good way to start the new year. Never would he have imagined a few months ago trying to involve someone he didn't even know, let alone under false pretenses. Hopefully, what Natalie was suggesting would work. He didn't need or want someone's hurt feelings on his conscience along with every other worry that came with this new business venture.

Finally, he turned to Natalie. "I'll need the spread by mid-April at the latest, so we need to work within that timeframe. By then, I'll have moved back to Chicago, likely staying at Mom and Dad's until I can get settled into my own place. I'll do the mentoring gig, spend a day or two with her on technique and business stuff. You just get her there. Everything else?" He pointed at her and furrowed his brow. "Leave to me."

"Yeah, of course. You're a big boy. Besides, why would I want anything else to do with it? Except the eternal indebtedness part."

"Do you really think this'll work?" He shot her a glance.

"It will or it won't. My money's on a little honeybee though!" Natalie smirked and double-tapped her chopsticks in the air to drive her point home.

Chapter Two

Carly

Chicago—Mid-April

The plane taxied down the runway after a turbulent flight. As soon as the captain gave clearance, Carly Kirkpatrick impatiently texted her part-time business partner Jessie to remind her of the planning session for one of their June weddings. She should have been there to conduct the meeting herself, but this was a chance she had to take.

Carly knew Jessie usually kept her phone in her back pocket and was always quick to reply.

This is your 3rd text. I've got sticky notes on my fridge, BR mirror, and car dashboard. Promise, I won't forget. Stop worrying and have fun!!!

How had her life come to this? How had she convinced herself that traveling from small-town Alabama to lakeside Chicago for a business weekend with a complete stranger had been a good idea?

She could have called it research, or a creative brainstorming meeting, but it was more like a desperate hope for professional resurrection. Over the top, really.

Carly's photography business was going nowhere at warp speed. She knew she had the talent. A "keen eye for artistic detail" had always been her photojournalism professors' compliment of choice back when she'd been a student at UT-Knoxville. She'd even once been featured in the Life section of *The Tennessean*—well, alongside three other students who also had keen eyes for artistic detail.

The business end, though? The fresh, unexplored fiscal ideas? The moxie to think she could survive in a world where everyone with a smartphone could potentially become an amateur Ansel Adams? That was where she faltered and the sole reason behind why she'd shored up her courage and made the trip. The only option she had to give her business a fighting chance and keep Jessie onboard and their calendar lined up with work.

But now, after landing in the Windy City, too far for comfort from her cozy house in the little Southern town of Camden Grove, her second thoughts were multiplying.

Outside the airport, a nipping spring gust nearly took her breath with it, a full ten- or fifteen-degrees difference from the balmy temperature at liftoff in Birmingham.

Tilting her head, a stray auburn curl swept into her eyes, making her wish she'd pinned it back before she left. She could hear her mother's voice now. *Keep that ungov'nable hair out of your eyes, Carlotta June. You want to be able to see what's coming, don't you?*

Carly's hair had always been a source of maternal scorn, especially growing up when she refused to sit long enough for braiding or smoothed-back ponytails.

She'd proved to her mother long ago, though, that her hair tended not to be the most unmanageable thing about her. As a child, thrusting her chin in the air and demanding to be called *Carly only* had been a curt effort to avoid standing out as the product of her parents' deep Southern heritage—bloodlines that had originated in the lowlands of Scotland and had migrated over the centuries to the Talladega and Madison counties of Alabama.

Carlotta was the name of her father's favorite aunt, and June—an equally significant name of some long-dead matriarch on her mother's side—left her parents pairing the two, to her chagrin, in an eternally annoying Southern designation that echoed over the hills when they'd call her in for supper. She never had understood why people double-named their children.

Now on the doorstep of thirty, she'd mellowed since childhood, though her best friend Ava still occasionally accused her of a little good-humored sass. Regardless, she tucked her wayward lock of hair behind her ear and silently conceded that she definitely wanted to see what was coming in the next forty-eight hours.

Approaching one of the waiting taxis, she handed the driver her carry-on to stow in the trunk and slipped into the backseat with her chunky camera backpack at her side. She pulled up her Notes app for the address and settled in for the twenty-five-minute drive.

The city's closed-in landscape left her a little claustrophobic and wistful for home. No cotton fields waiting to be planted. No farmhouses with trampolines sitting within sight of a rusty pickup. Too little greenery. Even the variable overhead traffic marquees had no sense of community like they did in Alabama. She'd seen one en route to the airport this morning near Birmingham that read: "Textin' while drivin'? Aw, cell no!"—a line she could imagine a handful of her mother's relatives saying. She drew in a deep breath to lighten the heaviness in her chest.

"First time to Chicago?" the driver asked.

"Yeah."

"Fancy part of town you're headed to. Here on business or pleasure?" He spoke fast, as if he had no time to talk but his job demanded it of him anyway.

"Business. All business."

"Too bad. You won't be far from good museums, restaurants. And there's always Wrigley's. Cubs play St. Louis this weekend. You're not catching any of the games?"

"No." A little too nervy for heavy conversation, she kept her responses short to match his speed. That, and the last place she'd want to go would be a baseball game. Anything but baseball.

"Scalpers should hit the streets a few hours before game time. You can pick up a ticket then."

"Not much of a fan, but I'll keep that in mind."

"I figured you for a sports photographer. Lot of you types are in town for that. Cardinals are our biggest rival, you know."

If he only knew. Covering sporting events was what had caused her to meet Hunter Matthews a few years back when they were both in college. And *he* had been the biggest mistake of her life, something she'd been trying to forget.

"How'd you know I'm a photographer?"

"The bag. It's a dead giveaway." Avoiding a turning car, he cut the wheel to the right with the finesse of a Nascar driver.

She looked down at the black Nikon backpack on the floorboard, a little flutter of butterflies in her stomach. Maybe she'd taken too big a step. She hadn't done anything this daring in a long time, not since those college days when meeting new people seemed adventurous and blind dates were a rite of passage. Those days were fortified with the collective courage of friends, though. Here in Chicago, she was completely on her own.

She nervously twirled a lock of hair around a finger and persuaded herself it would all be worth it to revive her business. She'd spent the last couple of months, albeit online, messaging with the girl who had set up this training weekend. And, though she couldn't say she knew her contact well, she had at least come this far based on the gut feeling that everything was on the up and up.

Regardless, whether she was leaning into the fear or leaning into the fire, she was riding headlong into the next couple of days, and she might as well get ready for it.

As they pulled onto Michigan Avenue, she looked up at the towering buildings, mountains of glass and steel that created block-shaped shadows against each other in the afternoon sun. Along with the driver's claim that she was headed to the fancy part of town, the mix of well-manicured corporate buildings and posh storefronts at least left her feeling like she'd be in a safe neighborhood.

The wandering pedestrians in the shade of the high rises gave no signs of sharing any of her kind of worries. With briefcases in hand and cell phones glued to ears, their walks bore the signature of boredom, like no one in this part of town had any business being overly concerned about anything. As they drove further down the street to her destination, she said to herself, "What am I doing here?"

"What's that?" The driver's eyes met hers in the rearview. His bushy brows, reflecting midway in the mirror, looked like two lined-up fuzzy caterpillars, the kind that determined the length of winter where she came from.

"Sorry, nothing. Just trying to decide if I made the right decision coming here." She had no idea why she thought to share that with her driver. Nerves obviously loosened her tongue.

"It's never a bad call to come to Chicago." The man's eyes narrowed against a grin she couldn't quite see. "Loosen up and enjoy the trip. You might find something here you like."

He pulled up to the curb in front of a high rise. The gold, scalloped edge of a pine-green awning, cupped over a revolving door, flapped against the breeze like a half-dozen waving hands there to welcome her. "This is one of those luxury condo buildings they put on the billboards. Most of my fares from the airport stay at the Hampton or the Hyatt."

Though he didn't ask directly, his comment implied that he wondered the same thing Carly was asking herself. *What are you doing here?* He didn't wait for a response, and she was glad. Instead, he put the car in park and, with a quick check for traffic, came around to open her door.

After collecting her carry-on and paying her fare, Carly glanced at the apartment number on her phone for the eighth time, then rounded her shoulders and entered the building.

The main interior garden lobby of the Emerald on the Lake had all the vibes of luxury living in the city. Even the tenants, scattered here and there in the plush leather furnishings of the open lobby, looked like models for Versace.

From the concierge desk, a tall man with thinning hair and a pleasant face greeted her. His rich baritone voice vibrated across the counter. "Well, we haven't seen you here in a while. How are you? Miss Marla, isn't it?"

"Oh." She raised a hand to her chest. "I'm sorry, you must have me confused with someone else."

His forehead creased in surprise. "My apologies. Don't think I've ever forgotten a name. Memory like a steel trap. That's why they hired me, you know."

She smiled. "I've never been to Chicago, so it definitely wasn't me. But I'm really impressed. Some days, I'm taxed to remember my own name, much less anybody else's."

He cocked his head and looked at her from the corner of his eyes. "Alright, then. Who might you be, and how can I help you?"

Feeling a little awkward, she bit her lower lip. "You can call me . . . Bee."

"Bea as in Beatrice?"

"Bee as in Honeybee."

"Well, I will *not* forget *that* name." He chuckled. "And you can call me Addison. What may I assist you with today, Miss Bee?"

When she turned the phone to show him the apartment number, he squinted and paused. Something flickered in his eyes that she couldn't quite pin.

Then, he said, "I do believe Mr. Radcliffe left for Europe early this morning. Are you sure you have the right address?"

It was the first time she'd heard the real name of the tenant she'd be visiting. She filed it away for safe keeping, even though her knowing such information would be against the terms—terms she had set.

The agreement had been that they'd use only the online names they'd established in the photography forum. No identities. No personal details. Business only.

Jessie had teased her about being overly cautious. She said she understood why Carly would be careful. The mentor didn't necessarily have to know *her* name and details. No need to share certain things, in case this guy turned out to be creepy. But she also said she didn't get why Carly took it a step further by not getting *his* name and details.

She didn't understand that after Carly's breakup with Hunter, distancing herself from men gave her the safety bubble she needed to function socially. Knowing anything personal about this guy, or any other guy for that matter, simply made her more vulnerable, more open to caring. Personal details led to personal relationships which led to personal investment which led to disaster. She just needed a good mentor and an honest businessman, and only for a weekend. That would do.

"Yes, I'm sure it's the right address. I checked it twice. We were supposed to meet here today."

"Well, then, perhaps it's the young Mr. Radcliffe whom you'll be meeting. I'm certain someone will be there to welcome you." The man pointed to a row of elevators in a corridor to the right of the desk. "Take any one of those to the 12th floor and make a left."

"Thank you." She hefted the camera bag onto her shoulder and pulled the carry-on behind her. *I'd better not have made this trip for nothing. If he took off and left, knowing I was coming . . . ugh!* She'd been stood up before, but not after traveling from three states away.

The glass elevator ride to the twelfth floor offered a bird's-eye view of the lush greenery cascading from planters on the interior balconies of each tier toward the lobby below. It reminded her of the roadways back home where the summer kudzu vines swallowed up trees, light poles, and fence posts in a patchy green blanket. Had she not been tired, she might have been tempted to hike the twelve floors to avoid adding to her nervousness from her fear of heights. Instead, she stood close to the button panel and turned away from the view.

With a left out of the elevator and a short walk down the hall, she stood outside door 1208, shifting from foot to foot, alternating between reasons she *shouldn't* be here and nagging thoughts about why she *should.* Thoughts of Jessie sitting back home in Alabama with her texts and sticky notes reminding her about their few solid bookings pushed her to stay.

As she rang the doorbell with one last look over her shoulder, along with one final thought about darting back to the elevator, she straightened her back while she waited.

He had to be successful at *something* to live in a place like this.

After a few seconds, he opened the door. She paused for a good, pregnant second or two. She hadn't expected to see someone quite as . . . painfully handsome as the man in front of her. "H-hi," she stuttered. "I'm, uh, the photographer."

Framing a set of cornflower blue eyes, his eyelashes were tantalizing. She'd never noticed a man's lashes before, but his somehow softened his face and her angst enough for her to reason that she probably could've landed in worse places. That, and the fact that he had the sculpted physique of a triathlete gave her sufficient pause to feel better about her decision to come.

He smiled. "Then I guessed right. And you're very punctual."

Awkwardly, she extended a hand. "Sorry, I'm, uh—"

"Honeybee?" He interrupted and took her hand in his. "PhotoMajex. But to avoid weirdness all weekend, how about we just ditch the online personas and you call me Jex. It's a nickname, too, if it makes you feel any better."

She had no idea if that was even close to his real name. But assuming that he was a Radcliffe and knowing he had a nickname did give her an advantage—two small details about him when he still had none about her. "Well, yeah, about that. I still think it's best if we keep a little distance, but you can call me Bee."

He grinned. "Come on inside, then. It's nice to finally meet you, Bee." He took her carry-on and led her from the foyer. She couldn't help but notice his longer mane of dark, caramel-colored hair leading down to a nicely trimmed fade. That steered her to survey his broad set of shoulders as he walked ahead of her.

Her eyes fought against her as she tried to take in her surroundings instead. Furnishings and drapes didn't have the same magnetic pull.

As they stepped into the open room, she did notice a bar island and the kitchen to the right, and beyond that stood the most eye-catching feature so far— a long window making up the exterior wall, overlooking the city below. Though she had no desire to step close to the glass, she appreciated, at least from a distance, the view to the east—Lake Michigan smiling at the curve of a shallow inlet.

His camera stood at the window, poised on a tripod with a long-range lens at the ready. She noticed he was a Nikon fan too.

She cleared her throat. "I spoke to the man at the desk downstairs. He thought you'd left for Europe this morning."

"I wouldn't have stood you up."

"Good to know. I mean, that we're still on schedule." She fidgeted and turned again toward the window, eager to avoid an awkward silence. "It's an amazing view."

"Yeah, this is my parents' place. My dad's the one going to Europe. I'm just staying for a few weeks while he joins my mom overseas. They like to travel."

She raised her eyebrows.

"Ah, sorry, no personal details, right?"

"Right." She nodded. "I know that's probably asking a lot."

He raised a hand. "Not at all." With a turn, he set her bag inside the door just at the entry to a short hallway. When he came back, he pointed a thumb toward the kitchen. "If you're hungry for a snack or something, feel free. The fridge and pantry are stocked. We should be set for the weekend."

"We? Um, wait, I thought I had use of the whole apartment."

"Of course you do. I'm pretty quiet, but you might hear me in the mornings if you're a light sleeper. I usually get up early for a workout or to take a run. My bedroom's down the hall there." He pointed, then finger combed his hair. "Wait." His expression changed, understanding seeping into his eyes. "I'm sorry. I thought you understood it would be the rental of a room *in* the apartment. Not the whole apartment." His eyebrows slowly rose.

Carly's face warmed. The weekend travel expenses had taken a toll on her bank account, but looking around, she could see what he meant. The whole place would have probably rented for four times what they'd agreed on. "Maybe I should see about getting a hotel room. It's my fault, really. I just wasn't thinking, you know, that we'd be sharing a place."

"Good luck with that. Especially anything close by. April's a big convention month here. That and St. Louis is in town for the Cubs and Cards face-off this weekend. Rooms are likely scarce. I probably had three or four people I could've rented yours to if I'd been looking. I hope it's not a problem. I'm pretty harmless." He smiled, then stepped across the kitchen to the textured, steel refrigerator. "Drink?" He pulled a couple of Finé water bottles from the door-in-door and held one out to her.

"No thanks." She'd never had a bottle of water that expensive in her life. Deer Park with ice crystals was a luxury where she came from.

"For later then." He set the extra bottle on the counter and turned the other up for a swallow, his corded neck pulsing as he put away half its contents.

She glanced at him as he capped his bottle. Trying to clear her head and think of what she should do next, she reasoned that he *seemed* safe enough. She didn't typically bet on looks before employing common sense, but being easy on the eyes worked in his favor.

"Tell you what." His face softened. "I get that you're reluctant. I've got a sister. I'd want her to be cautious too. How about you stay for dinner? At that point, if you want to make different arrangements, I'll help you see what's available around town. And if you decide to stay here, you can pay half tonight and half when you leave. That way if you don't feel like you're getting your money's worth or you're uncomfortable, it won't be a total loss. Deal?"

She paused, her stomach on the verge of growling. "Dinner sounds good."

"Alright, then. I'll give you some time to yourself to catch your breath. I've already ordered us some takeout from my favorite Italian place. Pasta, some salad, soups, seafood. I think I covered most of the menu. Hopefully, something will sound appetizing."

"You shouldn't have done that. I didn't expect you to feed me while I'm here."

"It's nothing I wouldn't do for anyone else who comes to visit."

"So, you . . . entertain a lot of women, then."

A smirk slowly stretched across his lips. "Don't get the wrong impression." He folded his arms. "I'm just hungry for Italian, and I like to talk over good food. You don't have to worry about the tab. My parents own the restaurant." He grimaced. "Sorry, did it again—personal information."

"Yeah, I now know you have a sister *and* parents." She exhaled slowly and smiled.

He returned a smile, emptied his Finé bottle, and tossed it in a recycling bin. "Anyway, why don't you take a minute. You're welcome to rest in the bedroom if you want, and, oh, if you'd like to take a swim, there's a rooftop pool. It's enclosed until the end of May and heated. My mother keeps a few new suits in the guest room closet, if you need one."

Carly hesitated. "Your mother keeps new swimsuits in the closet?" *Wonder what a woman like that would think about swimming in the strip pits in cutoffs and a t-shirt.*

"She has something of a fetish for being ready for guests, but yes, tags still on them, I promise. Feel free to take one. She'll never miss it." He leaned against the counter. "And dinner should be here in about an hour. We can talk business then."

"Thanks." Eyeballing the water bottle he'd offered her moments ago, she slipped it from the countertop as she passed by and turned toward her room.

"Hey," he called. "I hope you enjoy this weekend. Depending on what you're looking for, I've got a few business concepts that might help you. With any luck, we can accomplish something profitable in the next couple of days."

She nodded, smiled, and turned back for the guest room. Just before rounding the corner, she glanced back. He had leaned against the window and bent his head to the camera mounted on the tripod she'd seen when she first arrived.

When she entered the bedroom, she locked the door behind her and let out the phobic breath she'd held from watching him lean against the twelfth story window. Popping open the water bottle, she took a long sip and inventoried her situation.

Yes, she'd just agreed to dinner with a man she'd never met. Yes, he was acutely handsome. Yes, she had a room for the weekend, in an extremely nice apartment. With a replay of the last fifteen minutes in her mind, she realized that, no, they weren't laced with creepy vibes. No ringing bell of intuition warning her to run. Yet.

Jex seemed like a decent enough human being. He *looked* like a professional, had all the equipment. *Boy, does he have the equipment,* she thought. Images of the last few minutes, like candids in one of her photo shoots, clicked to life in her mind.

His smile when he opened the door.

His fingers combing through his hair.

Those eyes, blue as any blue she could remember.

She shook her head. Admiring from a distance—that's all it would be. That and hopefully getting a good enough vibe from this guy to spend the next two nights down the hall from him without feeling completely paranoid or awkward.

For a moment, as she let the cool water quench her thirst, she actually felt hopeful that this would be the break she needed, the answer to breathing some life into her business.

First, though, maybe she'd take that dip in the pool.

Chapter Three

Jex

He heard the guest room door lock click into place. Standing at the window, Jex noted that the view below looked much different than the snowy afternoon in December when he and Natalie had put plans in place for this very moment. He drew in a deep breath.

Before he'd even opened the apartment door, he told himself not to visibly react, since this woman was supposed to be the spitting image of Marla, but he hadn't expected this. Bee looked so much like Marla Fairchild that it hurt. Ordinarily, taking chances wasn't on his list of things he worried about. But seeing this girl? Now he wondered if he should even go through with the plan.

Natalie had told him it would work, but his sister had been known for her pie-in-the-sky ideas before. He certainly didn't expect to find that Natalie's description had been so spot on.

As he gazed out the window, restlessness rose in Jex's chest like a rogue wave, some unnamable hybrid of apprehension and attraction he hadn't adequately prepared himself for.

"Just someone needing some business advice," he whispered under his breath.

Over the next few minutes, he tried ineffectually to focus on the light dancing off the ripples on Lake Michigan, but his thoughts kept turning back to his weekend guest.

This woman obviously had high hopes of putting her business on the map. And honestly, the map in Smallville somewhere in the South shouldn't be too hard to hit. Despite her privacy hang-ups, he could tell she was a Southerner from a few loosely hidden, long vowels and dropped consonants. Subtle as they were, her voice gave her away with its pleasant cadence.

He was still surprised that getting her here had worked. Natalie had no doubt sweet-talked and finagled—what she did best. And somehow Bee believed he was the answer to at least some of her business troubles.

Truth was, he had no problem passing along some professional advice. He had been at the top of his game, and not too long ago. As a digital engineer who had an interest in marketing the products he made, and the fortitude and financial backing to study both hardware and software, he'd bolted from a potential career behind a drafting board the minute he'd earned enough certificates and diplomas to say he was legit.

With an entrepreneurial spirit and a juicy trust fund from his grandfather, he'd branched out, sunk his teeth into photography, and begun making his own contacts. The good fortune of having a diverse education had led him to some top gigs.

Then his company, PhotoMajex, was born—a business and industry solutions finder specializing in commercial products from software to hardware and a few things in between. When business was slow, Natalie kept him plugged into side jobs in food, architecture, and aerial photography.

He'd done plenty of the usual gigs—high-end weddings, headshots for actors, writers, and business types—but that had proven boring. Specializing had taken him to new places, and when Natalie graduated with a business and accounting double major, they began to partner—her taking on the office work and some of the marketing while he dedicated his time to the creative side of things. After that, work picked up; the gigs began finding him, making a return move to Chicago more feasible.

Jex squinted as the late afternoon sunlight reflected off the water below like a sheet of broken glass. The walkers traveling the Emerald Greenway ambled along, appearing unconcerned, with their dogs and strollers and small children. He envied their apparent easygoing way of life.

Since his breakup with Marla last September, nothing really seemed easy. In fact, the whole landscape of his life had changed.

After Marla had stoked their last trivial disagreement into a full-on argument, he could no longer turn a blind eye to her selfishness. The only answer for him was a complete change. From relocating to Chicago to realigning his career and future relationship goals, he'd been the caterpillar in the cocoon turning into goo. He only hoped the butterfly would emerge somewhere down the line. The fact that his father's voice played on repeat in the background, ushering him to come back to Chicago to assume his role as CEO of his restaurant dynasty, had compounded the matter. *It's all waiting for you,* he'd said. *Yours for the taking.*

Seating Jex at the head of the board of directors' table would have been his father's way of keeping decision-making leverage without having to be in the executive's chair day in and day out. Jex had no desire to be someone's stooge, not even his father's.

Thoughts, having gained the momentum of a small storm, settled just as quickly as they'd stirred when his phone rang. A headshot of his sister—a candid he'd taken while they were together at Christmas— smiled up at him from the screen.

"Yeah," he answered.

"Well, aren't you the voice of sunshine today. Did she make it?"

His eyes followed a couple of fast walkers weaving past other pedestrians below. "About a half hour ago."

Before Natalie spoke again, the door to the bedroom opened, and he turned, tucking the phone to his chest. Bee stepped into the hall wearing a near-sheer tunic with what he assumed was one of the guest swimsuits beneath it. He'd have to thank his mother later. His guest had toned, honey-beige legs that stretched out from beneath the tunic, and she'd pinned her hair up, a few auburn curls floating along her face as she approached the living room.

"Sorry to interrupt. I decided to take your suggestion and swim a few laps before dinner. I need to work out some muscle kinks from being on the plane. Do I need any kind of key or password to get to the pool?"

Jex forced himself to look into her eyes instead of letting his gaze linger down her slender frame. He almost forgot to speak. "No, no, just, uh, take the elevator or stairs to the top floor. You'll see the signs. They keep towels stocked in the poolside cabinet."

She hesitated. "What *is* the top floor here?"

"Sixteenth. Three flights up."

"Okay. Thanks."

"Yeah, sure. Enjoy your swim."

Bee crossed the living room and stepped out the entry door before he remembered that Natalie was still on the phone. He jerked it to his ear. "Sorry. I had to tell her how to get to the pool."

"Are you smitten yet?" Natalie's smugness seeped through the connection.

"She's been here for less than an hour, and you're asking me that?"

"You want me to dig around and find out more about her for you?"

"No. As it is, I'm paranoid I'll say something to tip her off." He glanced toward the hallway. "I don't want to scare her away before we even get started."

"You'll be fine. Now that she's there, you just need to give her something to work with. You know, make her comfortable first, then ask for her help. It won't be half as intimidating once she gets to know you a little. Order some take-out. That's the way to *my* heart."

"Yeah, it's already on the way, but so far, she's sticking to her guns about not sharing personal information. Makes it hard to get to know each other, don't you think?"

"That's no excuse. She's perfect for this job, so crank up the effort a little."

Jex thought about when he'd opened the door earlier, how he'd almost stuttered when he introduced himself. Beyond her auburn hair, green eyes, and swimsuit-model build being so similar to

Marla's that it was remarkable, she seemed like a genuinely nice girl, poised even if she was cautious. And though he hadn't really known what to expect before they met, the differences in Marla and Bee almost immediately became as stark as the similarities.

He shook off his thoughts. This was business, and this new girl could very easily pass for what he needed. He just had to find a way to help her with her own work and, in the meantime, put her enough at ease to get her to model for him.

When Natalie's voice faded back into his awareness, he realized she was giving orders. "I expect a full report on Monday. Capisce?"

"On a need-to-know, sis."

"And I need to know it all. Chat later."

The phone went silent, and Jex slipped it back into his pocket. *Full report, hmph.* He just hoped he could break the ice and get down to business, and fast. A weekend wasn't a lot of time for the ground he needed to cover.

Chapter Four

Carly

As Carly had hoped, the swim loosened the tension in her neck and shoulders.

With each lap, she felt a little closer to her old self, not just that girl relieved of her muscle kinks. Moreso, the one she'd been a long time ago, who'd once been brave enough to take some chances on herself. The girl she'd been before Hunter.

Her best friend Ava often told her she still hadn't regained all her sass. She wondered if this might be the first in a long line of steps to recovering faith in herself—the faith that had wavered when a cute blond she'd found in Hunter's arms so quickly became her replacement.

She put away thoughts of the past and grinned. Maybe this trip would be the beginning of her return to some sass.

By 7 pm, Carly had returned to the apartment to freshen up before dinner. After a quick shower and pinning up her towel-dried hair, she straightened her shoulders and opened the guest room door. Just beyond the formal dining room, she heard jazz music coming from the terrace. Jex had set an outside table with a steaming spread of Italian food, and the light from the glowing patio heater and outdoor lamps set a cozy but professional mood.

From her spot at the door, she surveyed the terrace before joining him. The table sat comfortably twenty feet away from the building's edge. And the tiled wall luckily gave her enough of a barrier between herself and the open air beyond it to stave off her phobia.

Having a meal with a man on a terrace above Lake Michigan seemed strangely romantic, something she hadn't expected would occur during a weekend workshop. As Jex bent over the table arranging bread in a basket, she stepped outside, taking in a second glance. He'd changed shirts, putting on an indigo sweater that played up the carved angles in his arms and chest.

"What a way to welcome a guest. A relaxing swim. A hot meal. And this view." She nodded past the terrace, trying to convince herself that she could side-step her discomfort long enough to eat dinner. If not, she may have to share something personal with Jex, and she didn't intend to do that.

He smiled, then redirected his attention to the basket. "You get those kinks worked out?"

"Actually, I did." Carly rubbed her arms against the evening chill. Fortunately, she too had changed into a sweater. When she turned toward him, he averted his gaze and clapped his hands together. "I think everything's ready. I put water on the table, but would you like something else to drink?" He nodded toward the kitchen. "Maybe some—"

"Water's fine, thanks." She hadn't meant to cut him off, but the butterflies in her stomach left her quick-spoken.

"Come on out, then."

When she crossed to the table, Jex pulled out her chair. At first, she thought maybe he was planning to sit there himself. Then, she realized he was being polite. Hunter had never made a chivalrous gesture in his life. The contrast left her both surprised and a little embarrassed that she hesitated before sitting.

As they began to circulate the dishes, her hunger caught up with her. The mouthwatering spread of Italian food was a little fancy, a far cry from the skillet-fried chicken, field peas, and mashed potatoes at most Southern tables, but it smelled delicious and tasted divine enough to draw out a satisfied sigh when she tried the fettuccine.

He smiled. "Good, I take it?"

"I didn't realize how hungry I was. This is a slice of heaven."

"Glad you like it. I'll be sure to compliment our chef the next time I see him."

Their discussion steered over the standard conversational terrain, first toward innocuous things like the weather, the taxi ride from the airport, and her evening swim. Then it dwindled to silence.

Before things became too awkward, she took the lull as her chance to dive into why she'd come to Chicago in the first place. "So, where should we begin? With business, I mean."

He passed the breadbasket. "I've been thinking about that. You know, it'll be hard for me not to ask you questions about yourself this weekend"

What was he doing? He knew the boundaries. She'd been clear enough.

"When I'm getting to know someone, I usually ask about where they went to school, what their hobbies are, how they order their steak." He rolled a fork full of fettuccine.

A thread of mischief played across his face and caught her off-guard. She laughed. "And how I order my steak would tell you something about me?"

"Absolutely."

"I give. Do tell me your theories about steak preference."

"You're asking me to let you in on the universal, top-secret, male method of nailing a woman's personality type."

"Oh, I see. You're pretty confident we're that nail-able." She let some of the South drip from her voice like a piece of honeycomb.

"Okay. Here goes. If a woman orders a steak well done, she's a no-nonsense type. Likes things complete. She's usually thorough and painstaking in whatever she does."

Carly grinned and nodded. "Medium?"

"If she orders medium, she's a fence-rider. Likes to keep up with the status quo. She's never the boat rocker, but always the bailer."

Leaning back in her seat, Carly's smile broadened. "Medium rare?"

"Oh, the medium rare woman is a perfectionist." He pointed his fork at her. "She wants the supreme steak experience with just the right amount of flame. Tender, juicy perfection. And that's what she's after in life, unlike the rare-steak woman, who walks on the wild side, isn't afraid of adventure, and tends to make the best of her mistakes."

"I find your beef psychology fascinating, but I'm afraid I'll have to disappoint you. I don't eat red meat and, therefore, can't be classified"

"See, it wasn't that hard to tell me something personal."

"Clever." She raised an eyebrow. "I'll have to be more careful."

"Here's an idea. How about we play a game?"

She took a bite of chopped salad and pointed her own fork back at him "I obviously can't trust you. You've already tricked me."

"Come on. It'll be fun. Do you remember playing two lies and a truth as a kid?"

"Yeah, except I think it was two truths and a lie."

"Ah well, I never had a reason to play it until today. Anyway, if we play it my way, there's not as much risk, right? You tell me two lies and a truth—"

She interrupted, "And you get one guess to determine which is the truth?"

"Exactly. Then eventually, if I get a couple of things right, we'll have something to talk about this weekend besides f-stops, shutter speeds, and photo ops."

She cut her eyes at him, "And what if I tell you all lies?"

"Then it's gonna be an interesting weekend. I'll have to pull out all the stops. F-stops or otherwise." He gave a cheeky grin.

"Okay, you first."

"Hmm. Alright." He paused for a moment. "Let's see here. One, I hate heights."

Carly shifted in her seat.

"Um, two, I'm left-handed like my dad, and three . . . I have never tried brownie batter."

Carly cocked her head and squinted. "You're lying about the heights."

"How do you know?"

"We're on the twelfth floor, and you leaned against the window earlier."

"Observant."

"And everyone's tried brownie batter, so I'm guessing that's a lie. But let me see your hands, just to make sure."

He raised his hands, one gripping a fork and the other a spoon, above the table.

"Ink marks on the outside of your hand. Definitely left-handed."

"Impressed." He nodded. "Okay, Miss Sherlock, it's your turn."

She folded her arms and thought for a moment. "Alright. *A*. I'm a vegetarian. *B*. My last phone call was to my big brother, Sam. And *C*. My biggest vice is over-planning."

Jex pressed his lips into a thin line as if contemplating his options. "You're not an over planner, or you'd have come with more than two bags. So that's a lie. You may or may not have an older brother Sam, and even if you do, I think you'd have withheld his name. I'm calling that one lie number two." He tilted his head. "Yeah, definitely *A*. You went the safe route since I've already figured out that you're not a steak eater and would've tagged you as a vegetarian after watching what you eat over the weekend anyway."

"Exactly." She smirked.

"Okay. Okay. I get it. No trying to drag anything out of you that you don't want to share. Guess we'll wait to see if you let your guard down as the weekend progresses."

The grin on her face softened. "So should we get down to business then?"

"I'd love to."

Chapter Five

Jex

Over the course of dinner, Jex talked to Bee about clientele and business priorities, marketing, and helpful craft courses. But the further the conversation went, the more roadblocks they found to any financial momentum. Limited funds and too few contacts were among the worst of her problems.

Once they finished the meal and cleared the dishes, Bee wanted to key in some notes about what they'd discussed, so they moved to the living room where she opened her laptop. But she seemed disenchanted about the whole evening. He could tell, once their conversation steered toward money, she became more discouraged.

Jex stole a glance at her from the kitchen. Even with her spirits dampened a little, she was attractive. After starting the dishwasher, he stepped toward the living room. "You know what I think? You're struggling with your direction."

"Well, that's kind of why I came to Chicago—for direction."

"No, I'm talking about the most basic stuff. Like, what do you want to take pictures of?"

Bee looked at him as if he'd just asked a question with the most obvious answer. "What do you mean? I want to take pictures of everything. Anything that'll pay me, that is."

"Exactly." He nodded. "Did you bring any spreads with you?"

She frowned. "I have a few on my laptop."

"Here." He took a notepad from the coffee table and jotted down his email. "Send me some of your layouts while I grab my computer."

"How many?"

"A good sample. Fifteen. Twenty." He noted the concern in her eyes and could feel her anxiety as he slipped down the hall for his laptop.

When he returned, he sat down beside her on the couch to share his screen. Close enough that their legs almost touched. "Okay, let's see here." He pulled up his email, imported Bee's files into an organizer as she sent them, and began to shuffle groups of photos into folders, marking them with category names. By the time he'd finished creating the categories list, he had a broad spectrum, from scenery to weddings, senior pictures to sporting events, headshots to architecture.

As they chatted about composition and lighting and whichever topics naturally came up, he pigeon-holed all of Bee's spreads into their respective folders. Half an hour later, he turned the laptop screen toward her. "Now, look at the numbers," he said. "What do they tell you?"

"What do you mean?"

"The number of shoots in each category folder." He pointed at the screen. "What do you see?"

"That I have more in some than in others?"

"Yes, but what patterns do you see?"

"I don't know. What am I supposed to see?"

He moved the mouse across the screen. "You're shooting more couples. Weddings. Engagements. Anniversaries. Even the prom photos. You lean more heavily toward couples. Why?"

She shrugged. "Because I enjoy people, I guess."

"Not just people. You like *couples*."

Bee shrugged. "Maybe because they're usually happy and fun."

"Okay, what other patterns do you see?"

"Scenery? And I have quite a bit of architecture. But I don't make money off that. It's more hobby stuff."

"Then why do you shoot those kinds of photos?" he asked.

"Because they're easy subjects. No red-eye to worry about. I can do filters or not. They don't cry like the little kids do when you set 'em in front of a stranger with a camera. And I don't have to edit for zits or bad hair."

Jex grinned. Her list of reasons and honesty charmed him as much as listening for her subtle accent. "Now we're getting somewhere."

He set the computer back on the table, turned to face her, and rested his elbows on his knees. "Why haven't you focused on architecture and scenery and couples, if that's what you enjoy?"

"My business name reflects that kind of thinking, because I've done a lot of wedding and engagement stuff, but I have to take whatever comes my way to pay the bills."

"And what's your business name?"

She cocked an eyebrow.

"Okay, personal stuff. I got it." He raised one hand in defense. "Fair enough, but I think once you really dive into what you love, the money will come."

"No offense, but that's probably easy for you to say." Her eyes surveyed the room. "I would guess you're more financially set than I am."

"Well, since we're not sharing, I can't tell you." He smirked.

She poked her tongue in her cheek, caught in her own trap.

"Anyway, I think you might be surprised at what specializing can do for you." He closed the laptop screen and looked at her again. "It's more than obvious that you're talented."

Bee shifted on the couch. "Thank you, but . . ."

"I'm not just saying that. You know it's true, right?"

A mild shade of pink tinged her cheeks, and he thought of Marla. Not because she would have ever blushed at a compliment. In fact, just the opposite. She *expected* admiration. He had to admit, Bee did resemble his ex. Features, expressions, even the pitch of her voice was similar, but for each hour that passed, she continued to emerge as somebody completely different from Marla. Where Marla would have breezed through her day with a designer bag in one hand and a credit card in the other, Bee seemed more practical, like she'd make the most of a dollar. While Marla laughed mostly at his expense, Bee, in the last few hours, had found the funny parts of their conversation and laughed *with* him.

Finally, she said, "I appreciate your compliment, but I—"

"Wait." He shook his head. "You *don't* believe me?"

Bee shrugged. "When business isn't that great, you begin to question yourself."

"Your content is solid. You've got an eye for contrast. The lighting is good. Your depth is on target. What are you questioning?"

"I don't know." She tried to change the subject. "What improvements do you see that I can make?"

Ignoring her question, he continued. "I can't force you to accept a compliment, but by the time you leave here, I hope I'll convince you that you've got something special." He really did see potential in Bee. Maybe that's what he'd have to do—make her a believer.

Before she could say more, he pulled his phone from his pocket. "I've got an idea. We're gonna do a shoot tomorrow." The thought of getting photos for himself slipped to the back burner as his idea took shape.

She leaned back on the couch. "Who're we shooting?"

"Just the two of us."

"Mmm, I don't know. If you're planning on taking pictures of me, I should warn you, I don't make the best subject. Besides, how am I gonna learn anything new if I'm in front of the camera?"

Jex scrolled through his phone contacts. "Let me handle the specifics, and you just show up wearing something . . . solid. No patterns. Do you have anything like that with you? Maybe in a red?"

"I have a white top and jeans, but my jacket's patterned."

"Hmm, I think I've got a burgundy parka around here somewhere. That would give some nice contrast."

Bee frowned. "Don't you think it would be a little big on me?"

"Doesn't matter. We'll just be using it for some color variation."

She looked at him skeptically. "Well, wouldn't it be better to shoot *other* people so we could work with technique and positioning?"

He waved off her question. "No worries. It's better without someone else around. We won't feel as much like we're on the clock, and we can take our time, enjoy the process."

Jex could tell by her squirming that this wasn't going to be an easy sell. "Tell you what. Sleep on it tonight, and we can finalize in the morning. That is, if you've decided to stay here."

"Sleep on what?"

"The guest bed." His flippant response did little to hide his amusement.

"You know what I mean. You haven't really given me many details about this shoot."

"I'll fill you in tomorrow. We'll talk about candids . . . oh, and the element of surprise. Yeah—" he thought for a second "—surprise is important for a shoot like this. So, are you staying?"

She looked at her watch. "I suppose so, since it's close to midnight. But I'm warning you, I keep pepper spray under my pillow, I know jujitsu, and my best friend is a swat team unto herself."

He laughed out loud. "Two lies and a truth?"

"Do you really want to chance it?" She raised an eyebrow.

His heart gave a little flutter when she smiled, rose from the couch, and traipsed toward her bedroom.

She really was beautiful.

When he heard the door close, he pulled up his contact list, and pushed the call button. "Trudy? It's Jex. I've got a favor to ask."

Chapter Six

Carly

Carly pulled her phone from her purse and noted her three missed calls—one from her parents and two from Ava. Though her parents were aware of the trip, she already knew she'd have some explaining to do to her best friend.

Leaving town before sharing with Ava where she was going and why wasn't typical for either of them. They'd had each other's backs since college, been one another's rescuers from boredom, binge study sessions, and bad dates for as long as either could remember.

While planning for this trip over the last few months, Carly simply thought she'd avoid adding to Ava's already full plate of worries and not mention it. That, and she thought she'd be back before her doctor friend had even realized she'd left.

Falling onto the lavish guest room's king-size bed, Carly blew a strand of hair out of her eyes and messaged her parents to let them know she'd made it. And because Ava would likely still be up, she tapped her favorites and hit the call button.

"You almost caught me going to sleep!" Ava never bothered with hellos.

"You mean you're getting some of that lately?"

"Side effect of exhaustion."

Carly plumped one of the pillows behind her. "Any new developments in the office drama?"

"Just more weirdness. Corbin's getting more suspicious by the day. I've decided to take your advice and do some digging."

Ava's office partner, Dr. Corbin Simmons, had initially taken a professional interest in Ava and brought her on as a colleague once she'd finished her residency. From there, he'd taken more personal notice, something Carly felt apprehensive about from the moment she'd met him several months back. Something about him just didn't feel right, and she worried about Ava getting involved with him on a more intimate level.

Then, when Ava shared that he'd begun to raise some red flags at the office, Carly spent the next several phone calls persuading Ava not to turn a blind eye.

"Just be careful." Carly melted into the pillow.

"You know I will. What are you up to?"

"Nothing . . . but sitting in Chicago."

"You're lying."

"Nope." Carly sighed. "Go find me."

They had both activated the locater app on their phones and followed each other as a safety measure ever since they had each developed the tendency to work late a few years back and the feature had become available.

Carly could practically hear her friend's fingers swiping at the screen.

"Michigan Avenue? Alright, Carlotta June, what in the world are you doing in Chicago?"

"It's business. I'm learning a few new tricks. I'm just here for the weekend. Then I'm back home. I'm trying to think of it as a professional workshop."

"So, it's a conference or something?"

"Not exactly."

"You're being evasive which might've worked back when we were first roomies, but not now. So, spill it."

"I'm here in some man's cushy high-rise apartment—in my own room, mind you—and I'm gearing up for a weekend work session. I've got to get some help, Ava, some new ideas, or I'm never gonna be able to keep my business going, much less keep Jessie on."

"But Chicago? With a complete stranger?"

Carly could hear Ava's concern kick up a notch. "He listed some convincing credentials on the photography forum that we're both on. And I did my homework. I verified. He seems professional, and he's nice."

"But you're staying in his apartment? Together? Since when was that a good idea? You don't do things like that."

"It's his parents' actually, and I thought I was getting it to myself. If you saw this place, though, you'd know why I could never afford the whole apartment. I've got a single bedroom until Sunday, and he's teaching me some stuff about the business. There's also a lock on the door, if that makes it any better."

"Which does you no good if he has the key."

"True, but you know how I get twitchy if something's off." She stood from the bed and slid a nearby desk chair beneath the doorknob, just in case. "No bad vibes yet."

"So, he's qualified?" Ava asked.

"Do you think I'd just shack up with any old guy with a Polaroid and a cute smile?"

"I hope you're not *shacking up* period."

"You know me better than that." Carly pulled the pepper spray from her luggage and tucked it under her pillow.

"But he's got a cute smile?"

"He's . . . well, he's gorgeous, but that's beside the point. I'm here for ideas. We're dissecting my business plan, and he's offering professional advice and some session tips. That's it."

"But if he's cute—"

"So you go from being my mother to my matchmaker in the matter of three seconds? Stop. You should know as well as anybody that I'm not in that game. My stint with long-distance relationships dried up with a certain player we both know."

"Baseball player or *player* player?"

"Huh." Carly huffed and sank back onto the pillow. "Hunter tried both and didn't do either one justice." She'd made no secret of her aversion to baseball in general and long-distance commitments in particular, all because of her train wreck of a relationship with a pro pitcher.

"You can't write off potentials just because baseball boy was a world-class jerk."

"Can't I, now?"

"And anyway, it's been what? A year?"

Carly closed her eyes. "Not long enough."

The thing with Hunter had started in college when she'd been the sports photographer for *The University Tribune* and did a cover story on UT-Knoxville's star player. The attraction was mutual, but after a couple of dates, their paths went in different directions for a time. When they reconnected a few years later, a steady relationship bloomed. Then, it wilted as she persistently frustrated his attempts to run the bases with her.

In the weeks before the relationship ended, she thought they'd come to an understanding that, despite the mutual attraction, they'd wait. For how long, she honestly didn't know. Turned out, it didn't matter anyway.

Just over a year ago, she'd blocked off a weekend to make a surprise visit to Atlanta where he'd been a first-year draft pick for the Braves. Walking in on him with the blond had been enough to torch the relationship and douse any desire to date since then.

As she ran a hand across the soft comforter, Carly prodded Ava. "You might take your own advice once you get away from Corbin, you know."

"No thanks." Ava sighed on the other end of the line. "If I weren't a doctor, I might become a nun. Men are too risky."

"You know it, sister."

As if on cue, they both parroted their old college catchphrase, "Out of the mouths of babes."

Sharing apartments, common life mantras, and their taste in comfort food over the years, they also shared relationship woes.

"So, what's his name?" Ava asked. "You know, in case I have to file a missing person's report."

"Oh, you mean the guy here in Chicago?" Carly rose from the pillow. "His name's Jex. Radcliffe, I think. At least, he told me to call him by his nickname which he says is Jex. And the doorman clued me in on the last name. Anyway, we're not using real names. Not yet. Nor sharing any personal details."

"Caution is good. Just do me a favor and come back home."

"Of course." Carly shouldered the phone. "I'll text you in the morning to let you know I'm still breathing."

When she hung up, she lay back on the bed, soaking up the room's luxury. The faint scent of lavender from the down comforter and plush pillows soothed her.

The place looked like it could be a photo from some posh lifestyle magazine, not one of her mother's Southern home and garden monthlies. And the closet? The one with the stock of spare swimsuits? It had obviously been the receptacle of more than Jex's mother's fixation on providing for guest swimmers. She had a collection of dresses, still new with tags, and shoes nestled in their boxes occupying three times Carly's closet space.

Must be nice not worrying about money.

Once she'd brushed her teeth and finished getting ready for bed, she slipped between the covers and sank into the comfort of the cool sheets. The events of the day played through her mind. Arriving at the airport . . . the taxi drive through the city . . . Jex opening the apartment door.

Just before she surrendered to sleep, the last thought she had was talking to Jex on the terrace. Those blue eyes . . . and that gorgeous . . . smile.

Hours later, when a humming motor activated, waking her from a sound sleep, Carly jumped frantically from her the bed, searching in the dark for her pepper spray. A short distance from the head of her bed, ivory linen drapes slowly accordioned open to the edge of the room, exposing a large sunlit window.

Squinting against the brightening light, she clinched the comforter to her chest until her eyes adjusted and she confirmed that she was alone.

Stupid smart curtains. Can rich people not do things manually?

When her breathing settled a bit, she stripped the covers back and looked at the designer wall clock staring at her like a mocking face. *Nine?* How had she slept until nine? Using every minute of this two-days' stay—getting her money's worth—was how she'd planned to spend the weekend, not sleeping it away.

A faint knock on the door caused a second jolt, and she hadn't even put her feet on the floor yet.

"Bee?" Jex's muffled voice echoed from the other side of the door. "You awake?"

"Y-yes, I'm up."

"Sorry about the drapes. I forgot to tell you about the timer."

She watched for the doorknob to turn, but it didn't. She noticed the shadow of his feet beneath the door and waited for them to move. They didn't.

"Listen." He paused. "I just got back from my workout. If you want to get ready, we can grab breakfast and get to work."

"Um, okay, yeah. Give me a few minutes."

"Sure. No rush."

After a quick shower, she chose a simple outfit from the three changes she brought—a form-hugging pair of jeans with a white button-up shirt and her most comfortable pair of low-top canvas lace-ups. She draped her jacket over the camera bag in case Jex didn't find that parka for her to wear.

Still unsure about his idea, she finished a simple application of makeup and stood in front of the vanity mirror, shoulders squared. If Jex thought this could boost her business, she had to at least give it a try.

Loosen up, girl. Focus on the fun.

Trying as she might to tuck away her reservations, she moved the chair from the door, grabbed her bag, and stepped quietly into the hall.

Rounding the corner to the living room, she saw Jex on the couch, filling his own small backpack from a stash of lenses scattered on the floor and coffee table. A deep red parka lay across a nearby chair. It must have been the one he wanted her to wear. Carly silently watched him choose equipment for the day and secure a portable tripod to the bottom of his bag.

When he fastened the last clip and brushed a hand through his hair, last night's pre-slumber thoughts came back to her full throttle. A little heat warmed her cheeks.

The dark jeans he wore fit him well, she admitted to herself. And his sand-colored sweater, likely half the cost of her car payment, gave a peek at a white t-shirt underneath. In other words, he'd chosen a more-than-favorable outfit and just enough layers to make any girl with a pumping heart take a second look.

Feeling a little underdressed in her Target-bought clothes, she shored up her nerves, brushed the front of her jeans in anxious strokes, and stepped closer. "You ready?" she asked.

As he stood and propped his hands low on his hips, he turned and caught sight of her. For a full couple seconds, he was silent. Then with a quick flicker of his eyes, he scanned her. "Wow, you look great."

The compliment left her reeling for a response. What should she say? *Wow, you look pretty amazing yourself. Love that cable knit. How about those jeans?* But all she could spit out was a quick "thanks." Quickly pointing to his backpack, she added, "Got all your stuff together?"

His eyes lingered a second longer. "I think so. I've pulled together everything we need. Oh, and I found that jacket for you." He circled the coffee table and picked up the red parka from the couch.

Setting her camera bag on the floor, she surveyed the jacket, then slipped it on. "A little roomy, but if you think it'll work . . ."

"It'll be perfect. Here." He stepped closer. "Let me roll up the sleeves for you."

As he worked on the jacket, she looked away, feeling a little awkward at his nearness.

"Now then." He backed away. "Yeah, that's exactly what I want."

She grinned self-consciously.

Still examining her outfit, he said, "You can leave your camera here, if you like. It'll be easier to travel light, and you can use one of mine, transfer any photos later."

"I don't know that I'd be familiar with your equipment."

He grinned. "Actually, that's part of the surprise."

"Are you sure about this?"

"Yeah, I even got an award in preschool. I was the best at sharing my toys."

His smile somehow eased her, and with a spreading grin of her own, she set her bag on the couch. "Since you're award-winning and all, maybe you want to share exactly what we're doing?"

"Not so fast. The element of surprise, remember?" He slipped on a black leather jacket, hefted the backpack onto his shoulder, and nodded toward the door. "Come on. We've got work to do."

Minutes later, they'd taken the elevator to an underground garage. As they rounded the corner from the elevator bank, a row of parked high-end Beamers, Lexuses, and Mercedes lined the concrete wall. Carly walked behind Jex and began texting Ava to check in as promised.

As they reached the far end of the garage, Carly, only vaguely aware of the row of motorcycles, assumed they were getting close to Jex's car.

Finishing her text, she barely took notice of the lockers along the wall in front of the parked bikes. That is, until Jex pulled out a remote from his jacket pocket, popped open the door to one of the lockers, and retrieved two helmets.

She vacantly tucked her phone into her jeans pocket and stopped in her tracks. "Wait, are you? . . . Are we? . . . Did you plan—?"

"To ride to the site? Yeah. It's not far. Sorry, I should have mentioned the bike. It's the only transportation I've got right now. My car's in the shop for servicing this weekend." He set his backpack to the side of a sleek, black Kawasaki.

"But I've never ridden on a motorcycle. Unless you count my cousin's moped down our driveway to the mailbox when I was a kid."

"Ah, ah, ah. No sharing of personal details." Mischief put a twinkle in his blue eyes. "It's not hard. Just hold on to me, and lean when I do."

What on earth was he thinking? She'd have to . . . hold him and sit . . . directly behind him. His body would be . . . like . . . between her thighs. Her heart sped up to match her anxiety level.

When he handed her a helmet, she turned it over in her hands until he took it back, turned the visor up, and slipped it onto her head, pulling the chinstrap snug.

"Too tight?" he asked.

"No. No, it's good. A-are you a good driver?"

"No, but don't worry. We won't be on long enough to crash and burn." He winked and straddled the bike. When he looked back, he added, "I'm just joking. I promise I'll take good care of you. Hop on."

As Carly mounted the bike behind him, he fastened his own helmet. Her heart pounded with the force of a percussionist driving down on a kettle drum. She tightened her jaw to bite back the anxiety, hoping that when she did hold on around his waist, he wouldn't feel her heart pounding against his back.

He picked up the bag from the concrete and handed it to her. "If you'll strap this on, it'll be easier to hold on if it's not between us."

Carly did as he said, and as the bike engine rumbled to life, she felt the deep bass resound in her core, like someone had quickened her heartbeat with a gong mallet. As he engaged the throttle, she grabbed him from behind, probably a little too energetically.

They exited the garage onto the street, and the hum of the motor rose in pitch. When Jex spoke once the ride began, the speaker in her ear caused her to jerk him tighter around the waist. He touched her hands reassuringly, as if he'd forgotten she was a stranger. "Whoa, there. I didn't mean to scare you."

The warmth of his fingers against hers left her skin tingling. Then, just as quickly, he set his hand back in place on the handlebar.

"We can adjust the volume if we need to," he said.

"No, sorry. It's fine." She tried not to raise her voice too much against the noise of the motor. "Guess I'm just a little jumpy."

"Relax. Showing you around the city will be fun." He pulled to a rolling stop at the first light. "Can I at least ask if you've ever been to Chicago?"

She paused and scanned the goings on of traffic and pedestrians around her. As she watched a runner with a German shepherd jog into the crosswalk in front of them, she answered, "No. This is the first time."

He flipped up his visor and looked over his shoulder. "Then I really do have a surprise for you."

She could see the smile in his eyes just before he turned to face the light and throttle the bike down the streets of Chicago.

Chapter Seven

Jex

Jex couldn't deny that he enjoyed the feel of Bee's arms around his waist, even though she was probably pressed against his back out of fear. And, though the day was turning out to be unseasonably warm, the mid-April air still nipped at him even with the short distance of their ride.

Despite it all, with each minute that passed, she seemed to get more comfortably seated behind him, her leans well-timed and becoming smoother with each turn. By the time they'd pulled into the lot closest to the dock, she'd loosened her grip and appeared more relaxed.

"You're a natural," he teased.

"How could you tell? From the gentle death grip or the steely composure in my voice over your helmet mic?" The sarcasm slid off her tongue like thick molasses.

After easing the bike into a parking space, he popped the kickstand and hung his helmet on the handlebar.

"Where are we?" She shook out her hair after unstrapping her own helmet.

He steadied the bike as she stepped off. "You like shooting architecture, right?"

"Yeah."

"I thought we'd take a ride around the city so you could see some of Chicago's finest."

"Why are we stopping here?"

Jex stepped off the bike and attached a lock to their helmets, then nodded to the dock behind her. She turned toward a flat-decked tour boat moored a hundred yards away. "On that?" She pointed. The tinge of surprise in her voice charmed him.

"We'll have some good photo ops since there are great views from the water. I can show you some lighting tricks too."

"Okay. I admit it. You *did* have a surprise. I didn't expect a boat tour."

He grinned. "Oh, this isn't the surprise. And trust me. You'll love it."

Trust me. Maybe those words rolled off his tongue a little too easily, he thought. His stomach lurched a bit when Bee so easily agreed. Not having shared everything about his motive for bringing her to Chicago had left him uneasy, like his deception lurked just under the surface, ready to raise its head and bite him if he didn't come clean.

He tried to shake off the feeling and tell himself that if they accomplished both his *and* her objectives, maybe there would be no reason to worry. But what did that involve? Only getting the photos he needed while instructing her on good business practices? Something about that still felt off.

Looking around the riverfront, he knew they'd pass some of the city's architectural monuments. If he could work those into his shoot and give Bee some new ideas, that was hopefully all it would take.

Months back, when Jex had first visited Hughley Photographics with Marla to propose his prototype, he'd noticed something useful. As they toured the building, things that were distinctly Chicago sat in every room: the four-starred city flag hung framed in the office lobby; a shadowbox display of 2016 World Series Cubs baseballs decorated a bookshelf; even a replica of the Cloud Gate Bean served as a paperweight on a conference table.

After Jex got the callback and the request for a photo spread with Marla, he knew if he could somehow get the shots he needed to satisfy Hughley, he could cement the deal by capitalizing on the man's love of Chicago.

In his gut, he knew taking his prototype out into the city was his real ticket.

Then, after the breakup and Natalie nudging him toward getting Bee as his model, it all seemed doable. And it still was. He just needed to keep focused on killing two birds with one stone.

Twenty minutes after they'd bought their tickets and boarded, the boat pulled from the dock in a slow groan and the tour guide began with preliminary instructions to the small group of passengers seated for the cruise.

Rather than taking one of the passenger seats, Jex turned to Bee. "I know a better place to enjoy the view. Come on."

He turned before she could respond, nodded to a boat worker wearing a captain's hat, and said, "We're headed up top, Ben. Got some shots to land up there, and the lighting's perfect right now."

The man nodded back and with a thick Yankee accent barked, "Yous giving my passengers ideas dey can go anywhere dey want. It's a liability, man."

Jex laughed. "And yet you still let me get away with it. Promise I'll be safe."

"You'd better. No need to be fishing yous outta the river today."

Jex led Bee to the front of the boat and toward a small set of stairs to the left of the control room. As they passed by, he could see the real captain at the helm inside the pilot house. Jex had gotten to know the man when he'd taken cruises in exchange for seasonal sets of advertising photos for the tour. The man nodded to Jex as they ascended the stairs.

At the head of the boxed cabin, a ladder led to the roof. He began to climb, but before he reached the top, he looked below and saw Bee stalled at the bottom rung.

"Come on." He urged her up with a flick of his head. "You'll like it up here." He could tell she was hesitant and a bit more than careful while holding the rungs. In fact, she seemed scared.

She bent her head to the breeze, then looked up at him. "Maybe we should stay down here. That guy back there seemed to think it was a bad idea to go up."

"It'll be alright. I've been up here plenty of times."

"Let me guess. Your parents own the boat?" She raised her eyebrows, anticipating his answer.

"Not quite. But I promise it's okay. Come on. Let's get set up."

She still didn't move. "Uh, I'm a little bit . . ." She shifted. "I'm afraid of heights."

"Oh, I'm sorry. I didn't—"

"No, I want to come up. Actually, I've been working on overcoming my fears."

Jex stepped back down the ladder. "Working on your fears, huh? And how are you doing that?"

"You know, climbing the stepping stool to change light bulbs and such."

"Are you really that scared?"

"I exaggerate . . . mildly. It's just that I had a bad fall once, when I was younger."

He paused a moment, trying to think how best to help her. "Well then, since you're working on your fears, Chicago is as good a place as any to step up your game. Are you willing to let me help you?"

She took a deep breath and shrugged. Her response came out more as a question than an answer. "Possibly?"

He held out his hand.

"You want to shake on it?"

"No, silly. Give me your hands." Still cool from the open-air ride, he positioned them just under his on the ladder's railing. "Hold on here with me, and I'll follow you up. I promise I won't let you fall. Take as much time as you need."

With his arms around her, he slowly ascended each rung in sync with Bee always one step above him. He could have focused on the chilly aluminum rail beneath his fingers or the sounds of the other passengers on the deck below or even the humming of the boat engine. But it was the sweet smell of jasmine from her hair that stirred him to distraction. As they reached the top, he was almost sorry when she crouched toward the center of the cabin roof away from him.

"That wasn't so bad, was it?"

She looked around. "Jury's still out."

"Did you fly into Chicago or drive?"

"I know what you're thinking. I'm not afraid of flying. I do usually take an aisle seat and ask to close the window shades, but I'm much better if there's a barrier between the air and me. Otherwise, my stomach feels like it's been shoved into my throat, and my heart starts fluttering like a hummingbird." She nodded toward the ladder. "So, thanks for being my barrier."

"One fear at a time." He stepped over the last rung and walked to the center of the roof.

"What do you mean?"

Reaching down, he helped her up from her crouching position. "Well, at least you've hopefully been able to put aside that other fear of yours about rooming with a stranger for the weekend."

"I'll let you know on Monday." She grinned and brushed off her pants.

"Fair enough. We ready to get started?"

She gave a tentative nod.

Within minutes, he'd unstrapped the tripod and set it on one corner of the rooftop at a low angle with the camera mounted. Crouching and bending his head to the viewfinder, he began adjusting settings. Bee continued to stand and watch from the roof's center.

"Do you know why I'm using this low angle?"

She folded her arms but didn't move from her spot. "I'm guessing it's so only the *sky* is reflected in the glass of the buildings instead of other buildings. It makes a nice clean shot."

"Yeah." He raised his gaze from the viewfinder, impressed. Maybe she knew more than he suspected. "We've also got the benefit of some clouds. They'll pull down the harsh light and give some cool reflection effects. Perfect day for pictures." He dialed in another setting then cast his eyes again on Bee looking up at the first passing building.

The tour guide's voice on the PA echoed through the canal. "Up ahead you'll see what was touted as Chicago's first air-conditioned office building. The Wrigley, constructed with a French Renaissance influence, belonged to the chewing gum magnate to house his corporate headquarters."

"Hey." Jex, still looking through the viewfinder, vacantly pointed toward his bag. "Can you dig into my backpack? I've got a case of filters. Tell me which you'd choose for shots against the background of buildings."

After she pulled her attention away from the Wrigley, he watched her from the corner of his eye carefully tread to the camera bag to find the filter box and study the lenses.

"I think a polarizer would be good. It'll manage reflections well enough, darken the sky a tad, and suppress the glare from the glass on the buildings."

He raised from the viewfinder again. "You've done dense cityscapes before, haven't you?"

She eased to the side where he sat and handed him the filter. "When you asked to look at my pictures last night, I didn't show you everything. If I had, you might've guessed what city I live close to."

"Clever." He grinned. "Do you think you'll ever tell me about yourself?" He found himself hoping she would.

"You already know some things about me. Just not everything. And to answer your first question, yes, I've done a couple of cityscapes, but Chicago's definitely a step up."

He leaned back to his camera. As he brought Bee into focus, now a few steps across the roof from him, he took advantage of the pretense of adjusting settings to enjoy the sight of her.

He admired her expressions through the lens—the angst of being on the pilot house roof fading as she took in sites she'd never seen before, excitement replacing dread as she began to study the massive buildings edging the waterway. They resembled hulking strongholds against a negligible moat, something she definitely wouldn't see in a small town.

He snapped a couple of test shots. Or maybe they weren't. Maybe they would be pictures he would enjoy later.

In one, she smiled and waved at some pedestrians on Michigan Avenue's overpass bridge. In another, she looked over her shoulder at him, and when she did, the mystery of being in the company of this woman whose real name he didn't know teased him like an unopened fortune cookie. Maybe he'd keep those two shots just for himself.

Her wavy hair blew away from her face, and she turned to him again. "You were right. This really is a great way to shoot the city. I had no idea. Are you almost set up?"

Ignoring her question, his conscience burned a little. "I'm glad you came to Chicago. This is kind of fun, getting to know you in a totally . . . anonymous sort of way."

She dropped her gaze. "Not that conventional, I guess, but I appreciate your help."

He rose and crossed the roof to her, his conscience wavering. Staring into her eyes, he wondered if he should tell her.

"Is something wrong?" she asked.

"No. I just . . . I've got a favor I'd like to ask you."

"Okay."

Keeping his eyes on hers, he reluctantly began, "Actually, I've got a confession to make too." He tried to gauge her reaction, but she didn't offer even the slightest twitch. "When I initially had the idea to do a shoot on the boat, I thought you might help me with a project I've been working on."

"If I can, I will." She tilted her head. "What do you need me to do?"

"I'd have to give you some personal details, if that's okay."

He watched Bee's eyes narrow as she considered what he was saying. "Okay. What do you need to tell me?"

As the boat came in sight of a couple of buildings known to the locals as the corn cobs, the tour guide wrapped up his discussion of the Tribune Tower and Trump Building and began to explain the history of the Marina City in his well-rehearsed spiel.

Bee, however, never averted her eyes from Jex. Finally, he drew in a deep breath and began. "A few months ago, I finished a design and build for a prototype of a new style of camera. I'm hoping to secure a contract for sponsorship and production with a big company here in Chicago."

"That's fantastic." Her eyes brightened. "You must be really excited."

"Yeah, it's a huge opportunity. My chance to begin building a dream I've had for a long time now. I thought maybe you'd consider working on a spread with me today to showcase that prototype. You're actually the perfect model for it."

Understanding slowly seeped into her expression. "So this was the idea you hatched last night."

He didn't answer but instead looked beyond her shoulder to another passing tour boat. If she knew this plan had been in the making for months, that'd probably be the end of it.

Bee didn't wait for an answer. "I don't think I'm your girl. Like I told you last night, I'm much better behind the camera than in front of it."

"That's what makes you ideal for helping me. I don't need a professional model, even though . . . well, you're very attractive and could definitely qualify as one."

She looked away.

Afraid he was saying too much, he quickly followed up. "What I want is someone who feels natural with a camera in her hands. You just happen to have a great smile and a beautiful face, and—" He stopped. "I'm sorry. I don't mean to make you feel uncomfortable. I think you'd be perfect, that's all. A few photos here on the boat would be a great start, and I promise that wasn't my sole reason for bringing you here. I have some business ideas to run by you today too. The biggest surprise is still to come. . . If you still trust me."

Bee hesitated, then glanced toward his backpack. Taking a deep breath, she asked, "So, where's this prototype?"

A slow grin spread across his face. He'd told her a little bit of the truth. And she was agreeing to stay, at least for now.

Chapter Eight

Carly

When Jex placed his camera in her hands, Carly held it for a moment, completely in awe. She'd never seen one like it before.

A left-handed DSLR.

She slid her fingers across the grip into the most natural finger-cradling position she'd ever found on a camera.

For as long as she could remember, she'd used right-handed everything—fishing rods, golf clubs, can openers. To slip her hand around a camera like this one felt like trying on a seamless glove.

"How did you come up with this?"

"That's privileged information, Miss Honeybee" He clipped a strap to the camera's body. "But I'll give you a hint. Left-handed, remember? And with enough design skills to be dangerous," he said playfully.

Nodding at the camera, he added, "A few people have tried with film versions, but until the DSLR came along, the designs were too clumsy. I've tossed the idea around for quite a while, kind of a mirror image of a standard camera. That's the simple explanation, anyway. It gets a lot more complex on the blueprint and development level." He glanced toward the camera. "What do you think?"

"Jex, I think it's ingenious. Can I try it?" He really was a professional with some serious skills. Who'd have thought she'd be fortunate enough to stumble onto someone with not only business sense, but a grasp of the inner workings of equipment? She'd definitely have to tell Ava about this.

"You bet." He pulled a flashcard from his backpack, popped it in, and attached a lens and filter for long-range shots. "She's all yours."

When he handed it back to her, Carly looked through the viewfinder, aimed at the receding "corn cob" buildings in the distance, and immediately began shooting. It was the most intuitive camera she'd ever held.

For the next hour, she pointed, clicked, adjusted settings, talked to herself, and even giggled once or twice. Occasionally, she turned and commented mostly to herself on the scenery beyond the boat's edge. Picture after picture, she became more comfortable with the camera, more at ease with the height from the rooftop, more relaxed with Jex.

The boat eventually made its way to what the tour guide below called Wolf Point, where the three branches of the river meet. As the guide called out various places of interest, she shot photos of the iconic 150 North Riverside Plaza, a top-heavy sky-rise, the core of which occupied a tiny half-acre lot. The mammoth building fit like the dull lead of a carpenter's pencil between the Amtrak to its west and the river to its east. To Carly, the structure looked impossibly balanced on its narrow base. "I can't believe they were able to put such a huge building on that small of a foundation."

"It's physics, and a few million gallons of water." Jex craned his neck upward.

"What are you talking about?"

He pointed. "Somewhere in the core of that building, there are a bunch of water tanks with upwards of 160,000 gallons of water in each of them. They slosh when the building moves with the wind to counter the sway."

"That makes me sick to my stomach to think about going up in a building like that. Sounds like a flimsy way to keep it upright."

Jex chuckled. "I hear it's deceptively stable."

"Is that what stability is all about? Having a fluid core?"

"Some would say being all gushy inside has its perks."

Carly held the camera back to her eye to avoid his doublespeak. "A synonym for fluid is also unsteady."

"Or it could be adaptable."

"Unreliable."

"Maybe adjustable." Jex seemed to enjoy their banter.

"Fickle."

"Flexible."

"Are we still talking about buildings?" Carly pulled the camera away from her eye.

"Doesn't really matter, does it?" He flashed a grin that produced heart-melting dimples.

The butterflies in Carly's stomach kicked their fluttering up a notch. Had Jex just been flirting with her? "How about we just take some photos?"

The butterflies went into a full-blown tussle. For Pete's sake, had *she* been flirting back?

Rounding out their tour with buildings like the throne-shaped Opera House, the Chicago Daily News Building, and the Willis Tower, they spent the rest of the boat ride reviewing the camera's thumbprints, snapping occasional points of interest, laughing, and talking. The conversation came easier as time passed.

Before long, the tour guide echoed a final approach to the dock they'd left from earlier.

When Carly heard the call, she looked at Jex. He'd already packed his tripod and camera. Now sitting a few feet away, he leaned back on an elbow and smiled at her.

She glanced down at his prototype in her hand. "I'm so sorry. I didn't mean to take up the whole time with your camera. It's just that . . . this is really incredible, Jex. You've designed something pretty amazing for people—"

"Like you?"

She pressed her lips into a thin line. "Obvious, huh?"

"I should have known when you pointed out the ink stains on my hands last night. It's a leftie problem—one that a right-handed person likely wouldn't think about. I'm learning all kinds of things about you, Honeybee."

Somehow that didn't cross her mind as a concern like it did when she'd arrived last night. After the silence stretched a second too long, she said, "You were wanting to take some pictures for your spread."

He laughed a little. "I already have."

"You did?" She vaguely remembered seeing him with another camera, but she must have been so wrapped up in his prototype that his taking pictures of her didn't really register.

"While you were taking your pictures, I was taking my own with my spare. I got exactly what I wanted—some of the best candids ever. They were perfect. I'll show you when we get back to the apartment."

Before Carly could respond, a voice on the PA that she recognized as the man with the captain's hat called from below. "Jex Radcliffe, we're now deboarding. This means yous and the pretty girl too."

Jex stood and walked toward her. When he came close enough to touch, he nodded toward the landing below. "I suppose we should go so Ben doesn't throw a gasket, but before we do, should we call it even?"

Carly cleared her throat. "What do you mean?"

"Well, *I* know you're a vegetarian, you have some fears, and that you're left-handed. And now, thanks to Ben, *you* know my last name, in addition to where I live, and some very intimate details about my prototype." When he took one step closer, he reached up, his hands tracing the collar of the jacket he'd requested she wear. "I think we're on a pretty level playing field, don't you?"

Her heart began to beat against her chest with the force of a hammer. Her mouth, cotton dry, opened, but no words came. The breeze off the waterway carried the hint of his musky scent as he slowly unclipped the camera strap from around her neck.

She could feel the heat rise to her cheeks and she stuttered. "I-I already knew it."

"Knew what?

"Your last name. Before today. The doorman at the Emerald, he told me."

Jex grinned, his face within inches of hers. "I'll have to have a talk with Addison. He can't be exposing all my secrets."

"Y-you have a lot of secrets?"

"Not really. I like surprises more than secrets." He stepped back. "And I have one more for you today. Come on."

By the time she'd let out the breath she was holding, he'd already pulled his backpack onto his shoulder and started down the ladder. He paused, motioning for her to step down with him. She lowered herself into the circle he'd created, and they descended together.

"How did you know I was starving?" Carly forked at her salad from a chic cafe a few blocks from where they'd left the boat.

"We never got breakfast, and I felt your stomach growling."

Carly blushed. Behind him on the bike, she'd been hanging on pretty tightly when they'd left the dock. "Well, this was a nice surprise. Catering to the vegetarian?"

"My sister likes this place. She's brought me here a few times, so I knew it had a vegetarian menu. Thought you might like it." He pulled a couple of napkins from a dispenser and handed one to her. "This still isn't *the* surprise, by the way." Lifting his fountain drink, he took a long sip. "I've been thinking about what we discussed last night. You know, specializing. What if you focused on shooting couples in unusual places, unique circumstances?"

"Isn't that what most photographers try to do? Take advantage of the scenery? How would that be any different or more specialized than any other photographer's work?"

"Capitalizing on scenery, yes. But how many times do you see photographers using the same boring places as a backdrop? There's always a market for something different. Think outside the box a little. How can you shoot and market the kinds of photos you want to take besides filling wedding albums for coffee tables?"

Carly shrugged. "I give. Tell me."

"Magazines? Advertisers? They're always looking for things like that. What about bridal fairs? And you don't even have to be local. There's a global market for stock photos. Maybe writers looking for book covers?" He peeled back the wrapping on his veggie hoagie and took a bite.

"I've never considered publication. At least, not on that scale."

"Why not?"

She snatched a glance at him as he sat back in his chair, then refocused on her salad. "It's a little intimidating."

"When someone sees your photos, what's the biggest compliment they can give you?"

"I guess when they say they like them."

"Wrong." He pulled his straw from his drink and pointed it at her. "It's when they have an emotional response. When they cry. Get angry. Gasp. Photos like that don't happen by setting someone in a wicker chair and telling them to smile. You want to see motion, depth, *e*-motion, when you see a photo. That, my Honeybee, is when the mediocre becomes the exceptional."

Her stomach fluttered a little when he called her *his* Honeybee. "And how do I do that?"

Jex's phone dinged with a text. He took a quick peek at the screen. "Right on time." He looked up and smiled. "We've got one more stop to make. Maybe that's where we can answer that question."

Just as she sidled up to the motorcycle, Jex faced her and pulled out a red bandana. He eyed her as his lips curled in a Cheshire grin.

"What?"

"This is for you."

She frowned. "And what am I supposed to do with that?"

"It's a blindfold."

"Nnnno." She began shaking her head.

"And here I thought you were beginning to feel comfortable around me."

"Don't you think it's a big enough challenge for me to stay on the bike without being blinded?"

He cocked his head as if to convince her. "This is a great way to really learn to ride. You'll begin to lean into the curves on instinct. But that's not the main reason I want to blindfold you."

"Why *would* you want to do that?"

"It's all part of the surprise Are you gonna let me have some fun?

"I thought you already were, hauling me around like a scared cat on the back of this machine of yours."

He tilted his head back, laughing, then held up the bandana.

"You're serious?"

"That's what my sister usually accuses me of."

The next thing Carly knew, she was perched blindfolded on the back of the motorcycle, Jex again sitting in front of her. When the bike jolted into gear, she grabbed onto his waist with the urgency of that same scared cat—now trying to avoid falling off the backend and completely forgetting that she barely knew who . . . or what . . . she might be grabbing.

The ride didn't take long, but after she gained her balance and began to *feel the ride,* as Jex said, she had to admit it was kind of fun.

With another sharp turn and a smooth roll stop, she heard Jex drop the kickstand.

"Do I take off this ridiculous hanky now?"

"No, not even close. We've still gotta take a walk."

"I don't think this was part of the deal." Though she couldn't deny she was having fun, walking down a city street with a blindfold on seemed a bit too ridiculous.

"You definitely agreed to the element of surprise by coming with me this morning. So, relax." He helped her from the bike, and once he'd checked her blindfold for gaps, wrapped her hand around his arm. "Hold on and I promise not to run you into any walls or let you fall off any bridges."

"A real bonus."

The whole adventure had given her what she and Ava had once called the "buzz of firsts"—that feeling when someone first rides a Ferris wheel or sees the ocean for the first time . . . or has their first kiss. That hummingbird in her chest settled inside her again.

As she walked, she had nothing prudent to focus on—no scenery, no architecture, no camera settings or equipment—only the cords of his muscles she could feel through his sweater. She tried to hold on without sending any weird messages. Too much of an arm squeeze and he might get the wrong idea. Too little and she'd lose him. Somehow, despite the awkwardness of it all, having a blindfold on and walking trustingly down the streets of Chicago on the arm of Jex Radcliffe didn't seem so bad.

A few minutes later, when they entered a building, she heard the echo of people talking across a large room. He steered her around an obstacle or two and then moved them straight ahead. "We're coming to the escalators. I'll tell you when to take a step."

"Oh, I don't know about—"

"Step!"

With a high, quick motion and unsure footing, she wobbled into his arms. Her hands landed on his chest, and she could tell by touch and the sound of his laughing that he was on the tread below her. They were descending.

"What are you laughing at?" She cuffed him on what she assumed was an arm. "You should let me lead *you* around a strange city blindfolded and see how light you are on *your* feet."

"Sorry." He snickered again. "Okay, maybe not so much."

"Good to know I could be your entertainment for the day."

"Guess I didn't realize how much fun this would be. We're stepping off in three, two, one, now."

Her exit was at least more graceful.

Next, she heard a set of doors open and Jex greeting someone.

"Hey, Trudy. Thanks for working this out and letting us steal away in your freight elevator. I owe you."

A gravelly female voice responded, "Glad you got my text and made it quick. You've got only a few minutes."

"No problem. We won't be long."

"This a new kind of dating tactic of yours?" Trudy said with a chuckle.

Jex pulled Carly next to him after she heard a set of doors open. "Just a surprise for my new friend here."

The woman smelled faintly of gourmet coffee and cigarettes. "I'll be up in a few minutes to reopen the floor."

When the elevator doors shut with a soft jolt, she felt the car moving upward. "Escalator down, elevator up. What kind of goose chase is this? And how many people do you know in Chicago?"

"A few, and be patient. Not much further."

After a minute, Carly huffed. "Slow elevator?"

"Something like that."

When she heard the doors open, he led her past a smattering of voices and around a turn. The voices faded as they rounded a corner.

With a few more steps, he stopped and took her by the shoulders. His touch sent a surge through her, the kind that caused her skin to tingle under his fingertips. "I'll help you sit down, here on the floor. I want you to keep your blindfold on until I'm ready. It won't take long."

"Okay. I suppose there's no harm in looking ridiculous for another minute or two." She braced herself as he helped her to the cool floor. Then, crossing her arms over her knees, she waited for Jex's surprise.

The whoosh and snap of tripod legs extending wasn't a foreign sound to her. Nor was the zip of a bag and click of the camera finding its place on the mount. The anticipation was killing her. A bike ride, a city walk, escalators, and elevators. Where on earth had he taken her?

After what seemed like a long wait, she sensed he was close. Very close. Enough that she could smell the hint of his cologne. Then he touched her shoulder again. A second surge coursed through her, this time sending a shiver of excitement down her arm that afterward she hoped he didn't notice.

"Believe me, you don't look ridiculous."

When he spoke, she felt his breath on her ear, and the tingle trailed down her neck.

"You know back on the boat when we talked about fears?"

"Yes." The fluttering of the hummingbird deepened in her chest.

"Let me be your barrier again. Before you take off your blindfold, I'll put my arms around you just like we did at the boat. I'll be between you and your fear. You're completely safe."

In the last few hours, something in her had shifted. She *had* begun to feel safe. When he encouraged her onto his bike even despite her fears, he taught her to lean with the curves, find her center of gravity. When he'd nudged her to go with him to the pilot house roof, he'd protected her climb. Something about this man allowed her to loosen her safeguards and live a little, and she was beginning to like it.

Carly hesitated only a second longer. "Okay."

"Ready?" She felt him ease into place behind her, his legs in line with hers, his arms finding their place.

She took a deep breath. "Am I?"

"You're safe," he repeated, his voice soft against her ear.

She reached up and loosened the blindfold. When it fell from her eyes, she slowly blinked. As her sight adjusted, her jaw went slack and the air caught in her throat.

Four feet past his shoulder was nothing but sky.

Chapter Nine

Jex

For a millisecond he worried that he'd overstepped a boundary. Maybe this wasn't such a good idea after all. She leaned into him and drew in another quick audible breath as he gently tightened his embrace. When she looked out into the blue, he held the remote for a series of rapid-fire shots. This time from the prototype instead of his spare.

Then, she found her voice. A whisper. "Oh, Jex."

He'd taken Bee 1,353 feet into the air.

The Skydeck at Willis Tower—what the locals still called the Sears building—sat on the 103rd floor. The Ledge, a group of four glass-encased observation boxes—one of which Bee now sat a few feet from—extended out from the building's exterior wall four feet into the air, leaving nothing but a thick, clear panel between the viewer's feet and the street, 103 floors below.

Taking cues from what little he'd learned about Bee in the last twenty-four hours, Jex was convinced that if she married her photography interests with her talent, she'd find all the success she could handle. But he wanted to show her that she could do more than just snap a good picture. He wanted Bee to see that she could create something truly breathtaking.

"Are you alright?" His lips grazed her ear.

She didn't reply at first. Then, "I think I am. . . .This is just . . . Wow."

Before removing the blindfold, he'd momentarily scrutinized the angle and set up the camera in the spot he considered ideal, focusing most intensely on her. As he studied her positioning—admired her, even—he realized he'd been wrong to think she looked like Marla.

The curve of her lips was fuller. Her smile more genuine. He thought about the look in her eyes when they were on the boat. They came alive when she was in her element. It had shown when she'd used his camera. He'd never seen Marla like that.

With his remote in hand, he continued taking pictures as she sat in front of the glass. "I wouldn't have put you out on the Ledge, you know . . . inside the observation box, I mean. I planned this before I knew you were afraid of heights, but then you said you were trying to overcome your fears. I thought . . . well, I was hoping you wouldn't mind sitting a few feet away from the Ledge if I were close by and helping to be your barrier."

Her chest rose and fell beneath her fingertips. "No. . . . This . . . really is amazing."

"We don't have very long here by ourselves. Trudy pulled a few strings for me to have the space for a few minutes, but I wanted you to see one of my favorite spots. I do a lot of thinking here. Sometimes, after hours, she lets me come and decompress."

"Quite a place to decompress."

"You could say that." He chuckled. "My sister brought me here a few years back after I had a falling out with our dad." Turning to the glass, he looked out into the sky.

Bee glanced at him, and asked softly, "What happened? With your dad?"

It was the first time she'd asked him something truly personal. He considered her question, then shrugged. "Langston Radcliffe's a hard nose when it comes to career paths. He's always had a plan in place for his kids. Unfortunately, his plan for me didn't match up with my own. He wanted me to slide in right behind him in the family business."

"And you didn't want that."

He shook his head. "I have no passion for what he does. I was trying to figure out what I wanted to do, and Natalie and I had a great brainstorming session right in that very glass." He pointed to the observatory in front of them. "That's where the idea for my prototype was born."

"Really? Right here?"

He nodded. "Sometimes, when I need to work something out in my head, she still nudges me back up here. Says I'm too caught up in my own narrow point of view and need a different perspective." He lifted his chin, gesturing toward the sky beyond the glass. "When I'm up this high, I pretend my troubles are all down there. From up here they're pretty small." He inhaled deeply. "Kind of strange I guess, but it tends to clear the mind."

He gestured toward the glass box. "Do you want to sit inside? A lot of people enjoy it."

She shook her head apprehensively. "I don't think I can do that."

"What if we eased only a little closer? No pressure. Only if you want to."

She looked tentatively from the glass to him. "Can we do this slowly?"

"I have an idea." Considering his camera angle, he reached to make a quick adjustment, then scooted closer to the edge of the glass and lay down with his head just along the lip of the Ledge. "Lie on your back, and slide here beside me."

Slowly, Bee closed her eyes, lay back, and gently shimmied next to him, her head still not inside the glass box.

"Just a little further."

"I don't know if I can do this." She gave a breathy laugh.

"Just pretend we're lying on the ground looking up into the sky. Here." He took her hand. "I've got you. Promise, nothing fluid or flexible or unsteady or unreliable here."

She caught the reference from earlier and laughed again.

A moment later, Bee had scooted to his side, and with backs to the floor, they lay with their heads inside the glass viewing room, their line of sight pointed up the building's exterior and to the sky beyond.

"You okay?" he asked.

"So far, so good. Should I open my eyes again?"

He laughed. "Sooner or later, that would be good." When she'd had a moment to catch her breath, he squeezed her hand. "Remember, you're safe here with me."

He turned to watch her expression as she took in the view. Reflections of the glass danced in her eyes and made him want to kiss her.

But he couldn't. . . . Wouldn't.

So why was he thinking about it?

He tried talking himself away from the thought.

Work. We're here for work. Two birds. One stone.

Rolling to his side, he said, "Now, I want you to slowly turn my way and look at me. Nowhere else. We'll get you used to it a little at a time."

Not thinking much about the photos he was after, he waited as Bee pivoted in slow, calculated motion toward him.

Work. That's all we're here for, showing Bee her potential.

"Stop there," he said. As he lay eye-to-eye with her only inches away, he smiled. "Having fun yet?"

"I never thought I'd be lying on the floor of a glass box, a half-mile in the air, with a complete stranger this weekend."

"You're not." His dimples deepened. "It's only a quarter mile, and by now, I seriously should rank a little higher than a stranger. I mean, we've slept under the same roof."

She raised an eyebrow, then failed to hold back a nervous giggle.

Their laughter faded. "This part wasn't in my plans either, but I'm glad we're here."

He had to refocus. *Work. Two birds. Maybe he should just focus on her. What could he give Bee in the next few minutes?*

"I want you to be perfectly still. I'm going to shoot us together at this angle. I want to show you what I mean by the element of surprise."

She glanced at the camera on the tripod above them. "You've been shooting all this time?"

"Not the whole time. Mostly shots of you. I usually don't shoot myself, so don't think I'm conceited. But I did want to show you with a few photos what I've been talking about. Are you good with that?"

Her eyes widened. "I . . . Yes, I'm good."

"Alright then." He gripped the remote. "Perfectly still."

Keep focused. What can I give to Bee?

Instinctively, he knew he had the potential for some great shots with his camera's angle capturing her expression, the backdrop of the city below, and the red jacket she was wearing. *His* jacket.

Everything was perfect, exactly what he was looking for. He tapped the remote again for a quick succession of photos and then stopped. Closer. He wanted to be closer.

He moved until her breath warmed his lips, then gripped the remote, absent-mindedly this time. The rapid-fire series of photos registered on his camera frame-by-frame like old movie stills.

"Don't move," he whispered. Without warning, he brushed his lips against hers—a feather against her skin—not enough to call a kiss, too much to deny the suggestion that it was. *Work. Pictures. Breathe.*

He squeezed the remote this time without warning when Trudy's gravelly voice scratched the air like a car driving on a pebble road. "Jex? You almost finished?" she called from around the corner. "I can't keep this closed off much longer." She stepped into view. "I've got people waiting."

Having worked at the Tower for years, Trudy obviously thought nothing of his lying on the floor. Scores of people had done all sorts of things at the Ledge—including jumping in the box, handstands against the glass, and lying down to take in the view, both inside the observatory and just at the edge.

"Yeah, of course." He didn't move. "Give me one more minute."

Trudy put her hands on her hips. "One." She then stepped out of sight.

When he first had the idea about visiting the Tower, he told himself it would be a good way to share his concept for Bee's business—one that she could easily pull off *if* she saw how it could work. *If* she'd give it a chance. He never dreamed, though, that when he staged his shots, every cell in his body would react.

"I-I guess we're out of time." Her voice barely carried to him.

"Looks that way." Trying to shake the feelings welling up inside of him, he quickly added, "But we didn't come this far for you not to see this." He backed up a little and with her hand in his, pulled her toward him. "Slow and easy," he said.

When she turned, stomach down, she laughed out loud, then drew in air at the sight below her.

"This . . . is one of the scariest . . . and most amazing things I've ever seen."

No longer conscious of a camera or an angle or lighting, he watched her, mesmerized, as she took in the view of the city below. "On a clear day, you can see four states from here. And since you're in Chicago for only a weekend, I guess this is your at-a-glance tour of the whole city."

Light from the sky glistened in her eyes as she took in the panoramic view.

She really was beautiful.

"When you said the 'element of surprise,' you weren't kidding." Her smile widened.

He pulled his attention away from her to scan the sights below. Cars, like beads on an abacus, slid back and forth along the thread-like streets. Despite the view, he thought about what had just happened and smiled. His lips still tingled from brushing against hers.

"Just wait till you see the pictures."

Chapter Ten

Carly

Carly's head was spinning. Holding on to Jex on the back of a motorcycle as he sped through the streets of Chicago was way more than she'd bargained for when she'd left Camden Grove.

And then there was the boat ride.

And Willis Tower.

And their kiss.

Or maybe she was kidding herself and it wasn't really a kiss.

Maybe it was just staging for the photos he wanted to capture, like an actor playing a part in a movie.

Was it just posing?

During the whole trip back to the apartment, that question kept running through her mind.

Jex tossed his bag on the couch when they came in the door, flipped on the TV, and plugged one of his flash drives into a reader, obviously eager to view their pictures on the big screen.

Carly removed the borrowed jacket and, at Jex's invitation, brought in a couple bottles of water from the refrigerator.

She sat next to him on the couch as each photo loaded. First, the ones from the boat—those she'd taken with the prototype—flashed in enlarged thumbnails onto the screen.

After a couple minutes of loading, Jex began the slideshow, scanning each picture with a critical eye. "These are really good." A few more slides in and the enthusiasm in his voice fully played out as he pointed at the screen. "Look at the composition there. You framed that shot perfectly. Lighting's spot on. And the reflections of the clouds in the glass of that building? Faultless. You've got a good eye, Bee."

When he turned to look at her, she smiled.

"What?"

She ran her fingers over the cold bottle in her hand. "It's kind of nice to meet someone whose love of photography runs as deeply as your own."

"Not hard to get excited when you find someone who knows how to take a good picture. That, and I guess I got a little charge out of you picking up my prototype and using it so intuitively."

After switching cards, the photos Jex had taken with the spare camera began to flash onto the screen. One by one, the slideshow popped up with picture after picture of her using his prototype.

She leaned back on the couch, watched the photos appear, and tried to think of something clever to say. When nothing came, she asked, "When're you presenting your camera to that company?"

"I'll send them over as soon as I can. I need to pull together the best shots, do some light editing. After that, I wait."

"And if they're approved?"

"With any luck, they'll unveil the prototype in three weeks at the company's spring awards ceremony."

Pictures continued to fade in and out on the screen. He watched them, making verbal notes to delete the doubles and a couple where her eyes were closed.

Then came close-ups of Carly without the prototype in the frame.

"You can toss those out too. Your camera's not in them," she said. "Were you dialing in your settings or something?"

"No, I took them on purpose. You look pretty captivating, don't you think? Happy, even."

Her face warmed.

"Am I making you uncomfortable?"

"No." She shrugged. "I guess I *was* happy. It was fun. I haven't really had much fun in a while." She took a long sip from the water bottle.

"I can't imagine why not."

Though it wasn't a question, Jex's expectant expression seemed to probe her for an answer. When she hesitated, he asked, "Why don't you have a boyfriend?"

"How do you know I don't?"

"I don't really. Nor would I understand why you wouldn't have someone waiting back home . . . wherever that is," he admitted. "But, at the risk of sounding bold, I'm going to guess I'm right."

"And what makes you so sure?" Jex's smile left her wanting to let her guard down.

"Well, first, during our truth and lies game last night, you mentioned a brother—real or pretend, I've not yet decided—but you didn't say anything about a boyfriend. And this afternoon, when we were at the Ledge, I got extremely close to you, and you didn't pull away, you know, out of loyalty to someone else. Anyway, you don't seem like the type to be untrue to somebody." He raised his eyes to hers. "So, was I right?"

She bit her lip, then answered, "I could tell you, but I'm still functioning on the premise that we're not sharing personal details. And what was that? Some kind of test? Getting close to me?"

He laughed but didn't answer. "You've spent a whole twenty-four hours with me now, and you don't want to give me even that small confirmation that I'm right?"

Carly smirked and took another long sip. After stalling enough to consider him, she set the bottle on the coffee table. "A little over a year ago, I came out of a bad relationship. So, yes, you were right. But pair that with the fact that there are a lot of crazies in the world, and I've been in the habit of keeping things safe and simple in my life. That's why I've insisted on not sharing personal information with you."

"Classed with the crazies, am I?"

"Call me paranoid, but it's safer if everyone's classed with the crazies until they're not."

Jex cocked his head. "So how do I win your trust?"

She shrugged. "That usually takes a bit longer than a weekend."

"I know you're scheduled to leave tomorrow, but I've really enjoyed today. What if we arranged for you to spend another couple of days here? Maybe we could see more of the city, and I could win some of that trust."

"But I thought you showed me all of Chicago today?"

"Only the bird's-eye view. We can see a lot more up close." He lifted his hand from the back of the couch and tucked a lock of hair behind her ear.

It was a simple gesture. Natural. Fluid even. When his fingers brushed her skin, she almost leaned into them, but then she stopped. "I should probably go back home. I've got a schedule to keep." She thought about Jessie and the few appointments they had on their calendar—too few to be an excuse not to stay. She knew Jessie could handle the sparse workload.

"Maybe between now and tomorrow, I can convince you to consider it. Besides, I'd really like to get your input on my final prototype spread. That'll take a couple more days for me to tack down, and we've got plenty more we could discuss about your business in the meantime. The possibilities are endless."

Rogue thoughts competed for her attention: how she felt when they were working together; the heartache she'd endured since Hunter; the fun she'd had in Chicago with Jex. The loneliness of the last year.

The possibilities probably *were* endless. Possibilities Carly both feared and desired all in the same moment.

"I don't know," she said.

His eyes searched hers. He added, "If it's the money you're concerned about, please don't be. I only charged you to begin with because it seemed bad form not to."

She stayed quiet. Jex finally raised his hands in defeat. "Okay, I give. I won't press you, but the option's there if you want it." He glanced up at the TV screen. "For now, let's take a look at the other pictures from today, the ones at the Tower. I think when we pull those up, you may see some things you haven't considered before. For your business, I mean."

Carly slowly nodded. The thought of what happened on the Ledge—or almost did— stirred in her again, nudging her from a carefully-guarded comfort zone like a tugboat pulling a ship from the harbor. "You go ahead and get them on the screen. I need to make a quick phone call."

"The friend with the swat team on speed dial?"

"Yeah, that friend." She grinned and rose from the couch.

Carly slipped into the guest bedroom and closed the door, pulling her phone from her pocket and tapping Ava's contact info in one swift motion.

By the time she reached the bathroom, Ava had answered the call. "Not a minute too soon. Were you on the river today? I was hoping you were floating downstream on a gondola or something and not face down at the hands of a serial killer."

"Chicago's pretty cool, but it's not Venice. Did you GPS me all day?"

"Of course not. Despite all the snags in my own life right now, I do still have one. I just checked in once or twice. Okay, maybe three times. Out of love and concern. So, spill it. Have you done anything I wouldn't do?"

Carly leaned against the bathroom counter. "You mean, have I done anything remotely exciting?"

"Is that some of your old sass I'm hearing? And, by the way, I'm not *that* boring."

"Look, I have only a minute, but yes, he took me on a boat tour of the city, and, Ava, the architecture was amazing."

"The architecture? You went to Chicago to spend the weekend with a guy we've determined is not a serial killer, and who you yourself said was a visual knockout, and you're telling me the architecture was the best part of the day?" Ava sighed. "Please say you've got more than that."

Carly wondered if she should tell Ava about the Ledge. She checked herself in the bathroom mirror, then said, "Well, he did . . . almost kiss me, or maybe he did kiss me? I don't know."

"What?" Ava's voice rose on the other end of the line. "Okay, I'm officially confused. Either he did or he didn't."

"He was staging a photo of the two of us, I think."

"Well, did it *feel* like a kiss? Did he follow it up with a look or words or a hug or something?"

"No, we were interrupted, but this whole day has been like something out of a book. He took me into Chicago on a motorcycle, we boarded a tour boat, he climbed with me to the pilot house rooftop, and he let me take a bazillion pictures with this new camera prototype he built himself. Then we had lunch, and he blindfolded me afterward and took me to the Willis Tower Skydeck."

"Wait. You climbed on top of a roof? And are you talking about the observation boxes at the top of the old Sears—?"

"That's it."

"But you hate heights. Did he know that?"

"Yeah." Carly brushed a curl from her face. "But somehow, he made it all . . . okay."

"If he watches chick flicks too, you should run. There's way too much good about this guy."

"I'll keep that in mind." Carly switched ears as she applied some Chapstick. "I can't talk right now. I just wanted to let you know he's asking me to stay a couple more days. What should I do?"

"First things first." Pragmatism resonated in Ava's voice. "Is he coming through on helping you with the business?"

"We're actually getting ready to talk more about that in a few minutes, and he's given me some ideas to build on already."

"And you feel like he knows what he's talking about?"

Carly clutched the phone between her ear and shoulder while she tugged her curls into place. "Yeah, he's helped me see patterns in my approach that I hadn't really paid attention to before."

"Do you want to stay?"

"I don't know." If she was honest, she really did want to stay, but doing that seemed so out of sync with how she'd lived her life over the last year that she didn't know if she was ready to admit the truth, much less act on it.

"Play it by ear then. See how the rest of the evening goes. But keep me posted. And promise me you won't stay too long. I need your help processing what's happening with Corbin and the whole office ordeal. He's been acting stranger than ever this weekend."

"Are you okay?"

"Yeah, of course. I'm just too close to the situation. I need someone who can see things in black and white."

"Funny," Ava said, "that's exactly why I called you. I promise no more than a couple of days extra at most. We'll talk later."

She tapped her phone to end the call and, for a moment, thought of Ava and how Dr. Corbin Simmons, on his best day, wasn't worthy of her. Ava was the most trustworthy person Carly had ever met, and if he wasn't reciprocating that trust, Carly would make it her mission to help Ava see that when she got back to Camden Grove.

In the meantime, she asked herself what she really wanted from this weekend in Chicago besides a professional booster shot. The hours she'd been in the city, those that excited her most, hadn't all been spent behind a camera or in conversation about business. They'd been the moments when she had connected with Jex, touched him—on the motorcycle, climbing the pilot house ladder, lying together on the floor at the Ledge. *Good grief, lying on the floor at the Ledge.*

Jex was definitely attractive, and a part of her wanted to stay. But her mind teetered between him and those still-raw memories of Hunter. She was *not* going to be played again.

No closer to an answer, she squared her shoulders and resolved to do what Ava suggested. *Play it by ear.*

Jex sat relaxed on the couch, arms stretched wide, as she stepped back into the living room. When he saw her, he smiled. "I think you're gonna be surprised by the photos at the Tower."

She raised her eyebrows with a thought. *That wouldn't be the first thing to surprise me at the Tower.*

He scooted to the edge of the couch and tapped at the laptop's keyboard as she sat down beside him.

When the pictures began scrolling across the TV screen, she first saw photos of herself, sitting alone, blindfolded on the 103rd floor of Willis Tower. As he clicked through the spread, the story unfolded like a spring crocus.

With each frame, the scene took on more breath and life, more story, beginning with the camera facing her. Then Jex came into the frame, close behind her.

Her heart quickened. She knew it was coming. The one moment frozen in her mind that she'd thought about continually since it happened.

The next photo faded onto the screen—her loosening the blindfold.

Then, the next—her expression at seeing the Chicago skyline, a mix of awe and something else. Not quite fear. No . . . the buzz of firsts.

She forced herself to breathe.

Next, they lay on the Tower floor together. Then facing each other. A run of multiple rapid-fire shots captured every nuance in her expression.

Finally, there it was. He'd caught the very second, the millisecond his lips had brushed hers. Looking at it seemed almost surreal, like the photo was of someone else, and she was a voyeur into their moment.

Jex tapped the laptop again, stopping the slideshow at that most critical photo.

She tried to swallow the air that had dried her throat.

"What do you think?" he asked.

"I-It's . . . well . . ." Her heart slammed against her chest. "It's an amazing shot." She couldn't stop looking at it, mesmerized by his lips, not a thread's width from hers. "Breathtaking . . . really."

She could feel his eyes settle on her. He whispered, "It's the perfect shot. And *that's* the reaction I want. Not what you'd get from perusing that coffee-table wedding album." He leaned back. "When you see a photo for the first time, and you can soak in the passion of that moment, that's when you know you've done something right."

She swallowed but didn't speak. He wasn't wrong. The lighting was perfect, almost ethereal. The angle of the backdrop—all the buildings visible through the glass beyond them—stretched out like a patchwork quilt. The contrast of his dark red jacket and the transparency of the glass worked magic. But all those things were merely good photography tricks.

And they weren't what made her knees weak. What caused her to lose her breath.

"Do you see it?" he asked. "This is what I wanted to talk to you about . . . for your business. It's an experiment I've been mulling over for a while now."

Carly finally peeled her eyes from the screen and turned toward Jex. When her head cleared, she began to understand. Reigning in all her thoughts that were running rampant, she managed to set her feet back on the ground and realize that their time at the Tower was simply him setting up an experimental shot at the Ledge.

"See," he said, "even though we're strangers, even though I don't know your real name, we pulled off a shoot that's not just intimate. It's . . . well, in your words, breathtaking. "

Carly looked away to regain her composure. She cleared her throat. "But I'm not sure I understand how that can help my business."

He nodded as if prepared to explain. "From the moment I met you, I've sensed that you're holding back—that you have a reserve of talent you haven't even tapped into because you're not stepping outside of your comfort zone."

The veiled compliment wasn't lost on her, but at the same time, she thought, *if he only knew what it took for me to suck up my courage and come to Chicago.*

She cocked her head. "So, you're suggesting I get uncomfortable at my job, and that's supposed to make me money? I thought the whole point was to get more confident as a photographer, more at ease with equipment and surroundings and staging so I can make creative decisions quickly."

"Yes, but confidence is built on adaptability. I'm convinced that stepping out of your comfort zone, and maybe even helping your clients do the same, can produce results that we can't even fully appreciate until it's captured in a photo. Results that cause people to react, like you did." He pointed at the screen. "Wouldn't *you* want a photographer for your big day who can capture that kind of moment? Think about how pushing past the norm, doing what we just did at the Tower, gave us this picture. And as the one behind the camera, if you start to experiment—even with photographing strangers—then applying what you learn in the field to people who *do* know each other will come intuitively."

She furrowed her brow. "You think I should shoot strangers in order to learn how to shoot people who know each other?"

"I think you should be open to new approaches, and maybe doing something exactly like *this* is a perfect way to do *that*."

"How did you come up with this idea anyway?"

He grinned. "I read about a study back in grad school. This psychologist conducted an experiment where he put complete strangers into an empty room together and asked them to stare into each other's eyes for four uninterrupted minutes."

She self-consciously broke eye contact with him. "And what happened?"

"He found the formula for immediate connection, and the experiment ended in his test couple falling in love."

"In four minutes?"

"No, but it was the beginning that eventually led to more."

She noticed him glance at the screen.

"Complete strangers can invoke a chemistry that people who've been together for years sometimes can't access. Capturing that chemistry is where we come in. With your talent shooting couples and your eye for interesting places, exploring this could give you an edge."

She tipped her head to the side, weighing his idea. "Let's say I did try to build my . . . adaptability skills. Taking pictures with strangers doesn't exactly sound like something people would line up at my door to book."

"Maybe not, but one look at the online dating industry tells me it's not impossible to get clientele. Last year alone, it topped 600 million in revenue."

"A figure you just happened to know?"

"I did my research." He glanced again at the screen. "And there are something like forty-five million dating app users in the U.S.

alone. Lonely people who are adventurous enough that I bet photographers like us could capitalize on it if we wanted to."

"I'm still not convinced that people would want to buy photos taken with a stranger?"

He shifted to more fully face her. "I'm not saying this way of shooting should become the bread and butter of your business. I don't even know if that's feasible. What I *am* suggesting is that if you open the door for magic, you're more likely to find it, and practicing something outside the realm of normal can be the turning of the doorknob."

He continued, "You may not sell a single photo if you put two people together who don't know each other, but you *will* begin to think differently. That's what you're after. The mindset shift is what'll bring in the money, not necessarily the experiment itself. Then again, you might stumble upon something that becomes the next great thing. At the very least, if you do try it, you could potentially get some marketing shots."

She glanced up at the photo frozen on the screen of the two of them, lip to lip, then turned back to Jex. "How would I even get started?"

He nodded toward the screen. "You've already got a feel for it, but to finetune, you could grab a photogenic friend who's single and willing to help. Then recruit as compatible a partner as you can find for her. But just make sure the two of them have never met."

She couldn't help but feel skeptical. "Okay. Let's say I get a couple of people to agree to this. Then what?"

"Then set up a shoot, maybe somewhere not so traditional, but definitely scenic. After that, do what you do best. But make sure there's a reveal where they see each other for the first time. You could even use blindfolds."

"That's a novel idea." She smirked.

"That's where the magic happens." He took a sip of his water. "Before, during, and after the reveal, you shoot like a shutterbug. Then, when the edits are done, use the photos to advertise. You might get more hits than you can handle."

"What if the chemistry isn't there? It sounds risky to me."

"The Dalai Lama once said, 'great love and great achievements involve great risk.'"

She grinned. "So, a Tibetan Buddhist would think this is a great idea."

"Don't you?"

She nodded at the screen. "How did you know you'd get that moment with me?"

"I didn't. But even without sharing personal details, it's pretty evident that we enjoy some of the same things, not the least of which is capturing exactly the right moment. And for me, that was enough to try the shot."

An experiment, she thought. Carly wilted a little inside. What had felt so exhilarating a few hours ago was just an experiment.

"Showing rather than telling you seemed like it would be more convincing." He shrugged. "I think it's an unexplored avenue with some tremendous potential."

All staging. She smiled tentatively, mentally kicking herself for misreading his cues. "Why haven't *you* tried doing this yourself instead of sharing it with me?"

"I was looking into it before I started work on my prototype, but I'm more into the hardware end of the business. You, though?"

Before she could answer, he added, "I think you could really find some success with this."

"I didn't have intentions of coming to Chicago to steal your ideas."

He waved a hand. "If you do this and it turns into something lucrative, I may have to come get mentoring from you." His dimples framed his smile.

He shut off the TV, and the image now emblazoned in her mind faded to black. "It's been a big day. We can talk more about business later. You wanna go with me to take a swim before dinner?"

She looked at the darkened screen again. This was a good thing, she tried to convince herself. At least now she knew it was business as usual for Jex. She turned to him, now clearer about their relationship. "As long as you're not a cannon-baller."

For a moment she couldn't believe she'd said that. Maybe Ava was right and some of her sass was coming back.

He laughed. "Guess you'll have to meet me poolside to find out."

Chapter Eleven

Jex

Jex had stepped into his closet, searching for his swim trunks, when his phone rang. Natalie's face flashed on the screen, and he swiped to accept the call. "Hey, Sis."

"You don't sound dejected, so I'm guessing our plan's working?"

"If you're talking about Bee helping me with the Hughley spread, we had a great session today, and I was even straight up with her beforehand, asked for her help. She took some impressive shots with the prototype, too."

"So, you told her she looked a lot like your former fiancée?"

"I didn't see a need to bring *that* part up."

Natalie sighed. "Just as well, I guess. Listen, speaking of the she-devil, Marla logged into the photography forum recently. Seemed like she was digging around for you."

"Why do that? She could just call if she wanted to talk to me."

"You two weren't exactly on the best of terms when she left, as I remember. Anyway, she started asking questions about Hughley, and that's got me feeling a little uneasy. It's like she's trying to network around you. How much did she know about this project?"

"She was at the first meeting, so she made connections there. If she's prodded around any, she could very well know as much as I do. You think she's got something up her sleeve?"

"Hopefully not, but I thought you might want to be on the lookout."

"Yeah, thanks, Nat. I'll do that."

With no natural segue, she asked, "Aren't you gonna give me any more details on little Miss Honeybee?"

"Well, um, she's great. Some real talent. And I think I've got her thinking about some new options for her business."

"Anything else?"

"What do you mean?" He knew his sister was digging, but he wasn't going to give any details without making her work for them.

"The obvious, Jex. Come on."

He sighed. "No, nothing more than business." His thoughts wound back to the last photo on the slideshow, to the single second he'd captured when his lips touched hers. His heartbeat ramped up. "I should probably go. She's here for only a few more hours unless she decides to stay a couple of extra days. We've still got ground to cover."

"Unless she decides to stay?" Her voice rose inquisitively.

"Yeah, I offered her the option, just so we could troubleshoot the Hughley spread and maybe talk through a few more ideas."

Natalie's sarcasm oozed through the phone. "Sure, yeah. You're falling like a rock in the water."

"Falling for what?"

"Her, ya goofball."

He sighed. "If you're finished, I think I'll go for a swim."

"She going too?"

"Goodbye, Sis."

"No, wait. I have to tell you one more thing. I've got to send you a release form."

Jex could hear papers shuffling on the other end of the line. "For what?"

"Honeybee. Have you forgotten so soon that she has to give permission for you to use her likeness in any of your commercial photos?"

"Oh, yeah. That."

"Yeah, that," Natalie quipped. "She's got to sign her real name though, so you'll have to convince her to share that little tidbit with you before she leaves."

"I'm working on that. Just send the forms to the printer here, and I'll ask her to sign."

Jex ended the call and set his phone on the bathroom countertop. While he undressed, questions about Marla began rolling through his mind. He wondered what his ex *did* know about his business with Hughley.

What's she up to? he wondered.

He shook off the distraction, pulled his swim trunks from a drawer, and suited up. Maybe a few laps would clear his head.

After finding the living room empty, Jex knocked on Bee's bedroom door, but she didn't answer. She must've already left for the pool.

The vision of her in the tunic she wore yesterday played in his thoughts, and he smiled as he headed for the elevator.

The Olympic-sized pool sat beneath the seasonal, glass-paned enclosure, imposing enough that anyone who didn't know better would have assumed it was a permanent fixture. A contracted maintenance crew would gradually remove it in a few weeks for the summer.

When Jex stepped past the entry door, he didn't see Bee at first and thought he may have left her behind in the apartment after all. He draped his towel over one of the loungers and moved to the water. Stepping onto the top rung of the pool ladder, he didn't hear Bee running up behind him until it was too late.

The unexpected shove came out of nowhere, and all he saw next was Bee's balled-up body splitting the water's surface above him and the bubbles rising in an effervescent gush as they both shoved off the pool bottom. When he emerged, he took in air and slung his hair away from his face. As the water cleared from his eyes, he turned, and Bee surfaced behind him, laughing hysterically after she came up.

Between breaths, he called out, "Here I thought you were all quiet and reserved. Holding out on me, were you?"

"I didn't say *I* wasn't a cannonballer." She cupped her hands and sent an arc of water straight across his face. When he shook it off, she'd already headed into a heated freestyle stroke toward the far end of the pool. He dived after her and came up, pushing toward her with his most efficient stroke, but she was much faster than he expected. Only in the last couple of meters at the opposite edge of the pool did he catch up.

After surfacing, he drew in a hard breath. "Where'd you learn how to swim like that?"

"Strip pits." Bee's breathing matched his.

"Strip pits?"

"Yeah." She swiped her hair away from her eyes. "We don't have rooftop pools where I'm from. When I was growing up, one of the local open-pit coal mines in my county was abandoned. After it filled with water, it was the teenagers' swimming hole. We used to race laps, and I was the strip-pit swim champ three summers in a row."

"What a title." He laughed. "Guess I'll have to step up my game then."

"Is that a challenge?"

He shrugged. "Why not?"

Before he could get ready, she yelled, "Go!"

Pushing off the side, she dug deep trenches into the water.

He took a breath and shoved off just afterward. Beneath the surface, he could see her attractive figure in the sleek sky-blue one-piece she'd chosen from the closet. The suit hugged her slender figure in all the right ways—a vision he chased as he skimmed the water behind her.

About halfway across the pool, he managed to get within reach of her feet. In three more solid strokes, he stretched closer to her knees. With a hard dig, he dived beneath the water and grabbed her waist, coming to the surface with her in his arms.

They both drew breath at the same time. When she opened her eyes, he laughed out loud as water streamed from her eyelashes. He held her tightly as she tugged against his grasp.

"You're a cheater!" she squealed.

"I was planning to win. That's all."

"By holding the competition back from the finish? Haven't you heard? It doesn't count if you cheat." After another couple of seconds, she stopped resisting so fervently, and he gradually loosened his hold. As she slid deeper into the water against him, they came eye to eye.

His labored breathing, in time with hers, began to slow. He took in the lines of her smile, watched the beads of water slide down her face. "I had a great time today," he told her. Not exactly the most earth-shattering comment, but the whole afternoon had been a breath of fresh air—the reassurance he'd needed that maybe dating again wasn't such a bad idea after all.

She blinked against the drops of water in her lashes, then looked into his eyes. "I did too."

"I almost kissed you back at the Tower," he admitted before he could stop himself.

"I know." She paused, started to say something, then looked as if she'd changed her mind. "Staging for the photo."

"No." He searched her expression. "I really did want to kiss you . . . like I do right now."

Chapter Twelve

Carly

With his lips close to hers, the tingle of Jex's breath against Carly's wet skin felt cool and tantalizing.

He drew her closer.

Her heartbeat quickened as he leaned in and left a whisper of a kiss at the corner of her mouth. Then, with the slightest movement, his lips brushed the other side, every graze building tension in her like the winding up of a clock.

When his lips finally fully touched hers, a current pulsed between them. The burst of a live wire weaving a feverish trail straight to her core.

Tender at first, then firmer, he left her more breathless than ever.

At first, she'd stiffened, every nerve inside her garnering attention, but now, she found herself in a strange, new place, melting like a heated candle into his embrace. Kissing him back. Her arms rose to his shoulders, her fingers tracing the back of his neck, touching skin she'd never touched, but relishing in the sensation of him as if she'd somehow found home.

She'd missed a man's arms around her. Missed the tingling feeling of being mutually needed. As if she were indulging in some luxury that had been withheld from her, she savored the taste of it all. The taste of him.

Then, just as suddenly as it had begun, he pulled away. Now breathless himself, he bowed his head. "I'm sorry. I shouldn't have—"

Carly shook her head, but no words came. Only awkwardness. With machine-gun speed, her brain immediately began firing a barrage of self-blame. What was she thinking letting him kiss her? She'd opened herself up to . . . whatever this was. She'd come here to make professional changes. And then this? "No, I'm sorry. I just—"

He raised his hand and touched her lips, silencing her. "It was me. I got caught up in the moment. I should never have moved in like that."

She stepped back. "It's okay."

He turned a little and cast his eyes away. "Let's just rewind a few minutes, forget this happened, . . . enjoy a good, hard swim. I cut my run short this morning and need a few solid laps anyway."

She nodded. "You go ahead. I may take a break, sit poolside for a while."

"We're good, right?"

She nodded again.

He quickly added, "I'd still like you to stay this weekend. That is, if you want to. I hope I haven't given you the wrong impression."

She stepped to the pool's edge. "I don't want you to get the wrong impression of me either."

"We're on the same page, then." He smiled awkwardly. "Last I remember, I had the job of earning some trust. Hopefully, I haven't blown it."

At first, she didn't respond, the bombardment of self-criticism still ringing in her head. "It's fine."

His faint smile faded as he nodded toward the far end of the pool. "Good. I'll just get those laps in. When you're ready, we can order some dinner."

He turned as if a little unsure, then split the water with a dive. When he resurfaced, he was halfway across the pool, moving away in a dead heat.

Carly breathed deeply for the first time in what felt like ten minutes. Her eyes followed him as he glided through the water, watched beads trickle in the creases and curves of his muscles with every stroke he made.

When he turned at the other end and headed back in her direction, she knew that the protective walls she'd put up before she came to Chicago were now a little shakier.

Chapter Thirteen

Jex

In their remaining half hour at the pool, Jex had tried breaking through the awkwardness between them by talking about the boat tour and the little cafe they'd visited for lunch. For the most part, he thought it had worked. Bee had begun to ease into ready smiles once he'd finished laps and they'd talked poolside for a while.

He still didn't know what had come over him, what one thing had led him to kiss her. The race across the pool? The way she looked in that swimsuit? Her playfulness in the water? Maybe it wasn't just one thing. Maybe it had *all* caught up with him without warning. Ended in something he didn't see coming.

The kiss had scared him.

He'd never imagined having a woman in his presence for less than a day and getting close enough to kiss her. Was it because she looked so much like Marla? He shook off the thought just as quickly as it formed, realizing how ludicrous it was. The longer he was around Bee, the wider the gap between her and Marla became.

The thought kept resurfacing that they may have looked similar, but Bee was different . . . in all the best ways.

By the time they got back to the apartment, their conversation had settled into more comfortable chatter, like they'd been . . . friends . . . for more than a day.

As he opened the door, the printer at the corner desk in the living room spit out two sheets of paper.

"The office calling?" Bee nodded toward the sound of the printer.

"Likely my sister." Jex crossed the room and picked up the forms in the tray. "She's my VA. She helped set up your visit here. And this?" He held up the papers. "Is a release form. It gives me permission to use the photos I took of you in my spread and any of yours you'd be willing to contribute to the cause. But only if you're still good with that." He set the papers down on the table. "No pressure. Just a formality."

"I'll have to admit, when I left Alabama, I didn't expect to be the subject for a prototype campaign."

Facing away from her, he grinned a little, wondering if she'd even realized she'd let that little nugget about her home state slip.

"Especially after the editing touch-ups, which should be light, you'll see exactly how perfect you are for that spread. Anyway"—he nodded at the papers— "I'll fill out my part and pass it on to you when I'm done." He looked up at her hopefully. "The only thing is, I'll need your real name. Maybe you wouldn't mind sharing that with me considering we've gotten to know each other . . . a little better since you first got here."

She looked as if she were holding back a grin but didn't reply.

He eyed her as she towel-dried her hair. "I'll leave you to decide."

Though Jex suspected from the way they'd both been able to socially recover from their kiss in the last hour that she'd sign the papers, a nagging feeling left him wondering if he should tell her the whole truth about Marla and his need for a similar-looking model. That kind of news surely wouldn't lean in his favor after what had happened at the pool. Bee would definitely think he was out to scam her if she knew. But he didn't feel right keeping anything from her either.

"I think I'll grab a quick shower," Bee said.

"Perfect. I'll order dinner, and I think I'll follow you. I mean, I think I'll get a shower myself." Trying to over-correct, his next words felt hurried. "Then we can get to work after we eat. Have any cravings?"

"No." Bee grinned and turned for her bedroom, then called back, "You've done a great job picking so far."

"So, I must've earned a little trust then."

"Maybe a shred."

"I'll take it."

As Bee disappeared into the bedroom, Jex speed-dialed for Greek food, placed his usual order times two, and turned his attention back to the forms Natalie had forwarded.

He grabbed a pen from the desk drawer, and after filling out his information, he came to Bee's section. The thought of soon knowing her real identity sent a little shiver of an unidentifiable something through him. Maybe it was genuine excitement.

Ironic, he thought, that the whole time he'd known Marla, she'd been a fake—for the sake of selling her image—yet she'd used her real name. And Bee had been nothing but genuine. He had no doubts that he got exactly what he saw with her. Yet, he didn't even know her real name.

Before showering, Jex opened his laptop and tapped a few keys on the keyboard. The slideshow of photos from earlier began to play again. The differences in the two women became clearer by the second. And the more obvious they became, the more he found himself drawn to Bee. And the more convinced that full disclosure about Marla was necessary.

He rose, set the pen on the table with the release papers, and crossed the hall to her bedroom. Outside the door, he started to knock, then paused, then raised his hand to the door again.

Yes, he *would* do it. He would tell her everything. It wasn't worth the worry of keeping it from her or wondering how she'd react. Maybe it wouldn't be such a big deal if he just told her the dilemma he was in and shared how it all worked out perfectly for them to mutually help each other.

As he drew closer to the door, the whisperings of her shower spoke from the other side. He decided it could wait until dinner.

On the TV screen, he left the photos of Bee and the shots of the two of them at the Ledge playing in an endless loop.

Chapter Fourteen

Carly

After getting dressed, Carly stepped into the living room. The guest bathroom's rainforest shower, quite different from her water-conserving Delta back home, had refreshed her, and washed off some of the lingering angst from earlier.

Nowhere to be seen, Jex must've still been showering. She smiled at his earlier slip of the tongue and glanced toward the towering lakeside window. Stepping closer than she had since coming to the apartment, she eased toward the view. When she began to feel her insides rise into her throat, she turned away. Maybe she was just hungry, and her stomach was battling with itself for lack of food. She hoped that Jex had placed an order that would arrive soon.

On the table, she noticed the paperwork that the printer had spit out earlier. Scanning the forms, she noted that they all had typical, wordy legalese. Sooner or later, she'd have to get used to forms like these if she were to use her own client's likenesses for business purposes like Jex suggested.

After browsing the last page, she sat down at the table and twirled the pen, considering signing her real name in the designated spot. She thought about the weekend's events.

About Jex.

Pushing the kiss aside, she focused on those things about their time together that felt, somehow, sure. Because, from experience, she knew what she could gut-check as sure, led to people she could trust.

First, he was reliable. That was clear enough. Keeping his commitment to a weekend helping her hammer out some fresh ideas for her business was no small thing.

He was credible. Definitely knew photography inside and out, just as she had expected.

Considerate. She'd never foreseen him treating her to a day on the town or to helping her overcome one of her biggest fears.

He was also adventurous. The hour at the Ledge had proved that.

Exciting . . . and maybe even a little dangerous in an alluring kind of way. A man on a motorcycle always was.

And that kiss . . .

She shook her head to push back the memory.

Despite her efforts, she couldn't.

He'd stopped their kiss, though, maybe in consideration of her reservations.

At the end of this mental list, she cleared her mind and drew the bottom line.

Spinning the pen again, she really couldn't think of an excuse not to sign the papers. In fact, based on her reason for coming to Chicago in the first place, Jex had given her more direction to boost her business than she'd ever bargained for. She'd have enough to do when she got home to keep her busy for months as she implemented the new ideas.

Finally, she set the pen to paper, but before making the first stroke, Jex's phone rang. Since it wasn't her place, she didn't answer it but instead stepped to the hall and called out to Jex.

He cracked the door. "That's probably our food at the front desk. I'll finish dressing and go get it. Just give me a few minutes."

His being partially dressed on the other side of that door put a little heat in her cheeks.

Carly returned to the table and, after sitting again, tapped the pen against the paper in no particular rhythm. She could wait for Jex to finish up, but her stomach growled in protest. She could likely go downstairs and bring the food back up before he even had time to finish dressing.

On the elevator ride down, she smiled to herself and made a point of turning toward the glass so she could see the open space beyond. At first, her stomach rose as the elevator began its descent, but then, with a controlled breath, she took a step away from the door. *Small strides*, she thought.

When the elevator doors opened, she rounded the corner to the concierge desk with a little livelier step.

Addison stood behind the counter attending to a woman in a pink outfit, complete with a brimmed hat large enough to keep distance between her and anyone with the thought of getting marginally close.

As Carly walked up to the desk and the woman strutted away, her hat brim rode the wave of her steps, the air heavy with the scent of gardenia in her wake. In the bright pink suit, she looked as if she were a walking mannequin, proportioned with all the right measurements.

Carly stepped up to the desk, and with one glance, noticed an expression of utter confusion coloring Addison's face. He didn't speak at first and Carly jumped in to clarify. "Remember me? It's Bee. I'm just coming down to get the delivery you called about for Jex Radcliffe."

He continued to stare at her oddly, then looked past her at the retreating figure in pink. "Uh, of course. Just a moment. I'll step in the office and get it." As he turned, he looked over his shoulder again, confusion coloring his expression, then disappeared into a room behind the desk.

Carly wondered at Addison's strange look. After a moment, he returned with two white bags—one filled with to-go boxes and a smaller one, likely containing utensils and napkins.

"Thank you, Mr. Addison."

"Yes, of course." He frowned as if he were going to say something but thought better of it. He shook his head instead. "I kept the food warm. Hopefully, you'll enjoy it."

Something about the way Addison spoke felt stilted. He began to shuffle some papers behind the desk, suddenly appearing very busy. "You have a good night, Miss Bee."

She nodded and turned toward the elevators, wondering at his behavior.

One of four people getting in the elevator, Carly paid little attention to the others and entered the side closest to the keypad. She punched the twelve button, and to the back of her, the other passengers called out their numbers: one man asked for the third floor; another, the seventh; and the last—a female voice—demanded with a pompous tone, "Twelfth floor and make it snappy, please."

Not your bell boy, Carly thought. "Already pushed." She held in the Southern sass she'd ordinarily have dished out to anyone acting disrespectful and instead faced forward, enjoying the smell of Greek food wafting from the bags. The ride would be short enough.

When the second of the two men vacated at his stop, the doors closed, and she hefted the bag holding the food to a more comfortable position while she waited for floor twelve.

As the elevator dinged and the doors opened, the snooty-voiced woman blew past her and inadvertently knocked the utensils bag from her hand. The wide-brimmed, Pepto-Bismol colored hat looked more like a tire-sized, pink pancake than headwear. The woman never even looked back, never acknowledged the mishap.

Carly knelt in the elevator car in a huff of frustration to collect the utensils as the entry to the twelfth floor disappeared behind the closing doors. Before she could punch the open button, the car descended again. Her stomach growled, and so did she.

Chapter Fifteen

Jex

J ex finished towel-drying his hair and emerged from the bedroom in a fresh pair of jeans and a white t-shirt. He passed by Bee's door, but she wasn't in her room. When he stepped into the living room, it was empty. The kitchen and dining rooms were just as vacant.

For a moment, his heart rate accelerated. Had the kiss offended Bee more than he'd realized? Had she taken the moment alone to pack and leave?

After stepping back to her bedroom door and seeing a few of her things still there, he took a breath and realized that she'd probably decided not to wait for him and gone to the front desk for their food on her own.

While he waited, he gazed again at the photos left playing on the TV screen. He paused the slideshow at the picture of Bee and him in their near kiss at the Tower.

Man, that shot. Who was he kidding? The shot was fantastic, but it was the near kiss that set off the quiver of excitement stealing its way down his spine.

That *near* kiss . . . that led to the full-length one in the pool.

All the thoughts playing in his head kindled a spark that he hadn't felt in a long time. If he were honest, maybe he'd never felt it before at all.

He'd been attracted to different girls at different times in his life, and he'd even been close enough to Marla to propose marriage, but he still didn't know how it had gotten so far with her. When he spent time looking back on it, maybe she'd pushed the proposal more than he had, but dragging up those memories was painful, and something he'd rather avoid.

This thing with Bee, though, had come on so quickly. He couldn't deny that she'd stirred up feelings that he didn't yet know how to process. Maybe that was why he'd pulled back when they kissed. He wanted more. Craved more. But this time it had to be different. He had to slow things down to make sure it was real.

When the doorbell rang, he reigned in his thoughts, crossed the foyer, and reached for the door with a smile. "You must be as hungry as I—"

When Marla Fairchild came into view, she lifted the wide brim of her monstrous pink hat and cocked her head, a wicked grin spreading across her face. "Why, yes, I'm famished."

Jex's jaw went slack. "Marla, what're you doing here?"

She walked up to him, lifting his chin with the touch of a pink-gloved finger. "Close that, baby. It's not becoming of you."

Stripping the hat from her head and sending it across the bar like a well-placed frisbee, she strutted across the room, a few loose curls freely flowing from her up-do. Approaching the nearest barstool, she sat, spun to face him, and pointed to herself. "I am here to resurrect your career."

Audacity oozed from her like burning lava. Anybody could see that she had no lack of self-confidence.

Jex walked forward, at first tentatively, then with more determination, his confusion turning to anger. "Marla, I'm not—"

"You don't have to say a word. I know your photo spread with Calvin Hughley is coming due. I've been keeping up with these things. And, despite our untimely and unsavory breakup, I couldn't very well watch you crash and burn and not help you. I owe you at least that since we were engaged."

"You don't owe me anything. In fact, I don't *want* anything from you."

"Of course, you do." She spun away from him in the stool, stood, and caught sight of the image on the TV screen. Stopping dead in her tracks, she first straightened her neck as if something had struck her square in the face. Then she slowly turned to Jex, her gaze still glued to the screen. "And what might this be?" Her words were slow, deliberate. Enunciated.

Jex reached for her arm, and with a stern voice said, "Marla, you need to leave."

She jerked away before he even touched her. "Oh, no. I don't think that's going to happen until I find out exactly what's been going on here. And who is *that*?" She pointed at the screen as if she were calling attention to a mangy dog.

"It's no one you need to know about."

"She looks enough like me, with the exception of that big head, that I think I very well should know about her."

"Come on. It's time to go. I'll talk to you about it another time. Right now, I'm busy."

"With what?" She looked again at the photo on the screen.

Jex's eyes trailed to the screen too. Bee's lips, barely touching his, looked more sensuous than ever.

"Or maybe I should ask with *whom*?" Marla snapped.

Before Jex could answer, he heard a bag drop to the countertop behind him.

"Bee." There was a pause. "My name is Bee."

Marla spun around. At first, she stared as if mesmerized. Then she smirked. "Well, now. Aren't we just . . . analogous." She said the word as if it were soaked in lemon juice.

Bee looked at Jex. Her expression asked for an explanation. "I don't understand. Who is this?" A hurt-filled frown, born out of recognition, dulled her eyes. "You had another motive for inviting me to Chicago, didn't you?"

Jex felt the blood drain from his face. "No. Yes. It's not what you're thinking." Anxiety stuck in his throat like an unswallowed pill. He shook his head. "I just need to explain."

Marla capitalized on the moment. "Well, I see that Jex no longer has command of his manners. So allow me. I'm Marla Fairchild, Jex's former fiancée." She raised one gloved hand to her cheek and lowered her voice. "Just between the two of us, I'm still trying to decide if I want to take him back."

Jex cut in before she could do more damage. "Marla's leaving."

Ignoring his comment, she patted him on the cheek, never taking her eyes off Bee. "Hmm. The look on your face tells me this lovely man didn't tell you."

"Marla. Stop." Jex tried to intercede again, but Marla continued as if he hadn't spoken.

"Why don't I fill you in since I've recently become more privy myself. You see, Jex is getting ready to be honored at the next Digital Imagists Awards ceremony with his forthcoming prototype. You probably already know that though. He's quite the genius, but despite that, he didn't get all the kinks worked out of his production schedule. He obviously couldn't get me to do this photoshoot." She flourished one glove-clad hand at the TV as if she were a model displaying the winning lotto balls.

"So," she continued, "he had to get a temporary replacement. Looks like you were the lucky winner since the developers really wanted my face. I will say, I *am* quite surprised. He actually did a decent job of finding a *reasonable* representation of me." She looked Bee up and down. "With a little attention, you'd clean up."

Jex raised his hand as if putting it between Marla and Bee would shut Marla up.

"Stop." He clenched his jaw. The contempt seething from all the insults had already done irreparable damage. "Wait for me on the terrace, Marla. I'd like to talk to Bee alone."

"Silly man, of course I'm not waiting for you on the terrace." She waved a hand as if to shoo off his ridiculous idea. "And besides, there's no need. I've got a dinner appointment with Calvin Hughley. His driver's waiting for me as we speak." She strutted toward the door. "You two have a delightful time eating your Greek cuisine." She cupped a hand toward Bee as if to whisper but spoke in a regular voice. "He ordered that for me too. Not a favorite."

Scooping up her hat, Marla then stopped just short of the door and turned. "Oh, and Jex, sweetness, I'm so glad you won't have to stick with this one." She flitted a hand toward Bee. "Why, you'd have to Photoshop a whole new person out of her. Take out some size from that hair, add some color and definition to her cheeks. She looks absolutely gray in those photos. And as for the posing, she just doesn't bring experience to the table." She slipped the hat back on and tucked a curl beneath its crown. "Anyway, I'll be in touch so we can straighten out this mess you've made."

With the final nail driven, she strutted through the door, never bothering to close it.

When Jex finally dared to look at Bee, she stood at the counter, touching her hair as if she'd tuck it away underneath a hat of her own choosing, if an inconspicuous one were close by.

Chapter Sixteen

Carly

Jex spoke first. "Bee, I—"

"Stop." Carly pushed the bags of food across the counter. "Here's your dinner. It's still warm."

He brushed a hand through his hair, noticeably frustrated. "You have to let me explain. Let's sit down and talk."

She turned to go to the bedroom. "I think that time has passed."

Jex followed her. She didn't bother trying to close the door. He was on her heels, turning with her every turn, stepping in quick movement with her every step. "You don't understand."

"Exactly." She pulled her carry-on to the bed and opened it with enough force to rip the teeth on the zipper.

"I never planned for this to happen."

"Obviously." She crossed the room and raked free the few hangers she'd used from their closet bar. "I could see the surprise in your eyes when I met your fiancé."

"*Ex*-fiancé. And that's not what I mean." He followed her back to the bed. "Yes, you and Marla look alike. Yes, I needed help with the spread. *Your* help. But—"

"But what, Jex?" She faced him, holding back tears, trying desperately not to allow her eyes to betray her. "I trusted you, and you used me." Her arm brushed against him as she turned for the bathroom.

"You don't know the whole story. I wanted to be honest with you, but would you have really come to Chicago if I told you I needed a model that looked like my ex-fiancé?"

Carly shoved her toiletries from the bathroom counter into her overnight bag, then stormed back to her luggage, slammed the last of her things in the bag, and zipped it shut.

"Would you?" he persisted.

"No." She put a hand to her forehead. "Look, I appreciate the ideas you shared these last couple of days. You showed me a few things I didn't know, gave me some good business advice, but this is where it ends." She grabbed her jacket, backpack, and carry-on, and whisked past him.

Following her to the front door, Jex pleaded, "Bee, come on. Let me at least explain."

"My name is not Bee." She stopped but didn't turn around. "You know, I almost signed that release form a few minutes ago with my real name. I thought for a second that I could trust you." She hefted the backpack to her shoulder and tightened the grip on her luggage. "Goodbye, Jex."

Coming out of the elevator, Carly saw Addison stationed at the desk. He gave her a knowing glance and tipped his head in acknowledgment. At the very least, she understood now why Addison had mistaken her for Marla, why he'd given her such strange looks.

He'd probably kept quiet because his loyalties lay in tending to the tenants who paid his salary. As angry and hurt as she was, she couldn't fault him for that.

After a couple of minutes streetside waiting to hail a taxi, she sank into the backseat of the yellow cab and, with a shuddering breath, let the first gush of emotion engulf her.

From the time she'd walked in on Marla and Jex to the moment she'd caught the cab in front of the Emerald, she'd held back tears for a sum total of fifteen minutes.

Marla had come and gone like an Alabama tornado, Jex had tried to talk his way out of his deception, and she'd held herself together long enough to deny him the pleasure of seeing she was so deeply affected.

But now, she allowed the dam to break. Every gut-wrenching feeling she'd experienced just over a year ago with Hunter flooded back in. The lies, the secrets, being taken advantage of. She'd told herself that after the breakup with Hunter, she'd never put herself in that position again, yet here she was, in the back of a taxi driving away from heartbreak and being lied to. Again.

As they crossed the city, the scene with Marla played out in her head on a continuous reel, turning her stomach with every frame. She tried to understand what would possess someone to be as cruel as Jex—and Marla—had been to her.

Weirdly enough, she understood Marla. Spending less than ten minutes with her, anybody could size her up as a bubblegum-pink-clad narcissist. But in the two days she'd spent with Jex, for the life of her, she couldn't understand how she could've so completely misjudged him, so nearly let him into her life.

Taking every precaution, she'd let her guard down just enough to begin to care, and even for a fraction of a second thought they might've found something in each other to at least explore on a deeper-than-surface level.

She sat back in the seat of the cab and watched as the cityscape she'd seen from the top of Willis Tower passed from her view.

Funny, she thought, how from that Tower she'd worked on overcoming one fear only to once again make herself vulnerable to being hurt by another.

Pulling a wrinkled tissue from her backpack, she patted her face dry and drew in a deep breath. Her emotional walls began to reform.

She was going home.

Chapter Seventeen

Jex

The Mediterranean smells coming from the bags of food left on the counter turned Jex's stomach, then dissipated as one hour turned into two. Bee's words echoed in his head on repeat. *I thought for a second that I could trust you.*

He should have told her everything. The risk up front would have been easier than her now believing he was a liar.

He sat on the couch staring at the photo still displayed on the TV screen as the sky beyond the glass of the large living room window darkened to a light-polluted dusk.

When the phone rang, Jex ignored it as he had the previous calls before it. Two rings, three, then four. He finally answered.

"Jex Radcliffe, I was beginning to think you were dead. I've been calling for hours now. Where are you?" Natalie's snappy question did little to elicit any positive energy.

"At the apartment." His voice was abrupt and somber.

"You sound weird. What happened?"

He looked to the waterfront at a boat lit up on the lake. "Marla showed up today."

"What do you mean, Marla showed up?"

"She came here."

"While Bee was there?" Natalie's voice rose an octave.

"Yep."

"So, I take it things didn't go so well."

"Pretty much a total disaster."

"What did she say?" Natalie asked.

"Who? Marla? She waltzed in here like she owned the place and me with it, implied that she was still in the picture, that I needed a reasonable facsimile of her to do the shoot because of scheduling conflicts, and that Bee was the flawed, if necessary, replacement I should now ditch because she obviously didn't measure up."

"Seriously? How did you ever get mixed up with her?"

"I don't want to talk about that."

Natalie sighed on the other end. "And what about Bee?"

"She's gone. Left a couple of hours ago."

"Did you explain to her—"

"I tried, Nat, but she wouldn't listen. She thinks I lied and that I'm nothing but a bottom-dweller."

"But you didn't lie . . . did you?"

"Of course not. I just didn't have time to tell her about the whole fiasco with Marla or all the details about the Hughley project. I honestly had plans to tell her everything over dinner. I just didn't get the chance."

"I guess that explains why Marla's been poking around in the forum. She had a plan to come back around all along."

"Yeah, and get this. She's having dinner tonight with Hughley. Who knows what'll come of that."

Had Natalie been in the room with him, he knew he'd have seen fire in her eyes, the same kind currently burning a hole in the pit of his stomach.

She reigned her voice into business mode. "Okay. We can do damage control here. Let's just think this through."

"Bee's gone, Sis. She hadn't even told me her real name yet. We were just getting to that."

"Did she sign the release?"

"What does it matter? I'm not concerned about the release."

"We'd have a shot at this contract without dealing with Marla if—"

He slowed what he said next. "I don't care about the contract, Nat."

The connection went silent for a moment.

"You started liking her, didn't you?" Natalie asked.

Jex leaned his head against the window. "She's not like Marla, at all. I mean, yeah, they look similar, but Bee's . . . real."

"Oh, my stars. You *did* start liking her. How did I know that would happen? I called it, didn't I?"

He paused before responding. "Yeah, I guess you did."

"Okay, Jex, we've got to segment here."

"What are you talking about?"

"Divide and conquer. That's what I'm saying. You've got to separate your professional life from your personal life for a minute, or both are going down in flames."

"I'm not looking for ways to fail here, okay?"

"I know. I know." She audibly exhaled. "But let's just talk through this and figure out your next steps."

Jex could practically hear his sister's cogs turning, and though she was a natural-born problem solver, he wasn't in the mood to troubleshoot. "What do you suggest?"

"Business first," she said. "With Marla schmoozing Hughley, we don't know what's up her sleeve, so we'll have to ride that storm out until she makes her intentions known. My guess is she's still fully planning on making her mark on this campaign. Whatever her plans, though, you have to get that prototype in front of Hughley."

"I don't even know if it's worth it anymore."

"Of course it is, Jex. This is your big chance. You can't just throw it away."

"I never wanted to, but who knows what Marla's thinking?"

"Just wait a day or two. Knowing her, my money says she's gonna let you know. You've got to keep your head wrapped around getting Hughley what he's looking for. In the meantime, we'll work through any challenges Marla throws at us." She paused. "Promise me you're not giving up on this."

Giving up would mean Marla had bested him; not only used him as her step ladder, but threatened his dream in the process. "How are we supposed to make this work?"

"I don't know yet, but we will." After a moment's silence, she continued. "What exactly happened to you this weekend?"

Jex's thoughts went to Bee. "Let's save that for later."

"We could, but I know you too well. You're stewing on something. We might as well talk about it now."

He impatiently rubbed at the stubble on his jaw and sat back on the couch. "All I know is that I've never felt more at peace, more at home, than I did in the two days she was here. Somehow, she just fit."

"Fit into what? Your weekend? Your career? Your life?"

He sighed. "I don't know yet."

"Okay. Do you know for sure that she's gone? I mean, it sounds like she left before she could change her departing flight. Maybe she's still in the city or at the airport."

"You should have seen the look in her eyes. Even if she is still here, she wouldn't listen to anything I have to say."

"How do you know that if you haven't tried? Heaven help me for saying this, but get off your butt and go goose the throttle of that bike of yours. If she's all you claim she is, then you should try to clear the air with her."

"I don't know, Nat."

"Stop stalling. You don't exactly have much to lose."

Something in Jex's chest tightened. Maybe Natalie was right. Maybe he should've already gone after her. His breathing slowly increased, along with his heart rate as hope stirred inside him. He paced alongside the window, ran a worried hand through his hair, and finally asked, "Do you really think I could get her to listen?"

"Probably not, but who knows? You flash that Jexy grin at her, and you might get lucky. The point is you'll always wonder if you don't try, so go. Find her."

"I'll call you later." He tossed the phone on the couch, and in one swift motion jumped the ottoman like it was an Olympic hurdle. Snatching his jacket from the foyer closet, he didn't even check the door behind him to see if it was locked. Past the elevator, he took the stairs two steps at a time down thirteen floors to the basement. Within minutes, he'd tightened his helmet and spun out of the underground garage with the sound of his bike echoing down the avenue at high speed.

Jex took a gamble that Bee had decided to go back to Alabama instead of staying in the city, and with any luck, she'd arranged her flights out of Midway instead of O'Hare. It was closer to downtown Chicago, and with flights from either terminal equally expensive, he was guessing she'd have planned to save a few dollars on cab fares to and from the airport by traveling through Midway.

Minutes later, he exited the interstate and sped down South Cicero hoping by some miracle he wasn't too late. Approaching the airport, he leaned his bike into a curve and rounded into the terminal's daily parking lot. He claimed the closest available spot, threw down the kickstand with a hard jolt, and took off in a jog, undoing his helmet as he ran. Just inside the airport, the first open attendant he saw was at the Delta ticket counter. He approached her, tucking his helmet under his arm.

She had a pleasant face but gave the tired greeting of a worker on the last hour of her shift.

"How can I help you?"

He set the helmet on the counter. "I'm trying to locate someone I think may be flying out of this terminal. Can I get a passenger paged?"

"Of course. Do you know which airline?"

"No, I don't."

"What about the destination city?" the attendant asked.

"I don't know, but I do know she'd be going to Alabama."

"Delta handles a lot of the flights to Birmingham. I can make an all-call from here. What name?"

He bowed his head. "I know this is gonna sound strange. I just know her as Honeybee, but it's really important that I talk to her."

After an odd look from the attendant, she picked up a handset and conveyed the message over the terminal's PA. "Attention, please. Would a passenger by the name of Honeybee please report to the Delta ticket counter? Honeybee to the Delta ticket counter."

Jex thanked the attendant and backed away from the counter, his eyes peeled toward the concourse.

Chapter Eighteen

Carly

When Carly had arrived at Midway, she'd found a flight out of Chicago back to Birmingham via Atlanta. Paying an extra fifty bucks to secure the earlier departure wasn't in her plan, but neither was sleeping in the airport.

After settling into a chair at her gate, she tried to call Ava. She didn't know why. Ava couldn't do anything from Nashville. And Carly didn't really feel like wading through the details of her huge fail with Jex. Not right now, at least. But she was lonely. The kind of lonely that wants quiet company, that doesn't require heavy conversation but finds comfort when somebody cares enough to sit with you while you lick your wounds.

Unfortunately, Ava didn't answer.

She tossed the phone into her purse and sat staring at a stain on the dull gray carpet a few feet away.

"You look like you had to put down your childhood dog." The woman sitting across from Carly had a thick Southern accent that ebbed and flowed like a slow-rising tide.

Carly glanced up from the spot on the floor. "I'm sorry?"

The woman must've been in her late seventies. Her silver hair, cut in a fashionable bob, framed her face and softened the deep-creased wrinkles around her brown eyes. A set of half-frame readers sat perched on her nose, completing the friendly-grandmother look.

Working skillful but arthritic loops with a set of knitting needles, the woman's hands pulled at a strand of butter yellow yarn buried in a handbag at her feet.

"Sad, dear. You look sad. I've been sittin' here for the last fifteen minutes, and I don't think you've looked up from that Coke-cola spill on the carpet the whole time I've been here." She tugged again at the yarn. "My name's Lucille Brinkmeyer, but my friends call me Lucy. What's your name, honey?"

She almost said Bee, but the old woman's warm smile broke past her barrier. "I'm Carly. Carly Kirkpatrick."

"Beautiful name. Matches that lovely face of yours."

The woman's needles clicked together, and the sound oddly proved soothing. "Thank you." She tried to steer away from potential questions about her frame of mind and instead asked the woman what she was knitting.

"This? Oh, this is a chemo hat. I make 'em for the patients at the Cancer Institute in Atlanta." Her voice rose on the last two syllables as if she were asking a question more than making a statement. "It's one of the few things I'm still pretty handy with, even though my arthritis disagrees on occasion."

"I'm sure they're really glad to get them."

"The Institute? Yes. But the people comin' in for treatments? Not so much, I s'pose. It's one of those things nobody wants to have to wear, something that a patient comes to hate and appreciate all in the same stretch of time. At least, that's the way it was for me. I was diagnosed six years ago this Feb'wary." She grinned. "I lit my cap afire after I went into remission and my hair grew back a little. I looked like a little chia pet, but I didn't have to wear that dad-gum hat to keep my head warm."

The needles took up clicking again as she worked them between loops. "Anyway, this is what keeps my hands from atrophyin'. That and takin' care of my Warren." She nodded toward a hunchbacked little man browsing the literature section in one of the quick-buy shops across the way. "He's always after a new read. Would you believe he's a romantic? He loves a book with a little mystery and a good love story." She pulled the word 'love' out like a long string of taffy.

Carly watched the old man as he paged through a novel from one of the shelves. Something in Lucy's tone when she talked about him made Carly's heart billow a little.

"What about you, dear? What fills your time?"

Carly turned back to face Lucy. "Oh, uh, I'm a photographer."

"That sounds excitin'. But being from Atlanta, I can peg another Southerner quick as a snap. So, I imagine you're either just passin' through Chicago or here on a visit. Have you been takin' pictures in the city?"

"I did shoot a few photos, mostly a weekend trainin' of sorts." Carly could hear her own accent deepen in conversation with a kindred Southerner. "I'm headin' back to Alabama now."

"That must've been some solemn business. You look utterly dejected, dear."

Carly understood that the woman's observation might seem abrupt if overheard by someone else, but it was nothing more than the honest concern of a woman born and bred south of the Mason-Dixon. "Just . . . draining, I guess." She sighed and nodded back to the man at the book table. "How long have you two been together?"

"We married when I was nineteen and him twenty. That was fifty-nine years ago come New Year's Eve. We ran off together and said 'I do' at the stroke o' midnight. We've been runnin' off together and celebratin' new beginnin's ever since."

Carly smiled. "He sounds like a romantic."

"Yes indeed, new life, new adventures, new babies—we had five of 'em. And now sixteen grandchildren and four great-grandchildren. That's why we came to Chicago this weekend. One of our granddaughters graduated from medical school. It was wonderful to see all the family. Anyway, now I've got something new to celebrate right here. I've made a new friend."

"Don't know that I'd be much to throw a party over."

Lucy set her needles in her lap and folded her hands on top of the partially knitted hat. When she looked across the aisle at Carly with earnest eyes, her voice softened. "You know, sometimes talkin' to somebody you don't rightly know helps. What's got you so down, dear?"

"Nothing that a little time won't fix. I've been through it before, but I'm not planning on it ever happening again."

Lucy nodded. "Ah, would it be trouble with a man?"

"I don't have a man, so how can there be trouble, right?"

Lucy cocked an eyebrow. "Recent prospect?"

Carly hesitated, looked back at the stained carpet, and rubbed her arms.

"You don't have to say a word, honey. I already know the answer. Doesn't take an Einstein to figure out your heart's on the tender side this evenin'."

"So, do you have any advice for somebody whose biggest trouble is attracting an honest man?" For a minute, Carly couldn't believe she'd just handed her personal troubles over to a complete stranger.

"That's a tough one. Honesty's certainly essential, but—" She stopped, pursed her lips, and furrowed her brow.

Carly didn't expect there to be a *but*.

Lucy continued. "I s'pose I can leave you with only a cautionary tale—somethin' from my own experience."

The older woman rubbed at her boney knuckles before picking up the knitting needles again. "Back in my courtin' days, I was sweet on Warren for months. I mistakenly shared my feelin's with somebody I thought to be a friend. As it turned out, she was sweet on him too."

Lucy paused and focused on some long put-away thought. "Molly Ashbury. I haven't spoken that name in a while, but never will I forget that girl in all my livin' days." She tugged at the yarn. "Why, she built up the biggest story you ever heard. Told me all about how Warren was a ladies' man. And every time we went to a ball game or the skatin' rink, she'd pull out all the stops to prove it. 'Watch this,' she'd say. Then with a twist of her skirt, she'd truck right over to him and spend the rest of the night in a flirt-storm of her own making just to prove he was all about the girl in front of him." She chuckled. "I was so blinded by what Molly wanted me to see that I couldn't see the truth. Nearly shooed him away like a bitin' horsefly when I finally did get to talking to him one to one."

The lull and simmer in Lucy's voice brought smiles to Carly. "What happened?" she asked.

"Two years after we graduated, we were both home from college for Thanksgivin', and we bumped into each other at the soda stand. He asked me point-blank why I'd never given him the time of day."

Carly leaned forward in her seat. "And what did you say?"

"I just as plainly told him it was because I'd been warned about him. Said I'd watched him with my own eyes payin' attention to Molly. He laughed right out loud. Told me if I believed Molly Ashbury over him, I deserved to miss out on the date of a lifetime that he just so happened to have planned for me the very next day."

Her needles stopped clicking as she looked up at Carly. "I was put off, to say the least, but he just kept talking, kept ribbing me, and the more we talked, the more fun I had. It got me to thinkin' maybe I was trustin' the wrong person." She took up her needles again. "I've allowed him to spend the next fifty-nine years tellin' me 'I told you so.' It does a man's ego some good to be right about somethin' every once in a while, I reckon."

"Sounds like you two were made for each other."

"No question about that." Lucy winked. "Now, I don't know about your situation, but I'll tell you one thing I've learned. Somebody—and I don't recall who—once said there's two ways to be fooled. One? To believe what's not true; and the other, to refuse to believe what is. I've kept that thought pretty close to my heart over the years. It's served me more than once to remember it. Maybe it'll serve you too."

Over the PA, the gate attendant made the first boarding announcement. As a few nearby passengers began to gather their items, Carly sat still, once again staring at the stain on the carpet. What Lucy had just said sat on her conscience like a weighted blanket.

Had she been mistaken to so quickly judge Jex? She hadn't really given him a chance to explain after Marla walked in.

Lucy poked the needles into her bag as Mr. Brinkmeyer sidled up beside her with a newly purchased mystery novel in hand. "Looks like they're calling the old folks, and that's our cue, sweetheart," he said.

Scooting to the edge of her seat, Lucy wriggled to a standing position as she wrapped one arm around her husband's. With a quick point toward Carly, she began introductions. "Warren, I've just met the sweetest girl here. Her name's Carly Kirkpatrick. She's been on a visit to Chicago too."

"Howdyado." The old man tipped his head toward Carly. "My Lucy been keepin' you comp'ny? She does a good job of that."

"Yes, Mr. Brinkmeyer, she does."

"I was just telling Carly about our courtship." Lucy smiled.

In return, he nodded. "You told her how we made good of a bad situation then?"

They must've rehearsed the story many times over the years, Carly thought.

Lucy patted his arm. "You know I did."

"The best thing I ever did was talkin' her into believin' in me. She's been my reason to keep smilin' ever since." He chuckled.

The attendant made a second call for passengers needing assistance boarding the flight.

"We'd better get you on this bird and fly on home, dear." He took Lucy by the hand. "It's a pleasure to meet you, Miss Kirkpatrick."

Lucy reached down and squeezed Carly's hand. "I hope when you get back to Alabama, you'll find *your* reason to keep smilin'."

The sincerity in her eyes touched Carly.

She watched as the couple hobbled through check-in and disappeared onto the jet bridge.

What they had, she wanted.

Somebody she'd fly to see their grandkids with.

A man who'd share in the telling of a memory a hundred times like it was the first.

She gathered her carry-on and hitched her camera bag over her shoulder to board as the ticket attendant called the next group of passengers to the jet bridge.

"Attention, please." Another voice came over the PA. "Would a passenger by the name of Honeybee please report to the Delta ticket counter? Honeybee to the Delta ticket counter."

Carly froze. The only one who'd have her paged by that name was Jex. Her mind went into overdrive, first trying to fathom what lengths he'd go to in order to legitimize his lies, then battling with herself not to answer the page. From a place she didn't know existed, a place deep inside where faith in broken things resided, Lucy's words came back to her.

There's two ways to be fooled. One is to believe what isn't true; the other is to refuse to believe what is.

Was there a shred of a chance she was giving up on something that deserved a shot?

The gate attendant made the final boarding call.

Doubt barely winning, she scanned her ticket beneath the attendant's welcoming smile, boarded the jet bridge, and forced herself not to look back.

Aboard the plane, Carly took her assigned aisle seat. Her heart, hammering in her chest, played havoc with her brain.

Moments later, as they taxied down the runway, questions lined up just like the planes awaiting take-off.

Why the questions now? She didn't know, other than the fact that her last seconds on Chicago soil pulled at her to change her mind.

She looked out the window at liftoff. It was too late now anyway. She needed to focus on getting back home and back to work.

As the plane leveled at 30,000 feet, the pilot came on the PA and gave a muffled report of standard flight conditions and turned off the seat belt sign. Carly glanced around and saw the Brinkmeyers just to the side and slightly behind her. Already a few pages into his book, Mr. Brinkmeyer sat in the aisle seat contentedly beside Lucy, who had again taken up her knitting.

Most of the plane's seats were filled. However, the one beside Carly had remained empty—something which gave her relief as she was definitely not in the mood for a chatty neighbor.

A half hour into the flight, she had quietly and sufficiently vacillated from frustration to regret a hundred times. Maybe she should have taken the call back at Midway.

What if she'd left something behind at Jex's? Some camera equipment or something else important and he was trying to catch her? She *had* left in a hurry…

No, it was silly to even be thinking about it now. She should put Chicago in the past and move on.

Tiring of the mental ping-pong, she unbuckled her seat belt and stretched. Passengers were in various stages of scrolling through phones, watching movies, and playing on-board video games. A few in front of her were prattling about the weekend ball game.

Over her shoulder, Carly again noticed the Brinkmeyers. Lucy's knitting lay resting in her lap, her head now leaning on her husband's shoulder. Mr. Brinkmeyer sat with his cheek against his wife's hair, still engaged with his book.

The sight of them was a picture in itself…

A picture.

Of course!

This was exactly what Jex had been trying to teach her. She had the moment—the one that would make people emotionally respond—right in sight.

Opening her camera backpack in the empty seat beside her, she married the camera body to its lens and turned around.

Leaning toward the couple and with a lowered voice, she said, "Mr. Brinkmeyer, excuse me, but I couldn't help but notice something about you and your wife just now."

He set the opened book on his knee as Lucy stirred on his shoulder. He shifted slightly to accommodate her as she settled back into a comfortable position.

"You really would do anything for her, wouldn't you?" Carly said with a smile.

The old man nodded. "Anything."

"I hope to have that kind of love in my life someday."

"I'm sure you'll find it."

"Thank you, Mr. Brinkmeyer." She gave a nod toward her camera. "I was telling your wife earlier that I'm a photographer. I know this is an odd question, but could I take some photos of you two?"

Before he responded, she continued. "It's just that . . . while I was in Chicago, I learned something about capturing perfect moments. And I think what I see right now with you and your wife is one of those moments. If you'll let me take your photo, I'll get your address and send you copies at no charge."

The man glanced down at his wife. Carly could see the reluctance in his eyes. "Well, I hate to wake her. She doesn't sleep so well anymore, and—"

"Oh, no. I wouldn't dream of it. I'd like you sitting just like you are now. That's what makes everything just right."

He tipped his head to the side. "I suppose we could do that. I'm not much to look at, but beside this little gal—"

"You both look wonderful." Carly grinned. "Thank you, Mr. Brinkmeyer. I promise I'll just take a few shots. Do you think she'd mind?"

"Lucy? Oh, heavens no. She'd be delighted to help you." He nodded at the book. "And you just want me to keep reading?"

"That's it. Just like you were a minute ago."

He held up the book. "It is a good one, so shouldn't take much effort."

As he found his place, Carly raised her camera, pointed, and began clicking. "Perfect," she whispered.

Within a few minutes, she knew she had the set of photos she wanted. After getting their contact information and thanking the old man again, she turned in her seat and began scanning her shots.

The thumbnails of each photo as she clicked through them left her keenly aware that despite every questionable feeling she had about Jex right now, she'd just put into action everything he'd taught her—seeing people in unique settings and pulling out the intimacy. Only she hadn't introduced strangers to each other. She'd found lifelong lovers—two people, in all their flaws, who couldn't have been more beautifully or seamlessly matched.

When she set the camera back in its bag, her throat tightened. Jex had given her more than a few business remedies. He'd somehow shown her how to capture love in the most unexpected places.

Chapter Nineteen

Jex

J ex had sat in the airport for four hours watching people enter and exit the security checkpoint, hoping that by some miracle he'd see Bee. He never did.

When the terminal had been vacated of all but the red-eye passengers, he finally stood and walked out of Midway with the simple but profound regret that he'd not been completely open with Bee in the first place.

With each step he took from the terminal, his heart sank a little more. Something told him that this one negligent act would haunt him in the days to come. Maybe longer. Much longer.

In the parking garage, he straddled the bike and sped from the concrete structure with the crisp air buffeting against his face. He welcomed the sting, though it was no distraction from his frustrations.

The long stretches of interstate between Jex and home left him with time—brutal, brain-lashing time—where images played on repeat in his head. Flashes of those seconds in the last two days that had renewed him. The soft expressions on Bee's face when she laughed as they played their truth or lies game, when they lay on the floor of the Tower so close to one another, when they were together in the pool.

Then, like a knife cutting through paper, the memory of Marla stepping back into his life ripped through his happier thoughts. He hadn't realized how much his relationship with the woman had sapped his energy, nor how much two days with a complete stranger had re-energized him. But what was it all for?

Nothing.

Absolutely nothing.

Instead of going back to the Emerald, Jex sped toward the heart of Chicago. Moments later, parked against a curb on South Wacker Drive, he dismounted his bike and walked a few short feet from the entrance of Willis Tower. A vacant Starbucks patio complete with wrought iron outdoor tables and chairs waited under lonesome streetlights for the bustle of morning business traffic.

The curbside parking spaces were virtually empty but for a few cars whose owners no doubt lit up the occasional office window of the neighboring skyscrapers.

He thought of Trudy, how she knew him well enough that she'd have recognized another of his pensive moods and let him go to the Ledge had she been at work. But, by this time, if she had worked the day shift, she'd long been in her bed. Without her help, the cold, outdoor coffee shop chair would have to suffice as his thinking spot.

He chose an iron chair closest to the street and sat down, tucking his gloved hands into his jacket pockets.

The security guards at Willis Tower, including Trudy, would greet staff and visitors in a few short hours. He'd be gone by then, but at the moment, coming back to where he'd brought Bee somehow felt right, like a piece of his time with her lingered here in some quiet dimension waiting for him to show up and claim it.

He leaned back, his neck propped against the cold metal, and looked up. The observation boxes, barely visible against the light-polluted sky, stood above him—the beady eyes of a giant giving a condescending glance at an ant at the toe of his boot.

Looking from the street skyward had a completely different effect than what he'd always experienced from the Ledge above, gazing down.

From the ground, he felt . . . insignificant. Like what he'd spent his time on in the last year was so negligible compared to what he could lose if he didn't find Bee.

Marla didn't matter.

Hughley didn't matter.

And as crazy as it seemed having known her for only a weekend, nothing else really seemed to matter if Bee thought he was a liar.

After an hour or so, he slid away from the table with a determined shove, remounted his bike, and sped off in the direction of the Emerald.

Soon after he returned to his parents' apartment, the sun rose, but the morning light failed to drive away the sick feeling in the pit of Jex's stomach. It worsened after he listened to a voice message from Marla.

Her arrogance oozed through the phone as the recording played. "Jex, sweetheart. I'm willing to forgive our little misunderstanding, but you and I simply have to talk. My dinner date with Calvin Hughley was quite productive."

I bet it was.

"He's such an operator! I almost couldn't keep his hands off me. Anyway, as fate would have it, I *will* be the face of this project, so don't get any ideas about your new friend. Lucky for you, Calvin's completely unaware of the huge mistake you almost made by pulling in an amateur. I'll do you a favor and help you keep it that way as long as you get your act together."

Jex closed his eyes in frustration.

"Oh, and I've spoken to my attorney. To put it plainly, you'd be much better off re-shooting that photo spread with me than risk some unwanted legal bumps in the road if you choose to use your stand-in. I have to hand it to you, though, she does resemble me. Of course, she's certainly not as—should I say—well-put-together. Anyway, I wouldn't want a chance of any confusion among my network of professional contacts. Defamation isn't a tangle any of us should have to deal with."

She paused as if to let her veiled threat sink in. "So, mark your calendar, babe, I'll be in town in a few days to re-shoot. I've convinced Calvin to extend your deadline, so don't bother using his original target date as an excuse to put me off. You're welcome. I'll be in touch."

Jex threw the phone on the couch. Whether Marla and Hughley were truly on a first-name basis, he could only guess, but he wouldn't put it past her to do whatever it took to climb to the top of Hughley's list.

Stalking down the hall, he peeled off his shirt. By the time he reached the bedroom, he'd stripped to his shorts, stepped into the bathroom, and turned on a set of cranked-up hydro jets in the glassed-in shower. Lamenting the fact that just ten minutes earlier, a steamy rainwater trickle would have knocked the chill from his bones, now he only hoped to pummel away the grimy feeling left behind from hearing Marla's voice.

By 6:30 am, hair wet and dressed in jeans and a sweater, he'd put off the fatigue from staying up all night and was no longer willing to wait for what his sister would call a sensible hour. Standing at the window overlooking the lake, he speed-dialed her number. After two tries and a generous round of rings, Natalie finally answered.

"Are you in jail?" she grunted into the phone.

"No."

"The ER?"

"No, but . . ."

The phone clicked.

He redialed. She could forgive him another day. When she picked up the second time, he quickly jumped in. "We've gotta talk."

"What on earth about at this unholy hour of the morning?" she grunted again.

"I've got to find her. I need to find Bee."

"You called to tell me this, at six"—she paused— "thirty-six in the flipping morning?"

He ignored Natalie's irritation. "I missed her at the airport last night, and now Marla left this message that she's planning to run my life, not to mention ruin it. She wants me to re-do the photo spread with her instead of Bee, and now she's got a lawyer involved."

Jex could hear Natalie ruffle her bed's covers on the other end of the phone. "On what grounds?"

"She threw out the word *defamation* like it was a piece of toilet paper spiked on her stiletto."

Natalie huffed. "She doesn't have a leg or a stiletto to stand on."

"I know that, and she likely does too. It's the negative publicity that would be the nail in my coffin. Hughley would shut me down before I could even blink." He shook his head. "I don't even know if it's worth it anymore."

"Of course it's worth it. This is your dream. But getting Bee to sign over those photos doesn't look like the firmest prospect right now."

Didn't *anybody* get it? It wasn't about the signature or the photos of Bee anymore. Regardless, he didn't have the energy to weather Natalie's armchair analysis of his private life, so he changed the subject. "Has she been on the forum?"

"Bee? No, not a peep."

"There's got to be a way to find her."

"Did she give you any personal information at all?"

Jex looked at the lake's water, turning from gray to a muted blue as daylight spread across its ripples. "No. . . .Wait. . . .. Alabama. She let it slip that she was from Alabama. I wish I'd asked her more questions."

"Big state. Nothing else?"

"Nope."

"Good grief, then what did you two talk about all weekend?"

"Business, mostly. I did get her email. She sent me some of her files so I could help her pin down her best prospects for growth. From the look on her face when she left, though, I don't hold out much hope that she'd respond to me if I tried to contact her. "

"That's it? You talked about business growth? The whole weekend?"

"No, of course not. But that *was* the purpose of her coming to Chicago."

Natalie was silent for a moment. "What else did Marla have to say?"

"She's coming here in a few days and wants me to redo the shoot, *and* she convinced Hughley to push the deadline out."

"Perfect. This could work in your favor. I've got an idea."

"Care to enlighten me?" Jex asked.

"All you've got to do is bend to Marla's ego long enough to get through the ceremony. Tell ya what, take her through the shoot, get enough of a spread for the unveiling, and then send the spread to me. I'll get your montage ready. That'll at least take one thing off your plate."

"She's not the face of this prototype campaign, Nat."

"I get it. Just do the best you can and send the files to me as soon as possible. Oh, and send those layout photos of Bee too. And maybe those files you said she downloaded for you while she was there."

"What do you want with those?" he asked.

"I never did get to see a very big sampling of her work from the forum. I'd like to take a look. Maybe I can reconnect with her online if I have a better idea of what she shoots."

"Whatever." He drew in a deep breath and exhaled. "Nat, I don't know how much more of Marla I can stomach. Working for Dad is looking better all the time."

"You and I both know that regardless of the setup you'd have with Dad, that's not you. Listen, the minute this awards ceremony is over, you can focus on other things, like reconnecting with Bee. She probably just needs a little time. But right now, getting ready for that unveiling is your top priority. Meet with Marla, take a few pictures, and leave the rest to me."

"I think you want this more than I do," Jex said.

"Just don't forget to send me what I asked for. You do your job, I'll do mine, and it'll all work out."

Jex ended the call and tapped the phone against his stubbled chin. As unsure as he was about the coming weeks, he did draw a little comfort from Natalie's optimism. She'd found ways to pull him out of ditches before.

Chapter Twenty

Carly

Carly drove her car from the parking garage at Birmingham's Shuttlesworth International, paid her weekend tab to a sleepy-eyed booth attendant, and shortly afterward wove onto the parkway toward home.

She couldn't shake thoughts of Jex out of her head. Cranking up the car stereo, she tried, but even the crooning of her favorite country musician couldn't pull her away from the images of Jex coursing through her mind.

By the time she'd arrived back at her place an hour later, she'd mentally walked through the weekend from beginning to end at least five times, and Jex had been in every single thought.

She unlocked the front door as the clock on her foyer wall sounded its 2 am chime. Parking her carry-on just inside, she relocked the door and collapsed on the couch.

The weekend had been more than she'd hoped for with respect to business at least. If she could just look at the last two days for what they'd originally been intended, there was no loss.

She kicked off her shoes, hugged a throw pillow to her chest, and willed herself to re-frame her hours with Jex. He'd shown her how to organize her files to find her deepest photographic interests. He'd discussed theory and sales practices with her. He'd shown her how to capture the perfect shot based on the unfamiliar, the element of surprise.

As she continued to catalog her thoughts, those sweet moments he'd shared with her slipped quietly, easily back into her mind.

The ride on his motorcycle.

The tour of Chicago from the pilot house roof.

The trip to the Ledge. . .

Their swim together.

And their kiss.

Just before the clock struck the half hour, Carly exhaled a long, held breath and broke into a sob. Tightening her grip on the pillow, she reminded herself that she was safe in Camden Grove now and just needed to get back to work.

In the three weeks since she'd returned from Chicago, Carly had tried relentlessly to settle into her normal routine, but everything felt off.

Though she'd photographed a few of the local high school's year-end events and completed a couple of planning meetings for some June weddings she and Jessie already had on the calendar, she'd still been too under-motivated to push her new ideas into high gear.

In the meantime, light editing on the Brinkmeyer photos had led to printing a selection of her favorites to send to them. She'd also spoken to the couple over the phone with the request to use their pictures for her ad portfolio. *Baby steps*, she thought. They'd readily agreed.

To approach the whole thing professionally, she'd even developed a release form to include with their proofs and a brief hand-written note telling them how much she'd enjoyed meeting them. Since their flight home, she'd often thought about the Brinkmeyers, many times wondered if she'd ever have her very own "reason to keep smiling."

With morning pushing into and past the lunch hour, Carly addressed the couples' package with a Sharpie marker, dropped the filled mailer and marker in her bag on the way out, and almost made it to the door, but the phone rang before she could turn the knob. Ava's face popped up on the screen.

Carly cradled the phone between an ear and her shoulder as she set her things on the entry table. "You taking an early lunch?" she asked.

"I just needed to hear a friendly voice."

Carly could hear Ava sniffle on the other end. "What's wrong?"

A long silence left her without a doubt that Ava was crying. "Hey, are you alright?"

"I think Corbin's involved in something seriously illegal. So many things just don't add up, and I'm trying really hard to accept that if I don't leave, I'll be pulled into his trouble."

"What kind of trouble?"

"I don't know. Insurance fraud? Maybe? He's not communicating with me about some things he *should* be—numbers and codes and patient files—but he keeps blowing me off, like I'm being too uptight. He tries to smooth things over with dinner and flowers, but I *know* something underhanded's going on. I know it." Her voice broke.

"Ava, your instincts are always on target. If you think he's shady, you need to cut your losses."

"Do you have any idea how expensive it would be to start up a new practice on my own?"

Carly sighed. "In Nashville, yes, it would be exorbitant. But not in Camden Grove. Don't you remember when you were considering joining Corbin's practice? I tried to convince you then that this would be the perfect place to open a clinic, and it still is. Everything's cheaper down here—cost of living, real estate, insurance. And the nearest family practice is in Hartley. Do you know how many hypochondriacs alone would line up at your door the minute you put out a shingle in this town?"

"I don't know what to do." Ava sniffled. "My head's reeling."

Carly could tell her friend was scared, and that, in turn, scared her. Fear had never been on the list of reactions she'd witnessed from Ava before. Concern? Worry? Anxiety? Yes. But not fear. "Are you at work now?"

"In my car, getting ready to go back inside. My 12:30's already waiting."

"Then we need to talk about this more later. I know my dad could pull together some properties for you to look at. Foreclosure banking has been booming lately. He's had his plate full. He just told me that the old newspaper office is coming up for sale soon. I know because I wanted it for a studio."

"Then why don't you buy it?"

"Takes more money than I'll have for a while, but you could look at it. It'll go for pennies on the dollar."

Ava sniffled again. "So, I'm supposed to just pull up stakes and leave? Just like that?"

"Why not? You sound scared, and if you think your partner may be into something illegal, it's time to act." Carly paused. "Promise me you'll at least think about it. I can put Dad to work on it the minute you give me the go-ahead. You wouldn't be signing anything just by considering your options."

The phone went silent for a moment. "I still don't know."

"You don't have to know. You just have to move."

"I don't suppose looking could hurt," Ava conceded.

"Perfect. We'll talk more when you're not at work."

"Thanks, Carly." Ava perked up a notch. "Before I go, are *you* doing alright?"

Carly knew her friend was changing the topic to pull herself together. It had been Ava's practice since her parents had passed away back in college—divert attention and suck it up.

"Doing great," she lied.

"How's it coming with all the new ideas from Chicago?"

"Oh, okay." When she'd first come home, Carly avoided talking to Ava about the whole disastrous ending to her stay with Jex. After unloading just enough with Lucy Brinkmeyer at the airport, she'd decided that because her friend had enough to worry about in her own world for the moment, she'd share only that it had been a productive trip, and that whatever had heated up between her and Jex had cooled.

A week later, when Ava called her on her sullen mood, Carly again put off telling her for a while, but the conversation eventually worked around to the difference Ava saw in her again. That's when she gave her a little of the story which led to a little more. Her friend had a way of pulling details out of her by degrees.

Ava sighed on the other end of the line. "I know you've got a lot on your mind too, trying to keep a photography business running and still working through what happened in Chicago." She paused. "We're a pair, aren't we? But there is a difference."

"And what would that be? We both have untrustworthy men in our lives."

"Maybe. But I'm finding all the evidence, and you're just going by the impressions that some chick with a fashion fetish has fed you. Not a reliable witness."

Carly grinned. "And here I thought you went to med school, not law school."

"All I know is that since you've come back, you seem just as unsettled as I am, professionally *and* personally."

Carly leaned against the door. "I guess I am. Every time I think about my business, I now see Jex's face."

"So, contact him."

Carly bit her lip. "I'm so conflicted, and I don't know why."

"I've got that answer." Ava continued, "A year ago, when you found Hunter with that other girl, there was no denying he was cheating, and because of that, you closed out of that relationship like an account for a stolen credit card. But with Jex, you don't have all the answers."

She knew Ava was right. "I was just beginning to think there was something between us, but when his ex-fiancé walked into the picture and staked her claim, it felt like the whole Hunter scenario all over again."

"That doesn't mean you have all the facts. If Jex was dishonest with you, you still need to get some closure or figure out your next step. You're not doing yourself a favor by not getting answers."

"I don't know." Carly put a hand to her forehead.

"You don't have to know. You just have to move." The echo of Carly's earlier advice to Ava struck a chord, and they both found room for a half-hearted laugh.

"Speaking of moving, you've got a patient waiting, and I have something to get to the post office."

"Chat later?" Ava asked.

Carly gathered her keys and purse from the entry table. "Chat later."

No closer to an answer, she grabbed her things, blew a lock of hair from her eyes, and opened the door.

A woman on the other side jumped back, one hand raised to knock and the other dropping the phone she'd been holding. It clattered against the threshold at the same moment a text notification sounded.

"Oh, hello." The stranger bent down for the phone. "Sorry, I wasn't paying attention. I was just texting my brother."

Carly frowned. "Can I help you?"

"Yes, I'm hoping you can. My name's Natalie Radcliffe. You and I have messaged over the photography forum."

Recognition set in, and Carly's thoughts went into overdrive.

"I helped plan your visit to Chicago a few weeks back. I'm Jex's sister. Can I come in?"

Chapter Twenty-One

Jex

As Jex boarded the tour boat, Ben, the same worker who'd greeted him and Bee weeks ago, called out to him from the pilot house. "Yous making rounds again, Jex?"

"Last time for this shoot, man. I promise."

"Not the same girl you brought last time, is it?" He snickered.

Marla scowled at the man as if he were growing a third eye. "Of course not. He's working with a professional now."

Jex bit his tongue. Marla had made his life a nightmare since she'd come back into town. Getting a spread of shots all her own had been her mission in the first week.

Attempting to ignore her remark, he turned to Ben. "Can we go up to the roof again?"

"Sorry, can't let you, man." Ben pulled his captain's hat level on his head. "Somebody on the tourist council heard about yous and the other girl going up top last time. We got a liability warning. Can't take the risk of being shut down."

"No problem, we can go to the back of the boat and get some shots from there."

"I want pictures from the best vantage point," Marla demanded.

Jex had already started in the opposite direction before she had time to argue. "It won't matter," he mumbled to himself.

Clopping like a Clydesdale in the four-inch heels she'd donned for the occasion, she followed him at a choppy pace.

He wondered how long he could stomach being with Marla. Only twenty-two phone messages and the threat of legal action had prodded him to respond to her. And now, listening to her in person was like fingernails down his mental chalkboard.

Insisting on being in charge, Marla had chosen the day of the shoot and had made a series of ultimate blunders in the eyes of any photographer smart enough to wield a point-and-shoot. One, she'd worn the most outlandish plaid jacket ever sold—something that would not only draw the eye away from the prototype but battle with the geometric lines of the architecture they'd have as a backdrop.

Two, she'd also chosen the very brightest part of a sunny day for a session, and three, she'd worn eyeglasses—not sunglasses, eyeglasses—to make herself look smart, he guessed. Instead, the glare they caused looked like a set of high beams sitting on her cheeks.

One would have thought that with the modeling she'd done, Marla would have a better grasp of good conditions for a shoot, but not one of her choices worked in his *or* her favor.

After Jex set up his tripod, a few of the passengers watched from afar as Marla struck vogue-ish poses, and he took his first test shots.

A half-hour into the shoot the lighting was way too bright, the wind was kicking up, and trying to work the glare out of the glasses left him putting Marla in awkward poses. Nothing seemed to be panning out like it should. And from beginning to end, Marla's attitude pulled him deeper into a funk. He was so far from replicating anything inspirational—anything like he'd caught in the photos with Bee—that he finally quit and called it a wrap.

As he began packing up, Marla, with his prototype around her neck and her hands propped on her hips, snapped, "Wait! I didn't even have time to change clothes!"

"No wardrobe changes." He lifted the strap from around her neck. "Hughley will want simple shots."

"That is *not* my forte. Simple may have been your other model, but not me. You're lucky I came back to spice up this campaign. You may have a shot now that I sold him on giving you a solid chance. You owe me, you know."

Jex gathered his equipment and turned for the boat's exit ramp without responding.

"Where are you going? We're not done yet!"

"Yes, we're done. With all the editing left to do, I've got more pictures than I can handle."

Marla trotted behind him like a child on the verge of a tantrum, her heels clicking forcefully in his wake. "Well . . . call me when they're ready. I want to see everything before you send them."

Jex picked up his pace, leaving Marla shouting at him as he exited down the boat ramp.

After impatiently strapping his bag and tripod on the back of his motorcycle, he mounted the seat, started the engine, and wound out the throttle, letting the rumble of the motor drown out the remnants of Marla's voice grinding in his head.

Four blocks away, when he was sufficiently out of range, he stopped the bike in an abandoned parking lot, dropped the kickstand, and slung his helmet across the pavement.

He had thoughts of calling Natalie, but she'd only tell him things he didn't want to hear. He already knew Marla was his only chance to land Hughley's sponsorship, and he was keenly aware that she had him bridled like a trained horse, leading him around by the bit. Never before had pulling the deal off the table with Hughley been even a remote thought. This was the career break he'd been banking on for a long time. But giving Marla the satisfaction of making his business decisions made him sick to his stomach. He might as well work for his dad.

Still stewing, he walked over to pick up the helmet and would have left if his phone hadn't vibrated in his pocket.

Natalie's name popped up when he pulled it out. *How'd it go with Queen Marla?*

Jex texted back, *Don't ask. I'll send shots later. Ever reconnect with Bee? You've been quiet.*

Natalie: *Nothing to report. Sending the montage to Davis soon. See you Saturday.*

Jex: *I'd like to take a quick look at it before you send it on.*

Crickets.

Jex cocked his head. Natalie knew he would want to see the montage before sending it on to the program manager. Surely, she'd run it by him first. Any other time, she would've met with him a day or two before the event so they could tack everything down. It sounded like Saturday was the earliest he'd see her.

A minute longer and his mind trailed to Bee. He wondered if she'd thought of him, like he had her, a hundred times since she'd left nearly three weeks ago. His feelings, tangled like a Gordian knot, left him tired.

Finally, he strapped his helmet on, straddled the bike, revved the motor to a rumble, and spun out of the parking lot.

The sooner he could get past Saturday, the better.

Chapter Twenty-Two

Carly

Though confusion set in, Carly inched the door open wider and, with an unsure gesture, allowed Natalie inside.

As they made their way into the living room, she lingered behind, trying to process the fact that Jex's sister had come all the way from . . . Chicago?. . . to see her, not to mention that this woman she didn't really know had found her. "Uh, want something to drink?"

Despite her bewilderment, hospitality was pinned somewhere on the helix of Carly's DNA like a roadside billboard.

"Do you have sweet tea? I've always wanted to come to the South and ask for true Southern sweet tea."

"Sorry, no tea."

"Not a fan?"

"Not unless it comes from the local barbecue place." She set her bag and keys back down and motioned toward the couch. "Have a seat. I've got water or maybe some root beer, if you want that."

"Water, then. Thanks." As Carly turned for the kitchen, Natalie called, "I'll have to try that barbecue place sometime. You say it's here in town?"

"Wiggles' Place."

"Interesting name."

"Interesting owner." Impatient with the small talk, Carly returned, handing her the water, and sat down on the couch beside her. "I'll be frank. I'm a little confused and maybe weirded out that you've found me, and I'm trying to understand why you'd want to."

"Frank is my language, so we'll get along really well." Natalie grinned. "And I'll get right to it.

"First of all, my brother has no idea I'm in Alabama. In fact, he'd probably fire me, not to mention disown me, if he knew I were taking matters into my own hands. So, if you don't mind, I'd like to keep that little secret between the two of us for now."

That wouldn't exactly be a problem, Carly thought, since everything had ended in Chicago. "Fire you?"

"Virtual and/or on-site assistant. Depends on the week." She took a sip from the glass.

"And how did you find me?"

"Wasn't the easiest, believe me. But, given you let it slip while you were with Jex that you were from Alabama, that gave me a starting point. He also said you'd downloaded some files on his computer to discuss business strategies."

"I did, but what do my files have to do with it?"

"Please, don't get upset." Natalie bit her lower lip. "I took a look at your photos, and in the subfiles, I ran across a prom shoot and the name of a school. Hartley High," she said. "Once I found the town of Hartley, Alabama, I did a search for photographers in the area. That led to a dead end since there are no female photographers in Hartley. I figured high schools would surely pull in people who were fairly local to do a prom shoot, so I went to the map and searched for cities and towns close to Hartley—anything big enough for a traffic light. That's how I found Collin Grove—"

"Camden Grove," Carly corrected with an edge to her voice.

Natalie took a sip of water. "Mmm. That's right. When I searched for Camden Grove photography businesses, there you were, camera in hand, but when I drove from the airport this morning, I still had to ask one of the locals where I could find you since your address isn't on your website. Guess it's true that everybody knows everybody in a small town."

Carly stood and walked to the window. "So, you know my name?"

"Yes, I do, and, from the looks of your work, you've got a really good eye."

"Why are you here?" Carly turned to face Natalie, her voice sharpening even more. Something about someone going through her files and stalking her didn't set right.

"I'm here because I need your help." Natalie hesitated. "Because Jex needs your help. And I also think my brother has . . . feelings for you."

Those last words hit Carly with the force of a hurricane gust. She began to shake her head. "After what happened in Chicago—and I hope he's clued you in on that fiasco—why would you bother? Why would I have the faintest interest in helping him?"

"Jex said you were upset when you left." Natalie set down the water. "And yes, I know about Marla showing up in Chicago.

That's exactly why I'm here. Please." Her eyes seemed sincere. "Just give me a chance to explain."

Carly wanted to turn away. A ripple of anxiety coursed through her chest. When she'd stared at Natalie long enough for discomfort to set in, she looked away. "Fine. Explain."

Natalie eased back on the couch guardedly and just as tentatively began to recount the whole story in detail.

The history of Marla and how she'd come to be Jex's fiancé.

How they'd crashed and burned after a few short months and Jex hadn't dated anyone since ending it.

How Marla was a back-biting she-devil who, before their breakup, had also been a key entry point for Jex's prototype at Hughley Photographics, the place he was trying to get his foot in the door.

And now, how Marla was sabotaging Jex's entire career all due to her own narcissistic delusions.

The most surprising thing, though, was that Natalie had been the impetus behind getting Carly to Chicago in the first place. After running up on her Honeybee profile in the photography forum, she'd been the one to make contact and set up the whole thing.

"So, there it is, the back story." Natalie leaned forward. "And if anybody's to blame for the screw up of the century between you and Jex, it's me."

When she finished, Carly still had a head full of burning questions and enough cautionary angst to lock the brakes on Natalie's request for help. "Why didn't Jex just tell me all of this up front? He still played a part in all of this. Or why didn't *you* say something when you set it up?"

Natalie raised her hands. "I know. I know. I've had my brighter moments. But seriously, wouldn't you have thought we were totally sketchy if we'd asked you to come to Chicago to pose for pictures, much less stand in as Jex's fiancé?"

"Wait." The wheels in her head began spinning even faster. "What do you mean 'stand in as Jex's fiancé'?"

Natalie sighed. "Sorry, that's another part of the story I suppose I should tell you."

"Yes, you should, since all I know is what you've said today and what Marla so kindly threw in my face when I had the chore of meeting her. By the way, being put in my place by somebody who looks *a lot* like my own reflection was disturbing."

"I really am sorry that happened, but you got a good taste of Marla's true character and an idea of why I can't let her waltz in and take the reins on Jex's big shot." Natalie scowled, pointing at nothing in particular. "This would never have happened if it hadn't been for Calvin Hughley."

"I'm confused. How does someone else, who wasn't even there, factor into this equation?"

"He requested Marla specifically for Jex's project. And from where I sit, the guy's a skirt-chaser and expected Jex to involve her from concept to unveiling so that he could flex his clout for his own purposes, if you know what I mean."

"Didn't he know Jex was engaged to Marla?"

"Pssshhh." Natalie waved her hand. "Minor hiccup for a guy like Hughley. He even wanted her at the DIA awards ceremony, I suspect so he could steal her away from Jex, wear her as arm candy, and take credit for scoring the campaign baby doll in front of all the big names at the party. He's got an insufferable ego, that one."

She lifted her glass. "Thing is, Hughley would actually be a great match for Marla. She was using Jex just to get herself in front of someone who'd further her own career, and, in my eyes, Hughley is just as opportunistic as she is."

Carly's head pulsated with the truckload of information Natalie had just dumped in her lap. "So, when Jex and Marla broke it off, you two figured she was out of the picture, and thought it was a wise idea to drag me into his business troubles? Get me to show up as some kind of stand-in on the pretense that *he* would be helping *me*? That pretty much sum it up?"

Natalie pursed her lips. "Yeah, that's about right. Except I was more on board with the idea than Jex."

"A pretty low thing to do, don't you think?"

"I can understand why you'd be angry, why you'd feel used. That's my fault, and I own it. I guess I hoped that by coming here, I could explain, maybe help you understand why we—I—pulled you into this."

When Carly remained silent, Natalie continued. "Look, this sounds about as sappy as I'll ever get, but I wanted to see Jex get his life set up. I thought if we could put him on the map with this project, sans Queen Marla, we'd get him rooted in his career, and he could get past his history with her even quicker."

"And I was your answer for that?" Carly raised her eyebrows. "Someone who looks so much like his ex that we could be sisters? That doesn't sound like much of a way to put the past in the rearview to me."

Natalie slowly nodded. "It seemed like a good idea at the time. I took a chance—a pretty good one, I thought—after chatting with you on the photography forum. I knew after a couple of conversations, you were at least nice, not to mention smart *and* gorgeous."

Carly didn't even blink, despite the compliment. "Flattery isn't a fence-mender with me."

Natalie smiled. "I can respect that. I hoped you'd feel comfortable enough after spending some time with Jex to agree to the photo shoot and to signing the release forms, once he told you more about his situation. I didn't expect it to go further than that. And certainly not to the awards ceremony. I thought having you on paper would be enough."

"Then where did my posing as Jex's fiancé come in?"

"Like I said, having Marla at the ceremony was one of Hughley's demands. Honestly, *your* being there in her place would have simply sealed the deal for Jex and his prototype, but I figured if we had the photo spread and got Jex to the unveiling without Marla, we'd somehow manage to explain our way around that problem when, or if, Hughley pressed for answers. Now, though, that's all changed with Marla back in the picture."

Carly tried not to summon an ounce of empathy for Jex or Natalie, but when she thought of how smug Marla had been back in Chicago, her resolve softened a little. "And Jex? What did he think of this plan?"

"He was the last person to place any personal expectations on the weekend when you came to visit, but apparently, you two hit it off."

"If hitting it off means being lied to."

Natalie shifted, the uneasiness showing in her furrowed brow. "The evening Marla showed up, he was planning to tell you everything over dinner. Then she came out of nowhere and beat him to it."

Carly punctuated her stare with sarcasm. "You'll forgive me if I don't jump at the chance to believe you."

"He *did* try to help you that weekend, right?" Natalie asked.

"That's not the point."

"I get it. If I were in your shoes, I'd probably be ready to poke pins in a voodoo doll too. I'll be the first to admit that we both really screwed this up. But Jex? He's got a heart, and right now, it's damaged goods because of what happened between the two of you three weeks ago. If you really want to know, he was ready to throw it all down the tubes, but I pushed him to wait. You've gotta understand. Photography, and now this prototype, has been Jex's dream for a long time."

Carly *did* understand that. Talk of photography and dreams was a language she'd spoken for a long time. "I still don't get why you're here. Am I supposed to blindly trust in someone's good intentions? Say, 'Okay. Glad he wanted to tell me the truth. Wish his obnoxious girlfriend hadn't butted in.' Is that really what you came here to tell me?"

"I came because . . . I owed you an apology." She paused. "And because I think you know deep down that Jex really is a good guy. And even though I can usually handle things on my own . . . I wanted to ask for your help."

Carly folded her arms. She didn't know whether to laugh or to cry. The whole situation was absurd. How could this woman Carly'd never actually met come here in behalf of a man she barely even knew, and have the nerve to ask her anything?

"I get that it's pretty brassy of me coming here, but—" She pinched the bridge of her nose. "Look, you two agreed to keep personal information off limits, right?"

"Yes."

"Wanna know something else pretty personal about Jex?"

Carly lowered her gaze, curious, but not willing to show it.

"When we were growing up, my brother was expected to take over the family business."

Carly remembered the conversation with Jex at the Ledge, when he'd called his dad a hard nose, said he had no passion for following in his father's footsteps.

"His schooling centered around that path for a good while—marketing, management, accounting, yada, yada. Then, when it came time to buckle down and focus on his future as CEO of Radcliffe Enterprises, he froze."

"What exactly does your father do?" Carly asked with an edge still to her voice.

"Radcliffe Enterprises is a group of companies dedicated to marrying e-commerce and food. I'd be willing to bet that Jex had some scrumptious meals delivered to the Emerald while you were in Chicago, right?"

Carly thought of the Italian they'd ordered. The smells and tastes had been heavenly.

"Our father owns the company and some of the restaurants that make prep and delivery of those kinds of meals possible all over the city of Chicago. And not only there. REI operates in more than 2,000 cities, works with over 104,000 restaurants nationwide. There's probably even a few dozen here in Alabama."

Carly tilted her head. "So much for small business."

"Langston Radcliffe is anything but small-time. Four years ago, Jex finally broke the news to our dad that he wasn't taking over the family business, and for a while, their relationship was more than a little rocky. Dad threatened to cut him out of the will, though I kept telling Jex he would've buckled sooner or later. Our dad's old-fashioned and hard, but not heartless."

"What happened?" she asked, despite her will to appear disinterested.

"Jex couldn't care less about our family's money. He just wanted to keep the peace, so he struck a deal. He agreed to set aside his ambitions and take on the CEO role if he failed to build his own profit-turning business within a five-year time frame. And we're not talking small revenue. They had a number-specific agreement. Jex knew our dad would require a meaty performance report to justify backing off and supporting his dream."

Natalie scooted to the edge of the couch, now looking even more earnest. "My brother needed his signature stamp on something big. Building a dream from the ground up without the Radcliffe legacy to stand on? That's his style, and he knew nothing smaller would appease our father long enough to give him a guilt-free shot."

"So, the camera project is his 'something big'?"

Natalie nodded. "He's got a year left to make it happen. By my estimate, that's just long enough to get his prototype in place for production. That is, if Marla doesn't blow the whole deal to smithereens."

"Why would she do that? Doesn't she have something to gain from his being successful?"

"The girl's a loose cannon. And she's for Marla only. Jex was her easy ride, at least for a while. I have no doubt that she was stepping on his shoulders just long enough for him to get mired in the mud, then she'd find another dupe to grind her four-inch heels into. What's worse, if she thought it would make her look any better, she'd as soon throw Jex under the bus as smile at him. That's why she has no place in his business."

Back in Chicago, when Carly had her first brush with Marla in the elevator, the woman had proved that she had no consideration for anyone else. Knocking the restaurant bag out of Carly's hand without ever bothering to look back had likely been one of many times Marla had disregarded showing common courtesy.

The more Natalie shared, the more Carly found herself wanting to believe Natalie, wanting to trust that Jex had always had good intentions, but she didn't know if she was ready yet.

"Can you at least answer one question for me?" Natalie rose. "Was working with Jex a total loss?"

Glancing at the table where the Brinkmeyer's package lay, Carly exhaled. She'd never have met them had she not gone to Chicago in the first place, nor would she have ever thought to take those few magical photos of them sitting on the plane if Jex hadn't shown her what she was capable of. "If you're asking if I gained anything professionally while I was there . . . the answer's yes."

"Then is it that much of a stretch, if he was willing to help you, to believe that Jex never intended to hurt you? Could you go a step further and find it in your heart to help me prevent someone from sabotaging his livelihood?" She waited.

With her back now turned to Natalie, Carly propped her elbow on the window frame. She thought of Lucy Brinkmeyer's words of advice, heard the deep Southern drawl of the elderly woman's voice in her memory, and said, "Someone recently told me that there are two ways to be fooled. One? To believe what isn't true. The other? To refuse to believe what is."

"What I've told you is true, Carly."

"Can you blame me for being skeptical?"

"No, I can't," Natalie said. "If I were you, I may not have listened to me as long as you have."

Carly didn't speak for a long time, then turned toward Natalie. "I'll help you, but only on my terms. And don't make me regret it."

Natalie smiled. "I promise you won't, but we've got some serious magic to work. Ceremony's in two days."

Chapter Twenty-Three

Jex

F riday evening, Jex sat on the couch, laptop cradled on his outstretched legs. He stared at the photos of Marla, the ones he'd sent to Natalie for the montage. Everything about them was wrong. No one would deny that she looked like a natural-born model in *front* of a camera, but to have her represent someone *behind* it was a joke.

She wore her polished smile like the poster child for orthodontia, had shampoo-model hair—something her stylist likely spent hours on per week—and possessed a personality that shouted from each picture, "Look at *me*!"

Bee, on the other hand, despite the resemblance, was her polar opposite. Her smile penetrated his shell. Her hair fell like she didn't have a care in the world. And she never had to shout to command attention. She could secure his with merely an expression.

Admitting the differences made him even more irritated, though with himself or the situation in general he couldn't say.

Why would a campaign to sell a new-style camera body need someone like Marla as its model? Anybody would see the irony. He wanted his camera to come across as a real tool in the hands of real photographers, not some toy or prop under the nose of somebody better suited to sell swanky cosmetics or New York City runway clothing.

The phone rang again. He'd stopped counting how many messages Marla had left. She was likely livid that he hadn't consulted her before sending the photo spread. It was too late for her to make waves now, though. She'd have to be happy with whatever Natalie had compiled.

Unconcerned with Marla's backlash, he still felt nervous about whatever scheme Natalie had in mind for the unveiling. He knew his sister well enough to be on edge but kept reminding himself that she wanted this prototype to be successful as much as he did.

The tension in Jex's neck let up only mildly as he rose from his computer. He looked out the window into the distant ripples of Lake Michigan and tried to call Natalie for an update.

She didn't answer. Marla wasn't the only one leaving messages; he'd been trying Natalie all day.

The ceremony was less than twenty-four hours away.

And he needed some reassuring.

Chapter Twenty-Four

Carly

After a quick call to her parents and a voice mail to Ava filling her in with sketchy details at best, Carly boarded the airplane, wondering again if she was a glutton for punishment or just plain certifiable.

She had set her terms, though, and consented to return to Chicago only if Natalie agreed to keep her presence a secret until the right moment, one she'd determine herself. Until then, finding a way to see with her own eyes if Jex was lying about Marla was her objective. She'd decided she could make that call well enough at the awards ceremony, when Jex and Marla were together and she could watch them from the wings.

On the Saturday morning flight, with the predicated threat that she'd disappear if she suspected for even a second that Natalie had tipped Jex off, Carly flew first class for the first time in her life, and with Natalie by her side, fine-tuned a detailed plan for the evening, only a few hours away.

They'd found a common ground, a shared purpose of putting Marla Fairchild in her rightful place. It was a strange kind of mutual understanding that might even bloom into a full-fledged friendship . . . *if* she found that Jex really deserved her help. She could stand behind the fact that neither Marla nor anyone else had a right to undermine Jex's business. But she also needed to believe that he was over Marla. She could lend a hand, as long as it didn't get cut off in the process.

When they touched down at Midway, their strategy was well-honed, and Natalie wasted no time whisking Carly off before her carry-on wheels even had a chance to cool. They had a big night to prepare for.

"Take us to Four Seasons, please," Natalie directed the taxi driver as they slipped into the back seat.

"Wait, are you talking about *the* Four Seasons? The hotel?" Carly's voice rose a notch.

Natalie cocked an eyebrow. "Is there something wrong with that?"

"I-I thought a first-class flight was fancy enough. I didn't realize I'd be staying at Four Seasons."

"Don't worry. I reserved a suite there for both of us. Since you don't want Jex in on our plan, I couldn't very well take us back to the Emerald. And I decided against my place since we're on a time crunch and need somewhere closer to the venue. Anyway, this is my dad's treat."

"Does he know that?"

"No." Natalie waved a hand. "But he puts people up at Four Seasons for much less important causes than this. If things go the way we've planned and we can get Marla out of the picture tonight, it'll be worth every cent to him and everybody else in our family, whether he realizes it or not."

Once they arrived, Natalie led the way inside the towering building as Carly craned her neck in every direction, soaking in the lavish scenery.

After they dropped their bags at the front desk with the hotel concierge, Natalie threaded her arm through Carly's and led her right back out the impressive revolving glass doors. "We've got shopping to do and not a lot of time to do it. I called ahead at Leuster's—they're my favorite boutique—and told them what we needed. I took a guess . . ." She eyed Carly. "You and I look roughly the same size. Anyway, they have a personal shopper there, Fiona, who works magic in the fitting department. She's also got an eye for flattering colors and grade A taste in classic design."

They walked a short distance to a hip, luxury retailer with the name Leuster's spread across the contemporary-themed storefront window in a chic font. Just below it, in a boxier script, read the name Adelaide Fox, Curator. Weren't curators for museums or art galleries?

A little embarrassed to admit it, Carly had already begun to worry about the amount of money it would take to buy a dress in a place like this. Who was she kidding? She didn't even have the cash to buy a shopping bag from such a chichi shop. Even the air outside the door smelled expensive.

She blurted out, "Natalie, I don't have extra money for this."

"Will you stop sucking the joy out of our trip? Dress, shoes, accessories—it's all on our tab. But we've gotta hurry." She looked at her watch. "We've got an appointment back at the hotel spa at two, a mani/pedi at three, hair at four, and, oh, I hired one of Chicago's finest makeup artists to show up at our suite at five." She yanked open the boutique door and nodded her head expectantly, waiting for Carly to scoot inside.

"When you said we had some magic to work, I didn't realize you meant this."

Natalie shrugged. "A girl should always take advantage of a reason to pamper herself. I have a feeling, though, that the real magic's coming later. And it won't have a thing to do with makeup or a French manicure." She smirked.

Whatever that means, Carly thought.

Chin raised, she walked into the boutique to an enthusiastic store attendant welcoming her.

The excesses of posh shopping, spa treatments, and people fussing over every curl and hangnail had never been on Carly's radar when she'd agreed to return to Chicago. But she ultimately decided, at Natalie's insistence, that since it was all on the Radcliffes' dime, the experience might be a nice consolation prize if things went sour. She didn't see ever having these kinds of extravagances in her life again, so she decided to relax and at least try to enjoy it.

Once the last of the beauty specialists left for the evening, Natalie quickly snatched the garment bag labeled with her name and another bag with matching shoes and accessories and headed for the door.

"Where're you going?"

"It's time to get this party started."

"But aren't we going to the venue together?"

"I have to go to the Emerald, put Jex's mind at ease, and settle a few final details. I'll send a car for you though. Just be ready and at the hotel entrance at 6:45 sharp. I'll meet you at the ceremony. I promise."

"But you're not gonna tell him I'm here, right?" Carly reminded her.

Natalie mimed locking her lips and slipped out the door before Carly had time to think of any other questions.

In the last few minutes, the room had gone from bustling with beauticians to silent and with only herself for company. She blew a flat-ironed wave from her eyes that the stylist had previously tried to spray-glue in place. She'd never tamed her waves enough to wear them in a sleek, straightened updo before, but Javier the stylist insisted it was exactly the formal style she needed for tonight's occasion.

Without Natalie there, her nerves sprouted wings. And the closer to ceremony time, the more restless she became.

She convinced herself to step closer to the hotel window to watch the streets below, busy with evening walkers and shoppers. Why she thought that would help, she didn't know. The height from her suite window to the ground did absolutely nothing to settle her nerves.

She quickly nixed that idea and next picked up her phone to call Ava for a mini shot of confidence.

Six rings. Then voice mail.

After waiting for the beep, she began. "Hey, listen, I wanted you to know that I haven't abandoned you. And I hope you're not backing out on thinking about a move to the Grove. Anyway, if you got my earlier message, you'll know that I'm back in Chicago for a day or two. It's a long story that I promise I'll tell you once I'm back in town, but the short version? You were right. I need some answers." She sighed. "I'll talk to you soon."

By 6:18 pm, she'd flipped through all 172 channels on the hotel cable system in quick succession and looked at the wall clock a total thirty-two times.

Then, at exactly twenty minutes before she needed to be in the hotel lobby, Carly rose from the couch and went to unzip her garment bag. She'd put off getting into her dress until the last possible minute for fear she'd break out in a sweat.

Running a hand over the silky fabric of her evening gown, her thoughts slipped back to the store, hours earlier, when the flutter of butterflies setting off a hurricane in her stomach had really begun.

At Leuster's, she'd very quickly dismissed the first two dresses Natalie's personal shopper, Fiona, had chosen.

One, a black number with a neckline that plunged to the belly button, said rich Academy Award nominee, something she definitely would not carry off with any hint of confidence.

The second, a jewel-tone strapless style, made the lyrics to a classic song about a devil in a blue dress come to mind. On principle, she'd never worn a strapless anything before. Having something substantial to hold it in place may or may not have been a deciding factor; but knowing she'd be nervous enough that tripping might be a real threat, she convinced herself that she and everybody else could do without a possible major wardrobe malfunction.

As she waited for the store attendant to bring in dress number three, she cringed thinking of the cost of the first two, despite Natalie blowing it off. Leuster's was one of those boutiques that didn't bother putting price tags on its merchandise. No doubt, anyone who shopped at a place like that wasn't concerned with such things anyway.

Fiona then rounded the changing room corner with dress number three, and Carly's jaw practically unhinged. Somehow cost didn't faze her so much anymore. Immediately captivated, she held back her reaction as she ran a hand across the fabric.

Once she stepped behind the curtain and slipped it on, she fell in love. It fit as if it had been custom made just for her, and for a moment, she stared at her reflection, drinking in the indulgence sip by sip like lemonade on a hot day.

"Are you coming out anytime soon?" Natalie called from the other side of the curtain. "I'm dying to see!"

When Carly stepped out of the dressing room, Fiona gasped. "Oh, my word." Then she followed up with a high-pitched rush of babbling. "You're the first to try the Trey Gerardo designs. I was so excited to bring this one out to you. I just knew it would be perfect." She clapped her hands with a quick beat. "The faille is such a luxurious fabric. And the navy is perfect for your hair color and complexion. Isn't the neckline just exquisite? Oh, and look at that skirt. It falls so perfectly on you." Fiona circled Carly, brushing the fabric and straightening the skirt.

Carly finally turned to Natalie, whose face had been as blank as a clean page, and came to life with a flutter of her eyelashes, as if the shock were slowly beginning to wear off.

"This dress." She nodded. "It's the one. Good grief, we'd better hope Jex doesn't see you before he goes on stage, or we'll have to revive him with a set of de-fib paddles."

"Agreed. Totally agreed," Fiona crooned.

Carly stepped up to the three-way mirror and caught sight of herself again. A rush of warmth flushed her face. Yes, it was definitely the right dress.

Now, only a few hours later, as she prepared to make her appearance at the awards ceremony, she pulled the dress from the garment bag and pressed it against her. The same warmth filled her cheeks as the floor-length gown draped in floating waves around her. With hair, nails, and makeup done to perfection, for the first time, maybe ever, she felt . . . elegant. Completely elegant.

Chapter Twenty-Five

Jex

J ex stood in front of the living room window twiddling a black
bow tie nervously, his hair sleekly styled into place. He'd spent
the afternoon hours working out and swimming laps to stymie
his nerves. And he'd still heard no word from Natalie, which only
added to his stress.

Historically, when she'd gone missing for a few days, she was
earlobe-deep in some project or other that would make heads
spin and feet move. Like their dad, she knew how to make things
happen.

Maybe she'd convinced the ceremony organizer that they didn't
need the video montage at the unveiling after all. Despite the fact
that Marla would go into fits if that were the case, giving her airtime
left a sour taste in his mouth.

Either way, it would all be over in a couple of hours, and maybe
then he could breathe. At the moment, he felt deflated, like Marla
had squeezed him into a tight corner with no room for air. And

despite the few written-down words he'd prepared to share at the podium, he now wondered if he would even be able to summon the desire to say them.

At a quarter to six, the entry door opened, and Natalie let herself into the apartment carrying bags from some swanky local clothier.

"Where have you been?" Jex spoke through clenched teeth. "I've been trying to call you for the last two days."

"Did you ever doubt me, and haven't I taught you better? Anyway, no time to talk." She patted his chest as she walked past. "I've got to get ready. I just stopped by to pick up the prototype and to see if you were all set."

"To see if I'm all set? What about you? Did you get the montage finished and sent over to the program organizer?"

"Relax. It's in Davis's hot little hands. I've got you covered."

Jex followed Natalie down the hallway toward the guest room. "Okay, great. You could have let me have a quick look at it."

She didn't respond.

"So why are you taking my prototype?"

After hanging the garment bag on the closet door, she set the other items on the bed. "Do you really need one more worry tonight? The way I see it, the fewer things on your plate right now the better. I'll take the prototype, get it in your model's hands just before she takes the stage, and you can concentrate on your acceptance speech, bragging about your creative genius and such." She popped open a shoe box, pulled out a pair of heels, and dropped them to the floor. "Right now, I've got to get dressed, so scoot."

Natalie pushed him out the door and closed it behind him.

"Any special instructions for tonight?" he called through the door.

"Yeah, when I spoke to Davis earlier, he said he'll call you backstage a few minutes before they do the unveiling."

He could hear bags rustling from inside the room.

"You've got your speech ready, right? Put it in your pocket now so you don't forget."

He rolled his eyes. "It's already there."

"And plan on being a little livelier than you are right now. You're winning a pretty fabulous award tonight, you know."

"Yeah, I'll have to work on that."

"After Davis puts you on stage, Hughley will announce the award for Outstanding New Concept. That's when you'll come onstage and—"

"What about Marla?" Jex leaned his forehead against the door.

"What about her?"

"We're supposed to be sitting at a table together at the ceremony, and I'll need to tell her where to go."

"I could give you a few suggestions." Natalie's voice still rang clear enough through the door to deliver sarcasm.

"Seriously, Nat. What do I tell her?"

The door swung open, and she braced herself against Jex's arm as she buckled the strap to one of her heels.

He glanced at his sister once and then again. As no-nonsense as she was, she could still outclass the classiest. "You clean up alright."

"You're so salty. I look ravishing." She stepped into the living room and tossed her clutch on the couch. "Here." She turned. "Let me look at you."

After a quick scan, she smiled. "Not so bad yourself, but no showing up at the party crooked." She straightened his tie.

"I wish this were going down differently."

"Go. Accept your award and blow everyone out of the water tonight with your nerdy brilliance. And as for Marla, tell her I'll let her know where she can go when I get there."

Jex raised an eyebrow. "Don't—"

"I'll behave like an angel," she cut him off. "I'll give her all the cues—when, where, how. Trust me."

He sighed. "You know, you could've called me the last few days instead of leaving me hanging."

"I could've." She shrugged. "But then your faith in me wouldn't have been tested, and you'd ultimately not know how spectacular your sister is when all this goes off without a hitch tonight."

With a guarded grin, he leaned down and kissed Natalie's cheek. "I appreciate all your help getting me to this point, Sis."

Natalie patted his chest. "Good. I'm glad you see my magnanimous hand in all this." She winked, snatched her clutch from the couch, and pointed to the prototype case. "That the camera of the hour?"

Jex nodded. "That's it."

"Alright then." She shouldered the case strap. "I'll meet you at the McCormick."

"Wait. I thought we'd be riding together. Hughley's sending a car."

"You mean Marla hasn't demanded that the two of you arrive on the red carpet together?"

"I've avoided her calls. She'll make it there on her own, I'm sure. You can ride with me."

Natalie pursed her lips. "I have something else to take care of before the ceremony, but I'll meet you at the venue. Promise. I won't miss a thing. Text me when you're almost there."

Just before closing the door behind her, she looked back. "Jex . . . I'm really proud of you."

He grinned again. "Thanks, Sis."

Chapter Twenty-Six

Carly

At 6:35, Carly touched up her lipstick, gathered her clutch, and went to the hotel lobby. She walked differently, nearly floated as she entered the large room, the dress, the hair, and all the pampering having lifted her above her familiar existence and given her a little taste of the extraordinary. Conscious of a few turning heads, she waited near the concierge desk until a fit man in a black suit, likely in his fifties, approached her.

"Miss Kirkpatrick? My name is Harrison. I'll be your driver tonight." He offered her a card with his name and contact number and her destination—McCormick Place—printed fancifully on its face. He then extended his arm to escort her to a limo waiting just beyond the entry. "If I may say, you look absolutely bewitching this evening."

Carly smiled and accepted his arm. "Thank you, Mr. Harrison." No one had ever called her *bewitching* before.

The ride to the venue felt as if she'd just climbed inside a fairy tale. The limo was, without doubt, the largest vehicle she'd ever ridden in, aside from a school bus, and it was equipped with a television screen, a wet bar, and a darkened chauffeur's window just like in the movies.

This night wasn't a scene from a movie, though. It was real, and when her thoughts circled back to why she was in the limo in the first place, that made her nervous.

She didn't bother with the TV or the wet bar. Though taking the edge off her angst might have been welcome, she wasn't a drinker and, even if she were, she wouldn't have wanted any distractions from the experience *or* the end goal.

She moved closer to the chauffeur's window and rolled it down. "Mr. Harrison?"

He kept his eyes on the road. "Just Harrison is fine, Miss Kirkpatrick."

Of course, just Harrison. Didn't chauffeurs always go by one respectable-sounding name? Suppressing a grin, she leaned toward the window. "I was just wondering. Do you drive for the Radcliffes often?"

"When they're in Chicago, yes."

"So you've been around their family quite a bit?"

"Some would say."

"You know Natalie, then." She paused. "And Jex."

"I've associated with them a number of times when they've come to town."

"If you don't mind my asking, what do you make of them?"

"Ma'am?" His brow creased.

"I'm sure that seems like a strange question, coming from somebody you've never met before, but I don't know who else to ask." Carly watched the driver's eyes drift up to the rearview mirror.

"It's not really my place, ma'am."

"Harrison, I'm in a pretty vulnerable position right now, and honestly, I need some insight. You know the Radcliffes—at least better than I do."

From the reflection in the mirror, Carly could see the driver's eyes squint above what must have been a smile. "Yes, I suppose so." He drew out his response expectantly.

"As their driver, you'd have an idea about their character, right?"

"Miss Kirkpatrick, I've been driving for clients for over twenty years now, everyone from high-strung CEOs of Fortune 500's to their, let's say, overindulged teens on prom night. So, yes, I am a fairly quick study of character."

"Then what do you think of them? Please, I promise this conversation stays inside this car."

Harrison guided the vehicle to a stop along a quieter side street and turned in his seat to face Carly. "The Radcliffes are . . . above board, if that's what you mean."

"Above board?"

"They're hard-working, devoted people who also happen to be very wealthy."

"People can be hardworking and devoted to the wrong kinds of things though and be dishonest cheaters. Believe me, I've had that experience before."

"Ah." Harrison cocked his head. "True enough."

"You're probably hesitant to answer my question since they're paying for all this." Her eyes scanned the car's lavish interior. "But after tonight, I'll never see you again. In fact, I'll probably never see Jex again either." She quickly added, "Or Natalie. I just really need to know whether I can trust them."

"Ma'am, may I tell you a story?"

"Of course." Carly leaned back against the seat. "If you call me Carly."

Harrison nodded and continued. "A few months back, during the holidays, I picked up the younger Mr. Radcliffe from a car dealership. He was getting some custom work done while he was in the area for Christmas, and his father's secretary had requested that I take him back to the Emerald.

"When I arrived at the dealership, Mr. Jex opened the door and ushered a family of five he'd just met into the car. They'd broken down enroute from Milwaukee to Cincinnati for the holidays and had no extra money for a place to stay while their vehicle was in for repairs."

Carly shifted closer to the chauffeur's window. "What happened after that?"

"He pulled me to the side and told me to take them to his favorite hot dog place and treat them to a true Chicago-style hot dog, something the kids would enjoy. The couple had three little girls, stair-steps in age, and they hadn't eaten since their car trouble. Then I was to take them to the very same hotel you're booked in while they waited for their car repairs.

"When I returned the next day to take them back to the dealership, I learned that Mr. Jex had made arrangements for food delivery during their stay and paid for everything. Even sent in a few Christmas gifts for the family. He happened to include a generous holiday bonus for me." Harrison squinted as if in thought. "Miss Carly, he didn't know those people at all, but I suspect, aside from having a little Christmas spirit, he took pity because he has a bit of a soft spot for people who need help."

Carly thought about how she too had needed help, how he'd been her champion with his slew of suggestions to boost her business. "So, you do think he's honest, then?"

"All I can say for certain is that I've never witnessed another client make such a special effort to lighten somebody else's load. Often those who use my services are more wrapped up in their own lives than in offering a hand to someone down on their luck." He nodded. "The way I see it, honesty most often goes hand-in-hand with empathy."

As Harrison turned and again shifted the car into gear, he pulled off Lake Shore Drive and shortly entered a slow-moving cue of other limos inching closer to the venue's main entry.

Carly thought about what he'd said as she watched people dressed in their fancy evening gowns and tuxedos sauntering along the sidewalk toward McCormick Place.

The night seemed surreal. Only weeks ago, she was simply a girl from Alabama, wanting to take a good picture and sell it. And now, here she sat, dressed to the nines, riding to the photography world's equivalent of the Grammys in a stretch limousine. How she had gotten to this moment was dizzying.

In less time than allowed her to fully prepare, the limo door opened, and Harrison held out a hand. He closed the door behind her as she stood from the car and he leaned a bit closer to speak to her above the swarm of attendees. "Miss Carly, I hope I've put your mind at ease. And, so you know, even though you two look alike, if I were a betting man, Mr. Jex sees in you what he never saw in Ms. Marla."

Startled at his knowing remark, Carly turned to see Harrison's smile.

"How did you—?"

"Enjoy your evening, Miss Carly."

From the other side of a crowd, she heard someone calling her name and spun to see Natalie waving and moving through a sea of people. When she turned again toward Harrison, he was already on the other side of the car. Just before he disappeared inside, he tipped his head at her. It was just enough encouragement for her to cinch up her nerves.

As she made her way closer to Natalie, she noticed that the carpet really *was* red, and lined with people in dresses and costumes the likes of which she'd never seen in Alabama. The hum of conversations and flashes of cameras left her lightheaded.

Then Natalie appeared beside her, dressed in the cocoa-colored silk sheath she'd chosen at Leuster's earlier that day.

Carly raised an eyebrow. "Wow."

After a twirl, Natalie struck a self-assured pose. "I was going for a liquid chocolate aura. You know, yummy. Did I achieve it?"

"I'd say so, from the looks of all the eyes trailing along after you."

"And you? Mm, mm, mm. Owning that dress, my friend." She nodded toward the entry. "Come on. We'll have to gush over each other later. We've got to move inside before Jex gets here. He just texted a few seconds ago, and he's in the arrival line now."

Chapter Twenty-Seven

Jex

From the window of the limo, Jex watched the line of people at the curbside coursing toward the building's entrance. He pulled at the stiff collar and looked at his watch—still early enough that he could double-check everything with his sister and get seated before the start of the ceremony. He always did like being early.

Just as his car pulled in front of the main entry, he caught sight of Natalie and . . . was that Marla with her?

Before he could get a second glimpse, they disappeared into the building. A circumstance serious enough to force Natalie to associate with Marla was hard to imagine. His sister's dislike for his ex had been obvious from the moment they'd met.

He shook off the concern and told himself that maybe Natalie was just trying to make sure everything was set for Marla before the ceremony. Who only knew what energy that would take. He'd be sure to hear about it later.

After another few minutes of wait time, the car reached the entry, and his driver opened the door. As he stepped out, he took a deep breath. Paying little attention to the pomp and circumstance of those making a grand entry for the local press, he tucked his head down and moved into the crowd.

He had a mission—getting this night over with.

Chapter Twenty-Eight

Carly

Inside the venue, Chicago's elite traipsed through the room in their gowns and tuxes while waiters with trays of champagne flutes drifted among the attendees with the efficiency of graceful ghosts. Carly tried not to gawk at all the extravagance but followed Natalie as she maneuvered through the crowd, stopping only once to drop a quick hello to someone who greeted her.

After they made their way to the front of the banquet hall, Natalie slipped through a backstage door and pulled Carly inside. The behind-the-scenes event staff shuffled around like a busy team of ducks under the direction of a lead manager quacking instructions over a headset as he consulted a tablet in his hand.

Natalie weaved through the workers and led Carly to a concealed out-of-the-way spot just behind the curtain. An extra podium, a few chairs, and some panel tables occupied the quiet corner just out of sight from the banquet hall.

Natalie turned to Carly and squeezed her shoulders. "Okay, this is it. I'm sorry you'll have to wait here for so long before the program starts, but to avoid being seen, this is really the only option."

"No. That's exactly what I wanted."

"The prototype's in the case just behind the table there." She pointed out its location. "Just remember, once they announce the award for Outstanding New Concept, Jex will come up on stage, accept the award, and they'll start the montage reel. After it's done, you'll hear your cue—the dramatic pause in the music. At that lapse, you'll step into the spotlight and the music will crescendo right at your entrance. It's really gonna be amazing."

Carly kneaded her fingers. "And the camera's set up for the shots?"

"Let me show you." Natalie stepped to the case, opened it, and pointed to an attachment. "This works on the same principle as your flash. Just hit the power before you go on, strut across that stage like you own it, and start snapping pictures. Go out into the audience. They'll love it. They won't even have time to stop oohing and ahhing over Jex's photos of you in the montage before the candids you'll be taking of them will start popping up. They'll go wild. Everybody wants to see themselves on the big screen. Think the kiss-cam at a ballgame."

"And you don't think Jex will go off the rails when he sees his photos of me in his montage reel?"

"His back will be to the screen, and believe me, he's antsy about tonight. He'll be so plugged into his speech and the audience's response, he won't even pay attention to what's happening behind him. He'll never realize we changed the photo spread. Then when you start with the audience interaction, he'll go with the program because he's never known what to expect from Marla in the first place."

"Speaking of, what about Marla?"

Natalie peeked through the curtain. "She should be here any minute, but don't worry, our attorney's scoring a fat check for working this event. And, timed right, he'll deliver to Madam Marla her ego on a plate. She won't have time to spoil things because she'll be too busy picking her jaw up off the floor from all the legal threats he'll hurl her way if she doesn't vacate the venue."

"Timed right? Are you sure I'm not gonna be in the middle of a lawsuit?" Carly frowned. Rolling that scenario over in her head had become too frequent a practice since Natalie had first mentioned Marla's threats to Jex. It had caused her to second-guess her role in all this more than she cared to admit.

"Trust me, when my dad's attorney finishes with her, she'll be afraid you're the one who's filing the suit." She let the curtain fall back into place. "Looks like everybody's getting seated for dinner, so I need to go. Oh, and one last thing. Hughley will be at our table, close to the stage, sitting with Jex. When you go out into the audience, don't spend any time around him. He just needs to see you. That's it. He's a Neanderthal, and I don't want him getting any ideas. Once you're done with the stage show, we'll sweep you away, and we won't have to worry about him."

Carly took a deep breath. The butterflies in her stomach had erupted into a swarm. "Why did I ever agree to do this?"

"Because you've got class and spunk." Natalie smiled. "The class to help a guy you met only weeks ago launch his career when you have no skin in the game. And the spunk to do something totally nervy to make sure he's on the up and up. That scores big in my book."

"You're pretty confident he doesn't have feelings for Marla anymore, aren't you?"

"More than positive, but I respect that you need to see it with your own eyes. I'd be the same way." Natalie squeezed Carly's hand. "People are gonna love you, and I promise, before this night's through, you'll get the answers you need."

Carly smiled weakly as Natalie tucked her clutch under her arm and disappeared around the corner of the stage.

"Okay." Carly brushed the front of her dress, shoring up her nerves. "Let's do this."

Chapter Twenty-Nine

Jex

The round tables inside the auditorium, adorned with white linen tablecloths, each seated eight. Decorated with globe vases filled with low-cut calla lilies, each one looked like a miniature shrine with china place settings surrounding the centerpieces like they were pledging allegiance.

Jex meandered through the crowd, shook hands, and exchanged the standard pleasantries.

Hey Jex, haven't seen you in a while. Where you been?

Why, Jex Radcliffe, you look absolutely delicious. When are you going to sweep me off my feet and take me away for a weekend?

Radcliffe, good luck tonight. Hear you've got a real winner of a project in the works.

For every probe and question, every cougar wink and proposition, he moved a little more quickly. Scanning the crowd between interactions, he didn't see Natalie until he'd nearly made his way to the front of the auditorium.

Across the room, he waved and caught her attention. As he laced through another bevy of people, he finally reached her. "Glad to see you made it. Is everything ready?"

"All set." She looked past his shoulder and then around the room.

"Did you come in with Marla?" Jex asked.

"No, of course not."

"I could've sworn I saw—"

"Come on. We need to get to our seats. They'll be serving dinner soon, and I'm starved."

Natalie had never been shy about eating, and tonight appeared to be no exception despite all the glitz and glamor. At least they'd have a five-star meal. That might be the only highlight of the evening.

As they made their way to the appropriate table front and center of the stage, Jex pulled out a chair for his sister and continued to keep an eye on the crowd for Marla.

Most of the attendees wore conventional evening gowns and tuxedos, but a few ensembles ranged from flashy to tacky. As he unbuttoned his jacket and slid into a seat, Jex's attention trailed to a display gaining attention across the auditorium—Marla making her entrance. She definitely weighed in on the flashy, if not tacky, side of the spectrum. With all the flare of a showgirl, she compelled the crowd to part to accommodate her extravagant dress.

"There she comes, the devil herself." Natalie's sarcasm dribbled out like water from a soaked sponge.

Heat rose to Jex's face, and not the kind that came with excitement or attraction. Totally the opposite, in fact—embarrassment.

In long, slow strides, she moved toward their table with exaggerated grace. First, the bright sapphire-blue headdress caught the eye. Then, the feathered collar. Finally, the emerald green dress itself, with a train of peacock plumage the length of a small banquet table. Jex turned to Natalie. She pursed her lips and rolled her eyes.

When Marla arrived at their table, Jex stood. "Marla." His greeting was frigid.

"Jex, sweetheart. Don't you look dashing."

When he didn't repay the compliment, she deferred to Natalie. "And my, my, I didn't realize you'd be here, Natalie."

"I *am* his assistant. Remember?"

"Oh, right. You were his go-girl when I came to town last September."

Knowing Marla's feathers would soon be flying, Jex cut in and pulled a seat out between himself and the plumage. "I thought we'd talked about you going mellow on the dress."

Marla began to unbutton the elaborate feathered train from the bodice of her tight-fitting gown. "You should know by now that I'm not a vanilla kind of girl. And don't get your tux in a twist, I'm doing a wardrobe change just before we go on stage—something a tad more subtle. I just needed to make a memorable entrance. It's a marketing tactic. You should be thanking me." She raised a hand for one of the waitstaff who promptly arrived at her side. "Will you be a pet and take this to be checked?"

The waiter had no time to reply before she dropped the train in his arms, the feathers laying in a blanket across his face. After he wiggled out for air, the poor guy left, blowing plume fronds from under his nose. Jex glanced at Natalie to take a visual temperature. She was smoldering.

"Have you seen Calvin yet?" Marla asked.

"No, I'm sure Hughley's got last-minute things to take care of."

"Before he gets here, we need to set some things straight. I was disappointed that you didn't run those images by me before sending them on for the montage. I should have had an editorial voice." She waved at a gawking onlooker and brandished her bleached smile. "But c'est la vie. No time for petty concerns now. I'm sure whatever you've settled on will be second string to the real deal. And there are more pressing matters."

"Like what?" Natalie snapped.

Marla raised her hands in a narcissistic flourish and ignored Natalie's interruption. "We're creating an image in people's minds here. And in order to sell this product, you need to play the part, even though we've had a dissolution of our personal relationship. You should know that all eyes are on you right now because all eyes are on me. And the more we can be the darlings of the evening, the lovers for a love-hungry crowd, the more appetizing that little camera of yours will be to the right mix of people."

Jex looked away, his stomach now rolling. He could feel Natalie's stare and knew she wouldn't keep her mouth shut much longer.

"Now, to get started." Marla leaned in and ran a hand through his hair. "The suit flatters you." She topped off her chilled compliment with an unexpected and overdone kiss.

He had no time to respond before Natalie physically tugged him away from Marla's clutches. "Where did you come across your get-up, Marla? A Vegas swap meet?"

Swallowing the jab with a serving of disgust, Marla dabbed at her lipstick with her pinky. "I'm not as simple-minded as most."

"Funny. I always heard that a peacock had too little in its head and too much in its tail. That would explain why you're such an—"

Jex pinched Natalie under the table. "Look, here comes Hughley."

Marla turned and Jex widened his eyes at his sister.

When Hughley arrived at the table, he bowed, and Marla raised her green-gloved hands—one to Jex and one to Hughley.

"I now have my two preferred men, one for each side. Wonderful to see you, Calvin."

Hughley kissed her hand. "And you, my dear, look ravishing."

Natalie mumbled, "I can think of a few better adjectives."

Jex elbowed her this time.

"And you." Hughley leaned toward Natalie. "You must be Jex's assistant. I didn't realize he had such a deliciously stunning sister." As Hughley took a seat, Natalie offered a prim nod.

It was going to be a long night.

Chapter Thirty

Carly

Within a few minutes of standing at her post, Carly had drawn back the curtain to take a peek no fewer than a half-dozen times. She eventually caught sight of Natalie making her way to the center-most table in front of the stage.

Then she saw Jex.

He almost took her breath away.

His hair, perfectly styled, now looked more distinguished. His classic, black tuxedo brought out a polished side of him she hadn't yet seen.

Maybe it was the fact that she knew what he looked like underneath the suit that affected her so much. The still-fresh memory of him in the swimming pool a few weeks back . . . without the tux . . . made her stomach flutter. But seeing him, heartbreakingly handsome at a black-tie affair, brought her to the brink of feeling full-on jittery. Her pulse began to beat in her throat, and a now-familiar heat rose from her core.

A moment later, the crowd on the other side of the auditorium rustled with activity, then parted. Someone had entered the room. At first, she couldn't tell who it was.

Then she knew.

Marla sauntered across the floor, noticeably drawing all eyes to her.

Dressed in a green, feathery gown, she sashayed through the crowd looking like a . . . well, a peacock—a very extravagant peacock—the gown's avian theme underscoring those sharper features that Carly thankfully didn't possess herself.

After Marla had made her way to Jex's VIP table, Carly strained to see his reaction.

He nodded at her, and they sat.

Because a vase of lilies blocked her view, she could see only the back of Marla's feathery headdress and the stiff expression on Natalie's face.

In a moment, Carly saw a hand run through Jex's hair, and then they . . . *kissed*. Her blood began to come to a slow boil. A waiter with a serving tray passed between her backstage view and Jex's table at the most inopportune time, just as Marla was pulling away.

Did he lean in and kiss her back?

Was he smiling?

Playing with his hair would have been enough, but—what if he did return her kiss?

Between the waiter, the lilies, and Marla's ridiculous costume, Carly couldn't gauge anything.

She pinched the bridge of her nose as if to hold back her frustration. Maybe she should ditch Chicago and let Jex and his prized career land where they may. She *would* be entirely justified . . . *if* he had kissed Marla back.

But then, maybe it was all a part of the performance. Natalie had explained that he needed to keep to the status quo at least until the ceremony was over and the contract was signed. But could she deal with that—a performance—the whole night?

She peeked again through the curtain and saw a thick-chested man with salt-and-pepper hair, shorter than average, approach their table. He leaned in and kissed Marla's hand, all while smiling at her like a prowling cat.

Hughley, she thought.

His taking a seat next to Marla further confirmed who he was. Even from her angle, she could see Natalie bristle as he scooted in close to his prize.

Carly dropped the curtain and paced the little strip of stage between her and the tables, trying to calm her nerves, attempting to process what she'd seen.

This night was going to be excruciatingly nerve-wracking.

Chapter Thirty-One

Jex

As the evening ebbed on, Jex pulled at his collar occasionally and made governing eye contact with Natalie nearly every time Marla spoke.

An hour later, after their meal had been served, eaten, and cleared, the awards ceremony, now well underway, waxed and waned with droning speeches and bad jokes, all of which were a gift for Jex since it meant he didn't have to converse with Marla.

As the last round of applause trailed into audience mumblings, a program assistant approached the table with instructions for Jex and Marla to make their way backstage in fifteen minutes. Marla rose from the table. "I'll have to go now for my wardrobe change. I'll meet you backstage in a bit. We have people to dazzle." She leaned in to kiss Jex for the second time as he stood.

Hughley, having already had a few too many glasses of champagne, rose as well and nodded at her with a hungry smirk. "I'll be delighted to see what you bring to the ceremony."

Marla blew the man a kiss before sauntering off toward the exit.

Natalie then also stood. "Jex, I need to go to the restroom." More to herself than anyone else, she added, "I think I'm gonna puke."

"You won't miss the unveiling, will you?"

"Of course not. Believe me, I wouldn't miss this."

He watched as Natalie disappeared behind the exit doors, wondering at her weird tone. As Hughley nearly dropped into his seat, Jex eyed him and reluctantly sat down as well.

"You've got your hands full with that one, don't you?" Hughley grinned.

"What do you mean?"

"Marla. She's a little higher maintenance than you're used to, I can tell."

Jex didn't respond.

"I can see it a mile away. Pretty face, gorgeous figure, smile that'll stoke the flames. But she probably needs someone to take her down a notch. You don't seem to me to be that type."

Jex didn't know whether to be offended that Hughley had categorized him or flattered that he didn't merit being in the same class as him. "And you think someone else is a good candidate for that . . . *job*?"

Hughley smirked. "I've tamed a few mustangs in my day."

Jex could feel his patience growing thin. "I'm no longer with Marla, nor do I care to comment on her relationships. I will say this, though. She's not a horse, nor should you treat her like one. If you two mutually want to hook up, that's none of my concern. Just leave me and our business dealings out of it."

Hughley's bloodshot eyes widened. "Hmm, interesting new twist. I may just see about that." He again rose from the table and turned to Jex. "I'll meet you backstage in a few. You have an award to accept, my friend, and I may have a new acquisition to make."

When Hughley stepped away, a little heavy on his feet, Jex began to wonder exactly how much the man had had to drink.

He sat back down and waited a few minutes for Natalie to return, but she hadn't yet made it back before he got a hand signal from the assistant across the room that it was time for him to go backstage.

With one last scan of the audience, something felt off, like he was on a roller coaster slowly climbing the top of the steepest hill. When he started for the stage, he buttoned his coat and took a deep breath.

Ready or not, it was show time.

Chapter Thirty-Two

Carly

Bursts of laughter came and went with the table chatter, all of it while Carly waited in the wings, stewing and trying to sneak peeks of Jex.

As waiters cleared the tables and the awards portion of the program started, the backstage area came alive with activity.

The emcee offered a lengthy intro that Carly hoped wouldn't set the pace for the remaining presenters, or they'd be there all night.

Each award and presentation drew applause and occasional whoops and hollers from the few who'd likely taken advantage of the liberal supply of champagne.

Over the next hour, Carly talked to herself and watched for any clues she could gather from behind the stage curtain, waiting for her part in the charade.

But for every glimpse at Jex, no matter how fleeting, for every uninterpreted smile, her thoughts built on one another like a snowball of contradictions: first, confidence that this whole scenario was leading to answers, then doubt that they'd be answers she'd want to hear. She initially felt a fiery curiosity, like a driver passing a car wreck, followed by a self-imposed detachment like the same driver not wanting to get involved. Should she believe Natalie and Jex were honest or rely on the actions of someone who looked like an iridescent bird and who—despite their considerable resemblance to her—had taken pleasure in demeaning her?

Why did this have to be so hard? She continued to pace, her hands now worn out from the constant wringing.

As the fight in her head continued, someone on stage accepted an award for some accomplishment she didn't fully hear, but in the two-minute acceptance speech, the speaker thanked her co-workers with words that struck a chord. "I won this award because I learned to trust my team."

That single sentiment triggered Carly's memory of the conversation with Mrs. Brinkmeyer a few short weeks ago in the airport—the one in which Lucy had talked about having trusted the wrong person all along, nearly costing her a life of happiness with her Warren.

Carly stopped the handwringing.

She stopped the pacing.

Marla. I've been trusting Marla the whole time. Someone who had left her humiliated and angry. She had relied on signals from her instead of talking to Jex.

The realization dropped on her with the force of a load of bricks. She *wanted* to trust Jex. And maybe now was the time.

Carly ran to the curtain. Natalie had said they were saving Jex's award for last. It couldn't be much longer. One of the program assistants approached Jex's table.

Seconds later, Marla rose, kissed Jex again, blew a sickening smooch at Hughley, and strutted off. This time, Jex was turned to the side, obstructed from Carly's view even more than before. Hughley practically swooned and fell back into his seat after Natalie rose and left too. Both women exited toward the back of the auditorium.

"Okay, people. Get ready for the final segment." The program coordinator from earlier passed by Carly, squawking orders at his entourage in tow.

After a few minutes, the staff had each dispersed to their assignments, and Carly glanced across the stage. There stood Jex, taking his spot for the final presentation.

She quickly darted behind a stacked set of tables just out of sight but where she could still see the coordinator pointing and giving last-minute instructions.

Shoring up her nerves, she decided she'd approach Jex after the ceremony, tell him that she was wrong to leave. Until then, she'd have to play this off like she and Natalie had discussed or risk him flubbing the whole show.

As if on cue, the jazzy music track they'd selected for the evening switched to a pulsing new-age piece promising the audience something innovative and cutting-edge in the next segment.

Now, less than twenty yards separated her from where Jex stood across the stage. More handsome than ever, he also seemed uptight. Even from this far she could see his clenched jaw.

As the crew finished their prep, Hughley came up behind Jex, patted him on the back, and ushered him to another spot with quick access to the podium. Jex's bland expression seemed off, like he was less than amused. *Nerves*, she thought.

Emerging from the shadows, Carly peeked once more through the curtain at the audience in search of Natalie. In the back of the auditorium, along the main doors, a small commotion, the sound mostly masked by the music, started to unfold.

Marla, now donning a silver chrome tube dress, wheeled around like a loose-spinning top, wrenching her arm from the loose grasp of a well-dressed, silver-haired man.

The Radcliffe's attorney, she thought.

The stage lights and distance wouldn't allow Carly to see the man's face clearly, but his demeanor said that he had the expertise and patience to deal with Marla Fairchild.

He pointed toward the exit. Marla turned in a fury, jerking her head toward the door forcefully enough to knock free a few curls from her up-do, then stomped out, the object of her rage strolling casually behind her.

Back on stage, Hughley crossed the floor with an unsteady gait, taking his place at the podium—Carly's cue to get ready.

She stepped back from the curtain, opened the camera case, and lifted the prototype out of its cushioning. Once again, she slipped her fingers naturally around the body's grip.

As they settled into place, she realized that, in coming to Chicago, she'd found not only ideas for her business, but tools to make it truly her own. She wondered if Jex had a place in that picture.

With a deep breath, she readied the camera as the music died down and Hughley began to speak.

"Ladiez and gennelmen." He paused. The slight slur in his voice echoed across the hushing auditorium.

Carly swallowed the nerves that kept bubbling up.

"Tonight, I give you an ingeniouz invention. Hughley Photographics has a new toy." He flourished his hand in the air. "You might see it, that is if your eyes get past the beauty of who'll be diz-playing it."

He lifted an angular crystal trophy from the podium and wielded it in the air. "Ladiez and gennelmen, let's congratulate the man who'll be presenting this prototype and this year's winner of the Out-ssstanding New Concept Award. Jex Radcliffe."

Carly stepped back as Jex came from behind the curtain and entered the stage to an explosion of applause. He took the trophy and shook hands with Hughley who, with an unsteady gait, retreated from the podium and descended the steps into the audience.

As the applause died down, Jex gazed at the trophy. Carly's stomach took flight. He stood no more than a few steps from her and looked so painfully handsome that she wanted to fall into his arms, relive those few heart-stopping moments they'd had together.

"Friends," Jex began. "Have you ever felt like a misfit? Like someone else makes the mold and you have to simply fit into it? I have."

Carly wondered if Jex's opening question stemmed from someplace deeper than what tonight was about. She thought of the story about the relationship with his father that Natalie had shared with her.

"Because of that, I took a long, hard look at my life and made some choices. One of them was to develop something that breaks the mold. I've had a vision for a long time. One that involved taking something typical and making it into something extraordinary.

As a left-handed photographer, I always wondered what having a comfortable camera would feel like. Well, I can tell you tonight, it feels pretty amazing."

The audience again erupted with applause.

When the noise faded, Jex continued. "This product is obviously not for everyone, but it's definitely for many of us. So, for a moment, I hope you'll sit back and watch what magic can happen when you're comfortable with your creative tools. When you not only think outside the box but when the box ceases to exist."

With the crescendo of a drum roll, the stage lights dimmed, and the montage began to play on the big screen along with a stirring musical score.

Pictures of Carly began to flash on the screen, the photos Jex had taken while they were on the tour boat weeks ago. Shot after shot left the audience smiling, jaws slack, and a few even pointing at the images displayed in front of them.

Carly couldn't believe the crowd's response. She turned toward the stage and peeked through the curtain at the screen to see if it was really the pictures of her that caused such a buzz.

That's when she understood.

Even though she'd never quite enjoyed being in front of the camera, the magic in those images was the mark of Jex's genius. The angles, lighting, and even the cropping he'd done since she'd last seen the raw versions took her likeness to something with an energy and message all their own. He had the audience captivated.

Before the montage drew to an end, the last of the shots—the ones in the observation box at Willis Tower, the moments that literally had left her breathless—came up on the screen. She could still feel the needle-pricking tingle of excitement, thinking about the height where he'd taken her.

When the last image, the one of them lying on the glass floor above the backdrop of Chicago, flashed in front of the audience, it was the only one he and she both were featured in. She could tell that Jex, standing at the podium, watching his audience, still didn't realize why they were spellbound.

By the time he turned to the screen, it went black, and the well-timed signal for Carly's entrance cued up with the pregnant silence.

In the millisecond between his turning to the screen and her cue, Carly gripped the camera tighter, drew in a deep breath, and stepped from behind the curtain onto the darkened stage, her back to Jex.

In another second, the music built to a frenzy, and as the lights came up, the energy in the audience ignited like a fuel fire as the spotlight hit Carly.

From the podium, Jex cleared his throat with applause still sounding and announced, "Friends, tonight I give you my dream. Please welcome my assistant Marla Fairchild as she displays the DSLR Southpaw 2000."

The crowd, now lively with whistles and applause, drove Carly from her rooted position on center stage. She strolled to the top of the steps, working the audience with the same humility of a winning pageant queen. She waved, then brought the camera to her eye, pointed it at the audience at large, and shot the first live photo of the night.

As the image projected on the big screen, attendees went wild with applause, and Carly knew then that she had command of the crowd. It was a strange feeling. One she'd never even come close to experiencing before.

She stood and held the camera, scanned their faces, and soaked up their enthusiasm. When she saw Natalie along the far wall, she remembered her purpose. A quick thumbs up was Natalie's affirmation that Marla was gone. Now it really was show time.

She began her descent into the crowd, never turning within revealing range of Jex.

Her relief at making it to the foot of the steps without falling in her heels lasted for a sum of two seconds as she moved into the audience, snapping candids of the varied groups of attendees and waving to them between photos.

Each image displayed in real-time on the screen, and each table became more animated as she circulated the room.

After the third table, caught up in the crowd's energy, she mistakenly crossed Hughley's path.

That's when everything changed.

Chapter Thirty-Three

Jex

When he'd stepped out on that stage and accepted the award for Outstanding New Concept, Jex didn't realize that all the accolades in the world amounted to nothing when compared to the live responses to your work. He watched the audience, their expressions rapt, as the montage played behind him.

While he scanned their faces, he recorded what he saw for later—something he could replay for motivation during the days when nothing professionally seemed to go right. Everybody needed those kinds of reels in their reserves.

One thing that surprised him most, though, was Marla's stage appearance. She showed up for the presentation in a very classy, understated navy evening gown that actually complimented her instead of making her look like she needed plucking.

In fact, he couldn't have hand-picked a more perfect dress for the ceremony. She reminded him of the woman he'd originally met and fallen in love with over a year and a half ago the evening he'd stopped to help change her flat tire on Manhattan's Palisades Parkway.

She'd been on her way to some charity event. Dressed in a head-turning, black sheath, she had stepped outside her car after limping it to a stop along the roadside.

After stopping and a few minutes of conversation as he changed the tire, they'd exchanged enough information for her to know he was a photographer on his way to a shoot. She'd asked for his card and, after thanking him profusely for his help, said she'd be calling him for some professional headshots. She'd been much more amicable back then.

As the spotlight swung to capture her taking candids of the crowd, he shook off the thought. *People change.*

From the montage, he could see that the audience fell in love with Marla. That was the only thing he worried about. Giving her an inch meant sacrificing ten miles.

As she circulated the crowd, Jex alternated between watching the screen for the real-time candids she was shooting and watching the audience respond to her. He held his breath for the first shots, hoping that everything was keyed in correctly and that the automatic settings would do their job in the hands of an amateur. With variable lighting and movement, shooting would be tricky enough.

After the first few shots, though, he rested a little easier. Marla was actually taking decently framed photos, all while working the audience right into the palm of her hand.

The first table of attendees seemed mildly reticent, unsure of what to expect. The second became more animated when they saw themselves on screen. And the third behaved like total hams as Marla clicked the series of photos that published their antics like a digital billboard.

The audience devoured the attention, each table now attempting to draw her to them next. And Jex watched. Somehow, she carried herself differently than he'd expected.

Chapter Thirty-Four

Carly

The crowd continued celebrating with each photograph projected on the screen. Their energy was contagious. Only once did Carly face Jex from her spot on the auditorium floor, camera to her eye, zooming in on him with his trophy on the podium at his side.

If she were honest, she took the shot more for her own benefit. Seeing him through the viewfinder was a guilty pleasure, but as the image flashed instantly onto the screen, the crowd's noise level rose again.

The stage lighting had reflected Jex's cut jawline perfectly and left more than Carly charmed by his good looks. In fact, a few women in the back cut the continuous buzz of the crowd with sharp whistles. They clearly enjoyed seeing him too.

Caught up in the crowd's response, Carly made her way front and center of the VIP table, and within Hughley's reach. At first, he tugged gently at her arm, purring at her with compliments.

Camera still poised, she resisted. "Mr. Hughley, let me step back here and take your photograph. I'm sure everyone would rave at a picture of you on the screen."

"So, you think I'm handsome?" The man's breath reeked of alcohol. He tugged a little more insistently.

Carly ignored his question, gritting her teeth as he drew her closer. "I do need my hands to do my job, Mr. Hughley."

"I need my hands to do my job too, sweetheart." He jerked Carly into his lap and cackled, his warm, sour breath sending champagne exhaust up her neck.

Carly pushed him away, but just as quickly, he pulled her back.

On impulse, she drew back the camera and walloped Hughley's forehead. With a thud, the man grabbed at his hairline and, standing in a wobble, dumped Carly to the floor.

The music screeched to a halt as attendees rose from their chairs and Jex bounded from the stage into the crowd.

Chapter Thirty-Five

Jex

Between watching Marla circulate and work the audience, Jex had focused on the lighting and the camera's performance in a real-time projection scenario. When a side shot of him flashed onto the screen, he first felt a little self-conscious, but then smiled and pumped his fist in the air, rousing the audience's energy even more.

He then returned his attention to the screen, waiting for the next shot to appear.

He didn't notice until a reasonable delay that something was happening in the audience. When he turned back around, Marla was in Hughley's lap, the man's hands covering ground they shouldn't be.

Before Jex could process the whole scene or the urgency behind her movements, she'd clubbed Hughley in the head with the prototype, and he'd flung her to the floor.

Jex bounded from the stage, taking the stairs two by two. He pulled Hughley by his collar as Marla scrambled up from the floor.

"What is wrong with you?" Jex shoved the man, now wild-eyed and sobering up.

"Take your hands off me," Hughley growled. "Here I thought she was up for grabs."

"She is NOT *up for grabs!*" Jex seethed. "And don't you ever touch her like that again." Other than a now deepening disgust for Hughley, Jex didn't know why he'd felt the need to intervene in something Marla had made no secret of wanting. She'd practically drooled on Hughley as much as he had her. The man's audacity just rubbed him wrong.

From his periphery, he could see Marla clutching her dress and backing away. Without taking his eyes off Hughley, he put himself between them.

Hughley glared at him and then chuckled and brushed off his tuxedo. "You must think you're somebody, now that you've got your foot in a door." Hughley's words rolled off his tongue in fumes.

Attendees within range looked at each other in shock, no one willing to break the layer of ice now weighing so heavily on the scene. Hughley, still obviously affected by his blood alcohol level, rocked back and forth on his heels. "I'll tell you this much. No man who's as wishy-washy as you will ride on a nice, cushy contract under my company umbrella. You're a recipe for bad businezz. Go get your trophy off my stage and enjoy it, 'cause that's all you're getting out of tonight—a nice piece of crystal."

Jex shook his head. "You have no restraint or decency, and honestly, I don't see how you've made it this far." Turning to pick up his camera from where it had fallen, he pointed a finger at Hughley. "You can keep your cushy contract *and* your cheap crystal. I'd dump this camera in Lake Michigan before I'd attach your name to it."

A few people from the crowd gasped. Natalie, out of breath from pushing through the audience, emerged at his side. "What just happened?"

He looked around. "I'll explain later. Where's Marla?"

Natalie stared blankly at Hughley. "She's . . . gone."

"C'mon, we have no business here."

As Jex parted the crowd, pulling Natalie by the hand, Hughley called out, "There are better minds than yours, Jex Radcliffe. Much better minds than yours."

Chapter Thirty-Six

Carly

Carly had clutched the skirt of her dress and scrambled to her feet behind Jex when he'd stepped between her and Hughley.

She'd heard all she needed to hear. Amid the chaos of clubbing Hughley with the camera, Jex had confirmed exactly what she'd been afraid of all along. The pieces fell together perfectly. Jex and Marla *were* still together, and this whole charade had been Natalie's personal scheme to get Jex's fiancé out of the picture for good, both literally and figuratively.

Without waiting to see what came next, she shouldered her way through the crowd of people gawking at the spectacle that had just taken place.

Anger and embarrassment rose from her stomach in waves of nausea. She had allowed herself to become a key player in a setup that did nothing but open her up for another disastrous failure.

Why'd she do it? Why had she trusted Jex *or* Natalie?

Without taking time to catch her breath, she turned and elbowed her way through the gathering crowd to the exit, tears welling up in her eyes.

She jerked her clutch from the attendant at check-in and ran until she reached the street. After digging for Harrison's card, she made the call. She had no intention of waiting, though, and instead started walking up the street to get away from the McCormick. She could only hope Harrison would see her as he approached, or she'd have to hail a cab and top her night off with another personal expense just to add insult to injury.

With half a block already behind her, enough adrenaline pumped through her veins to walk the full three miles back to the hotel, but as she began to slow from a tromp to an aggressive stroll, the last thing she expected was a voice she faintly recognized calling out from behind her.

"You must feel really good about yourself."

Carly wheeled around. There she stood in her chrome-like tube dress, reminiscent now of a drainpipe, mascara smeared in patchy streaks down her cheeks. Had it not been for the difference in dress, they'd have been close likenesses, both the image of a disparaged woman.

"Did you feel like a superstar up there on stage?" Marla spat at Carly as if she'd swallowed coffee grounds. "That's where I was supposed to be, you know. Not you. Me."

"Stealing your show was not my idea of a good night, believe me."

"You're a liar," Marla yelped.

Fatigue setting in, Carly bowed her head. "You know, maybe I am. Maybe I've lied all along, from the moment I set foot in

Chicago, about who I am, about the values I represent. Maybe I've been too scared to be honest, because being honest takes guts I don't have right now." She put a hand to her forehead. "But my guess is that if you take a good long look in the mirror, you're doing the same thing. You think you've got to wear an extravagant dress or treat people like dirt to make yourself appear a little more valuable, a little better." She stopped, breathed, and looked tiredly at the limo pulling up to the curb. "The real truth, Marla, is that you're just a woman in a shiny party dress who was forced to miss the party. And you're no worse for having missed it."

Harrison put the car in park and jogged around it to open the door for Carly.

Stepping to the door, Carly then turned back. "But think of the bright side, Marla. You did get the guy. Last I saw him, he was back at the party defending your honor."

The last thing she saw through the darkened window as Harrison pulled away was Marla with folded arms, looking toward the McCormick.

Chapter Thirty-Seven

Jex

When they cleared the last set of double doors and made it outside, Natalie, who'd been in a near run to keep up with Jex, tugged at his suit coat. "We've got to stop. My feet are killing me. What happened back there?"

"Where were you?" Jex snapped.

"On standby with the equipment in case I needed to make adjustments to the shots on the screen. I saw you get the award, but after that, my focus was on the feed."

Jex set his camera on a nearby bench and loosened his bow tie.

Natalie followed him. "What happened?"

"Hughley! That's what happened." He paced, running a hand through his hair. "What an idiot I was to trust that guy! I got a bad vibe the first time I met him. My mistake was choosing to think anything good could come from working with him."

Natalie closed her eyes. "What'd he do?"

"When Marla crossed his path during the presentation, he pulled her into his lap and put his hands all over her."

Natalie's face went pale. "You're kidding."

"Not much telling what he'd have done if she hadn't hammered him with my camera. I was a little surprised about that, to be honest, but he got way too bold."

"Uuuuugh! The nerve!"

"He didn't get far. The knot on his head was already rising by the time I got to his table."

"Good for her!" Natalie's lips pursed in anger.

"So, you've become Marla's cheerleader now?" Jex turned away, still pacing.

"Not exactly *Marla's* cheerleader." Natalie continued. "Jex, there's something you should know."

Ignoring her, he growled. "I can't believe this. The biggest night of my career, and it ended this way."

"Jex."

"What?"

She took him by the hand and pulled him to the bench. "Sit down with me a minute. I need to tell you something."

Natalie's eyes clouded with concern. "You were supposed to find out after you got the award and the night was a big success, after everything was over."

Jex's response came slowly. "Find out what, Natalie?"

"I did something I thought would help your career, and . . . well, you didn't really know the full score the whole way through the ceremony."

"Meaning what?" His voice sharpened.

"Don't be mad. I did it for your own good."

"You did what, Natalie?" His stomach tightened as Natalie squirmed under his gaze.

"Look . . . I went to Alabama this week and brought Ca—" she paused, remembering her promise to Carly. "Bee. I brought Bee back to Chicago. That was her in there tonight. Not Marla."

"YOU WHAT?" Jex bolted from the bench. "That was Bee? That Hughley had his hands all over?" He started to walk away, then turned and came straight back. He blared, "How did you find—? No. You know what? I don't want to know." He pointed at Natalie. "You have done some careless, impulsive, thoughtless things, but this?" Turning away again, he buried his head in his hands. "What were you thinking?"

"Maybe that we would catapult Marla out of your life and save your career?"

He huffed and paced more. It was just like Natalie to take matters into her own hands. Even when they were kids, she'd charge in, set on saving the day when the day didn't need saving. What a disaster!

"Think about it, Jex. The montage? They were all your photos of Bee. And the one of you and her at the Ledge? That was the icing on the cake, the one that left the audience with all the feels."

"Wait. You used the spread of Bee?"

"Yes, and they loved her because they could see that you loved her first."

"What are you talking about, Nat?"

"Oh please, just admit it. You're in love with Bee."

Natalie's claim felt like someone had just knocked the air out of him. "I'm not . . . I mean . . . You can't think . . . Surely, she's . . ."

"Yeah, surely she's in love with you too, ya big lug, and it was all going perfectly until Hughley got sauced up and decided laying hands on Bee was within his rights."

He didn't know whether to be furious or excited or dumbfounded or frantic. "Why did you keep this a secret from me? Maybe I could've . . . I didn't even know you were planning the audience interaction."

"I know you didn't. It was all a part of the strategy. We figured if we could engage the audience and leave less to the modeling, it would sell the campaign. And we were right."

"But you could have told me that!" Furious, yeah furious felt right at the moment.

"Bee made me promise not to tell you anything. And honestly, it was a good idea. Doing this was risky. I was worried that if you were aware of the plan, you'd get even more nervous and flub the whole thing."

"Yeah, well, thanks for the glowing vote of confidence."

"She also wanted assurance that you and Marla were a thing of the past."

"What?" Dumbfounded. Now, he was definitely dumbfounded.

Natalie sighed. "Like I said, Bee's in love with you too. She just doesn't want to admit it. My guess is she needed the reassurance before she jumped all in."

Jex's eyes widened. "Oh no, no, no." The frantic feeling came barreling in full-force.

"What?"

Jex pressed an open palm to his forehead. "She was there when I spouted off at Hughley. She heard me."

"What did you say?"

"I told him that Marla wasn't *up for grabs*." He quoted himself with hooked fingers. "She probably thinks I meant we're still together."

Natalie pulled out her phone, dialed, and lifted it to her ear. She shook her head at Jex after a moment. "She's not answering."

He snatched the camera from the bench and thrust it at Natalie. "I've gotta go find her. Any ideas where she went?"

"Before we left the auditorium, she was already gone. But she's staying at our suite at Four Seasons. Maybe she went back there. Here's the key card." Natalie pulled the card from her clutch.

Jex started backing toward the street. "Go inside. Get my case and all the montage data. I don't want anything left . . . except for that trophy. Hughley can have that. And double check for Bee, just in case we missed her."

"Sure."

He started to jog down the street to meet a cab parked curbside, then, as a second thought, turned around and called out, "If you see or hear from her, call me."

"Do you want me to say anything to Hughley?"

"No." His stomach turned at the thought of him. "We're done."

"Hey!" Natalie called after him. "Are you gonna forgive me?"

Jex slid into the back seat of the cab without answering.

He couldn't lose Bee twice.

Chapter Thirty-Eight

Carly

The emotional exhaustion wrought from a night of total deception left Carly drained.

Harrison pulled away from the venue with the chauffeur's window still open from their conversation earlier in the evening. "So your night was a disappointment then."

It wasn't a question. More of a confirmation.

She figured most of his passengers, if they weren't too drunk or too aloof to answer, might have agreed, just to keep a social perimeter. Now sniffling, Carly said, "Harrison, I don't really think I can talk about it right now."

"That bad? Don't worry, then, Miss Carly. You certainly don't have to talk about it with me. Where would you like to go?"

Carly's voice nearly spurted with anger. "Why did he have to be so deceitful? He *and* Natalie. And I had this drunken, obnoxious octopus snatch me tonight and pull me into his lap all because I trusted both of them. It was sickening. I've never been so humiliated in my life. Here I was thinking Jex might even have feelings for me. Huh! That's what I get for being his showgirl, demo-ing *his* product all while he's pining over another woman. I can't believe I fell for Natalie's scheme."

Harrison, now paused at a stop light, stared at her in the mirror. "Miss Carly, I'm sorry you've had such a terrible night. And that I may have misled you. Would you like me to take you back to Four Seasons?"

She balled her fists into the fabric of her dress, realizing how furiously she'd rattled on to the driver. "It's not your fault. That's just how underhanded they are." She forced her breathing to slow. "Harrison?"

The driver's eyes met hers again in the reflection of the mirror. "Yes, ma'am."

"Have the Radcliffes hired you for the rest of the evening?"

"Yes, ma'am."

"Then, yes, could you take me back to the hotel and wait while I get my luggage, then drive me to the airport?"

"Of course."

"Good," she said, now biting back her emotions. "The sooner I leave Chicago, the better."

When Carly got out of the limo, she told Harrison she'd be only a few minutes. Already forming the notes in her head she'd write to Natalie and Jex, she wanted to make this stop a quick one.

Once in her suite, Carly changed into jeans and a pullover, slipped on comfortable shoes, and slammed all her things back into her suitcase. Deja vu, she thought.

Quickly, she scribbled two notes, using the hotel's stationery, and left them on the desk—Natalie's opened, face up; Jex's folded with his name on the outside.

She glanced around the lavish room, then gathered the now lifeless evening gown in her arms. She pulled it to her face, the satiny fabric cool against her skin, and breathed in its luxury, something she'd try to remember, even if it had been another disastrous evening.

Leaving the dress on the bed, she zipped shut her luggage and turned out the lights.

She just wanted to go home to Camden Grove.

Chapter Thirty-Nine

Jex

When he arrived at the hotel suite, Carly was gone, and the dress from that evening lay on the bed. He picked it up, her jasmine scent still lingering in its folds. That's when he noticed the notes on the desk.

The first was open.

> *Dear Natalie, Congratulations. You got what you wanted, the photo spread—signed, sealed, and delivered. I guess my consolation prize was finding out the truth about Jex and Marla before my head got too wrapped up in him. Too bad it wasn't before my heart did. Please give the other letter to your brother so I can tell him __my__ truth. Then leave me alone so I can forget that Chicago ever happened. —Bee*

Jex wadded up the paper, then closed his eyes. He dropped the letter on the table, his heart pounding in his chest.

He snatched up the second letter, opening it wildly.

> *Dear Jex, I came to Chicago for help, and you showed me ways of looking at things I didn't know existed. For that, I owe you my thanks. I regret some things, though. The day you kissed me, I let something happen that I vowed would never happen again. I started falling. That was my first mistake. Coming back to Chicago for more heartbreak was my second. I willingly signed over the rights to the photos. They're yours. But I did keep the rights to one thing—my heart. —Bee*

Chapter Forty

Carly

The airport was quickly becoming Carly's least favorite place.

Harrison had dropped her at the entrance closest to her airline's ticket counter and given her a genuinely empathetic smile before leaving her with his tip still in her hand.

Once inside the airport, she found the ticket lines full of out-of-town Cubs fans sporting ball caps and team gear. They still had adrenaline from the game pumping through their veins. A few Brewers fans, less animated, also occupied spots in the long lines.

Carly parked her carry-on at the end of the shortest line she could find. While she waited, she pulled out her phone. Three missed calls from Natalie. She pushed aside her irritation and tried to call Ava. Hearing a friendly voice right now would help.

After the fourth ring, Carly hung up without leaving a message. She'd try again after going through security.

Tucking a strand of hair behind her ear from her disarranged up-do, she could feel her empty stomach lurch. She hadn't eaten since having a few finger foods during the early afternoon spa session, nor did she have much of an appetite now. In fact, she felt empty through and through. Before boarding the plane, though, she'd have to force something down, or motion sickness would set in for sure.

Scrolling through her phone as the line inched forward, she didn't at first notice the woman weaving in and out of people, clearly in search of a particular passenger.

When the line moved forward again, she looked up and came face to face with Natalie.

"What are you doing here?" Carly fumed.

"I've got something to say."

"I'm trying to get home. I don't have time for this."

Natalie nodded at the rowdy group of Cubs fans in the ticket line in front of her. "Looks like you'll be waiting for a while."

"The line's moving."

"Then I'll get a ticket with you."

"What? No." Carly stepped to the side. "Just leave me alone."

"I can't. Not until I tell you what just happened." Natalie's voice softened. "Look, give me five minutes."

A man donning a Cubs hat, in line where Carly had been standing, interrupted. "I'll save your place."

"See? You won't even lose your spot."

Carly tightened her jaw. "Two minutes. You've got two minutes." She turned to the Cubs fan. "Thank you."

"Perfect." Natalie grabbed Carly's carry-on and rolled it to a close-by bench. "Sit." She patted the seat. "Please."

"A minute forty-five." Carly plopped down. "Now, what do you want?"

"To tell you what really happened and how it's completely different from what you *think* happened at the ceremony tonight."

"It's pretty plain to me. You used me, and it backfired for both of us."

"That's not what happened. Yes." Natalie gave a quick nod. "I wanted you there to help Jex. And I told you that up front. Yes, it required your signing over the rights for us to use the photo spread of you. But what you witnessed at that ceremony was a man who happens to have a sense of decency tell a man with no morals at all that the woman he tried to grope was not a piece of meat. What you observed was chivalry, not his commitment to another woman."

"He thought I was Marla, and if you ask me, he made a pretty emphatic claim that she was 'not up for grabs.' That sounds pretty committed to me."

"But don't you see?" Natalie touched Carly's hand. "He wasn't saying she was *not* available, but instead that she was not a toy for Hughley to handle." She sighed. "Jex would have done the same for any woman. He's just that way."

"But they kissed, twice."

"No, *she* kissed *him.* Playing hard to get with Hughley, I'm betting, so he'd want her even more. And that, no doubt, was what stoked his fire in the first place."

"So, you're telling me that Jex and Marla aren't together?"

"That's what I've been trying to tell you all along."

"And he didn't kiss her back tonight?"

"Could you not see his face? He was practically shoving her away from the table when she left for her wardrobe change."

"All I could see was a vase of lilies and that peacock headdress of hers." Carly sat back in the bench. "How am I supposed to trust you? How am I supposed to believe that he's not with Marla right now, consoling her over the stunt we pulled with the attorney? I'm still half expecting to be sued, thanks to you."

Natalie pulled her phone out. "Take a look at this, will you?" She tapped the screen a couple of times and turned it to Carly. "What do you see?"

Carly delayed a moment, then looked at the phone. She drew in a frustrated breath. "Looks like Jex's award."

"You're right. And it's still sitting on the podium, exactly where he left it. Before I came to search for you, I snapped a picture of it because I wanted to at least have a visual reminder that he got close to taking one of those stinking DIA trophies home."

"What do you mean?"

"After you left, Jex completely renounced his contract with Hughley Photographics *and* the Outstanding New Concept Award. He left it all behind because of what Hughley did to you. And no, he didn't know it was you at the time, but he did it because of what he stands for. I don't know about you, but that's the kind of guy I'd want in my corner."

"He gave up the award? And the contract?"

"Everything. He left Hughley stuttering. Told him what he could do with his trophy. And if that's not enough to convince you, just know that I came all the way across town to stop you from getting on that plane when I could be at home soaking my feet right now." She sighed. "Why would I have an interest in finding you if we were just running a game? For crying out loud, everything's been burnt to the ground."

Carly's jaw went slack. She stared blankly at the lines inching toward the ticket counter. He'd given up his business, his dream, everything . . . for her.

Natalie gripped Carly's hand. "I guess my two minutes are up, and I honestly don't know what else to say." She tilted her head, her voice hopeful. "He's got eyes for you . . . Honeybee."

Chapter Forty-One

Jex

When he got back to the Emerald, Jex threw his tie and suit coat on the couch. He changed into some jeans and a Henley, threw on his jacket, and pulled a key from his nightstand.

He needed to ride, to figure out a way to straighten this mess out with Bee.

Slamming the door shut behind him, he headed for the stairs, thoughts barreling through his head at the speed of a runaway train. Within the space of the last hour, he'd thrown away his chance at establishing the career he'd always wanted and sealed his fate as his father's replacement.

But none of that mattered.

Because he had lost Bee.

He straddled his bike, and with a forceful rev of the throttle, it roared to life beneath him. Kicking it into gear, he squealed out of the garage with no confidence that he'd find peace of mind tonight.

The wind buffeting against him seemed only to stir the embers rising to a full-on blaze in his chest.

After an hour, he ended up at the foot of Willis Tower. He parked his bike illegally but didn't care. What was a ticket at this point but a welcome distraction?

City traffic had died down, and he walked over to one of the outdoor Starbucks tables, aiming to take a seat.

"What are you doing here at such a late hour?" Trudy, making late night rounds, stepped from the shadows with a lit cigarette. She looked official in her security uniform.

"You move to night shift?" Jex asked.

"Covering for one of the other workers whose kid's coming into town." She dabbed the cigarette out in a concrete sand tray and exhaled a plume of smoke. "What about you?"

"Just needed some time to clear my head." He nodded at the bike. "Took a ride and ended up here."

"Wanna come in? The evening shift just left. I could let you go up top for a while. I know how you like to solve the world's problems up there."

Jex bowed his head and offered her a dismal smile. "I can't even solve my own."

Trudy jerked her head in invitation. "Well then, sounds like a trip to the top of Chicago's in order. Go knock yourself out."

Drained and disheartened, Jex stepped into the building.

Chapter Forty-Two

Carly

The ride from the airport was excruciatingly slow. Traffic on the interstate crept to a standstill with a wreck blocking both inbound lanes.

While their driver found an alternate route, Natalie tried repeatedly to call Jex, but he didn't answer. "His phone keeps going to voice mail." She tapped her screen to end the call.

"Where could he be?"

Natalie shook her head. "Knowing Jex, he's off thinking somewhere, trying to sort through this mess."

"Thinking?" Carly perked up. "The day he took me to Willis Tower, he said that it was his favorite place to think. Maybe he went there?"

"Not likely if Trudy's not around. We could swing by and give it a try, though."

Carly took a deep breath. The thought of the Tower made her empty stomach that much queasier.

Natalie directed the driver on where to make their next stop, and within a mile of their destination, her phone rang. When she looked at the screen, she shook her head at Carly. "Hello? . . . Yes, this is she . . . Oh, yes, I must have forgotten it . . . Okay, thank you. I'll be right there."

After ending the call, she turned again to Carly. "I have to go back to the McCormick. Jex's case is there. In all the excitement, I left it behind. But we can drop by the Tower first."

As they pulled within sight of the closest of the Tower entrances, Natalie pointed. "Look. You were right. There's his bike. He must've come here after I sent him to the hotel room."

"He went to the Four Seasons?"

"Yeah. He was looking for you."

"Oh, no." Carly frowned. "He must've seen the letter." She tried to remember exactly what she'd written, tried to imagine what he'd think as he read each word. Her heart dropped.

"What letter?"

"The one I left for him on the desk. And one for you too. Letters I'd just as soon neither of you saw now."

Natalie raised her eyebrows. "I'm guessing you gave him plenty to think about then."

Carly looked up through the limo's sunroof at the Tower's columns of windows receding into the night sky. "Yes. A lot."

"Well, I don't see him anywhere, so I'm guessing if Trudy *is* working the night shift, she's already taken him up."

Carly swallowed. The inside of her mouth felt like cotton.

"Since he's around somewhere, maybe you should go up. The security guards make rounds on the hour. I know because Trudy complains about it every time I see her. If she is on duty, she'll let you in once she knows you're looking for Jex. She's got a soft spot for him, I think."

The driver stopped the car close to the parked bike. Carly's stomach began to fill with dread. "Wait. Don't you think you should go with me?"

"Jex is a little miffed at me right now. I'm sure you'd do better on your own. I can wait with you until we make sure Trudy's here though. Then I'll go get Jex's case while you talk to him."

"But—"

"Look." Natalie pointed. "There she is now. She'll check all the entry doors on the bottom floor. When she comes to this side, knock, and then tell her you need to see Jex. She'll definitely let you in if you catch her. Go on."

The driver circled the car and opened the door.

When Carly stepped out, she looked back. Natalie leaned through the open window. "It'll work out. I'm sure of it." She nodded Carly toward the entrance.

Before she had a moment to process her thoughts, the driver closed the car door and got back in, leaving Carly alone in the moon's shadow of Willis Tower.

While she waited for Trudy to come to her side of the building, she walked over to Jex's bike and touched the metal, as if it would somehow give her courage.

She paced along the sidewalk and craned her neck to look up the side of the monstrous building. The height of it reached nearly into the clouds. How was she supposed to get the nerve to go all the way up there by herself?

Maybe she should just wait for him to come down. Surely, he wouldn't be too long.

What if it wasn't even Jex's bike parked there? His wasn't one of a kind. Probably a couple thousand like it in Chicago alone. What if he was somewhere else?

Her speculations continued until one of the entry doors opened.

The woman she recognized from weeks earlier, dressed in a security guard uniform, stepped out the door, pulling a phone from her pocket. Before she'd fully engaged with the screen, she noticed Carly. "Hey, I know you. You're that girl Jex brought here a few weeks back."

Carly stepped closer. "Trudy, isn't it?"

"That's right. Good memory."

"Have you seen Jex tonight?"

"Funny you should ask. He's up top now. Seems a little down, if you ask me. Something happen between you two tonight?"

Carly dropped her gaze. "You could say that. Do you think he'll be down before long?"

"I'm here all night, so I'm guessing he'll be up there for a while too. He usually takes his time." Trudy glanced at her watch. "Tell you what, I don't ordinarily do this, but I've got my rounds to finish. I can't take you up myself, but if you want to go and see him, I'll walk with you to the elevator."

"Oh, I don't know." Carly waved a hand. "Maybe I should just wait for him to come down."

Trudy grinned. "Scared of heights, are you?"

"That obvious?"

"Not to most, but I see it all the time. Come on. I can get you through this." She led Carly inside as the limo pulled away.

Descending the escalator to the lower floor, Carly remembered the day she fell into Jex's arms when he'd coaxed her onto the escalator's top step. The memory stirred up the butterflies in her stomach again and maybe enough courage for her to follow through with going up to the Ledge without Jex's help this time.

After they arrived at the elevator, Trudy pushed the button and turned to Carly. "When you get inside, close your eyes and don't watch the floor number display. Stand there, keeping your eyes closed, and think of the most pleasant sights you've seen, say, in the last month. Focus on those for a couple of minutes, and before you know it, you'll be at the top. Sounds simple, I know, but it works."

The elevator door opened, and Carly hesitated.

Trudy held the door-open button and nodded. "Go on. I promise, you'll be fine. Remember, the most pleasant sights."

Carly took as deep a breath as she could and slowly exhaled. She stepped into the elevator, backed up against the wall, and looked at Trudy. "The most pleasant things." She nodded and closed her eyes.

When she heard the doors close, her breathing quickened, and her heart began to pound. "The most pleasant things." She breathed. "The best things. The sweetest, most pleasant things." She began to pant. "The best, most wonderful things."

Reaching like a drowning person for a lifesaver, she began to grasp at specific images.

Jex. She thought of Jex.

Jex, introducing himself.

Jex, looking at her pictures.

Jex, laughing at their truth or lies game.

Her breathing slowed, if only slightly.

Jex, on the tour boat, leaned back on his elbow.

Jex, sitting in front of her, on the motorcycle, so close.

Jex, in the swimming pool, the cords of his muscles pulsing in the water.

Now easing into a calmer rhythm, she thought of the way he looked with water dripping from his shoulders.

Jex, standing so close she could breathe in his scent, taste the anticipation of his kiss.

When the elevator doors opened, Carly gasped. Bit by bit, she stepped forward, gathering courage for every inch she coaxed herself to move. The vast room was quiet and darkened, empty of the noises noticeable on a typical day.

As she took soft, reserved steps further from the elevator, she scanned the room. Beyond the glass-paned windows, she could see nothing but the amber glow from the city lights below. They cast a soft light through the glass and into the room.

She didn't see Jex and stepped tentatively toward a couple of the Ledge's observation boxes. Each of the four protruded into the city's ambient light.

When she rounded the bend enough to see the furthest glass box, she noticed the slightest movement.

Jex.

She swallowed, her mouth now sandpaper dry, and slowly eased closer. How could she tell him she was sorry? Sorry for being so overly cautious. Sorry for being so quick to accuse. For not trusting when he ultimately gave her no reason to doubt.

What would she need to say to convince him that she wanted to take a chance? A chance on them.

As she drew closer, she saw him standing inside the furthest box, his silhouette against the glass, as if drifting above the city.

She waited a moment. Then, she knew what to do.

Chapter Forty-Three

Jex

The headlights of the cars below lit up the streets like they were the arteries in the circulatory system of a city. It always surprised him how peaceful and slow-paced it looked at night. Much more tranquil than his own life was right now.

Here he was, a thirty-year-old man whose ambition to make his mark on the world had just led to his own professional ruin. And, truth be told, he was fine with it. Hughley and he would've eventually crashed and burned anyway. Better now than later.

After the news got around about what had happened at the ceremony, he'd have one course left to take and a father ready to plug him into a career he'd shrivel up in.

But that wasn't even the worst part. The woman he'd met only weeks ago, initially touted as a solution to his career problems, now held the answers for so much more.

Except she was no longer within reach.

She saw him as nothing but a liar.

How could he make this right? What could he do to convince her that if he'd ever told a truth in his life, it was this one? That he was falling for her.

He drew in a deep breath and leaned his head against the glass wall. It wasn't until he exhaled, his breath clouding the glass in front of him, that he noticed something. A motion from the corner of his eye.

Chapter Forty-Four

Carly

Quietly, Carly had stepped away to a table and picked up someone's discarded newspaper. After digging in her bag, she'd found the Sharpie marker, the one she'd used to address the Brinkmeyer's package, and once she'd scribbled her message across the newspaper, she took a deep breath and inched toward the Ledge, hoping there would be enough light for him to see the words, praying she'd have the nerve to deliver them.

She chose the observation box adjacent to Jex, knowing that if she summoned enough courage to step inside, he could see her.

Once at the edge that separated floor from glass, she almost turned away. Then with shaking hands, she opened the newspaper so her message was visible.

The most pleasant thing.
The most wonderful thing.
The best thing that's ever happened to me.

With her breathing now steadier, she closed her eyes and slid her foot inside the edge of the glass.

The most pleasant, most wonderful, best thing.

Eyes still closed, she eased her other foot inside.

Most pleasant, best, wonderful . . .

In slow, even, calculated movements, she placed the newspaper against the glass section facing Jex.

Best, most pleasant . . .

When she was completely inside the box, her message to him against the glass, she opened her eyes.

There he stood, suspended over an entire city, motionless, looking directly at her through the glass of their boxes.

The strange thing was she didn't even see the buildings below.

Or the tiny cars.

Or the threadlike streets.

Not the lights or the city fading past the limits of downtown Chicago.

Instead, fear drained from her—a vortex of relief . . . when she saw only him staring into her eyes.

Chapter Forty-Five

Jex

When Bee looked at him, his heart nearly ruptured. In front of her, against the glass wall, she'd placed a piece of newspaper with words hand-written in candid black.

My name is Carly.

When he stepped from his glass box and went to her, he rounded the corner and came face to face with the girl he thought he'd never see again.

A girl with a new name.

The glow of the city lights below illuminated her face and left him nearly weak.

"Carly?" He smiled. "That's a beautiful name."

"Please." She touched his lips. "Let me talk first."

Her eyes glittered as he took her hand in his.

"I first came to Chicago scared. Too scared to risk being vulnerable. And I made the mistake of not trusting you. Then I held onto that doubt when I came back with Natalie." She squeezed his hand. "I'm sorry. Tonight, you lost everything you've worked so hard for, and I feel like I'm partially to blame."

"You're wrong." Jex shook his head. "I'd have been miserable with Hughley. You're setting him straight was a favor."

"But if we hadn't altered the program, you still might have had a contract, at least."

"Yes, and I'd be exactly where Marla and Hughley wanted me, legally bound and much worse off than when I started."

"But what will you do with your prototype?"

"Let's not talk about that." Jex smiled. "You came back to me. That's what's important to me now."

He took the newspaper from her hands and stared at the curves of her handwriting. "Thank you for trusting me."

Carly looked into his eyes as if searching for reassurance. "Jex, I'm still afraid."

"Of what?" He pulled her close.

"I've fallen before."

He laced his fingers in her hair. "Then let me be your barrier."

When he touched her lips with his own, her arms encircled him, sending waves of energy through every cell. The newspaper fell to the floor of the Ledge as she returned his kiss, first achingly tender, each touch only a whisper of what he wanted. Then more resolved as if they'd both finally found that something in each other that had been long lost.

As they melted into an embrace at the top of the city, everything below them—the lights . . . the cars . . . the streets . . . all of it—ceased to exist.

Chapter Forty-Six

Carly

By the time they'd reached the Emerald, it was well into the early hours of the morning. They'd left Natalie asleep on the couch, covering her with a blanket, and Carly had wistfully kissed Jex goodnight at the guest room door.

With a few short hours of sleep behind them, she emerged again from the bedroom with her flat-ironed curls now having reclaimed their form around her face.

Jex stepped out of his room moments later, and as Carly pulled a bottle of water from the refrigerator, he slipped his arms around her, drawing her close. His embrace was warm and healing.

When she turned to him, her eyes took in his disheveled hair, and she stood on tiptoes to kiss him, tasting the faint flavor of mint on his lips.

"Good morning, beautiful. How's my honeybee?"

She melted into his arms. "Don't you remember my real name?"

"Um, Gertrude? No, Flora. Maude?"

She playfully shoved him away only for him to return, determined for another kiss. Gladly granting it, she eventually slid back. "Did you sleep?"

"Hardly at all. I had you on my mind the rest of the night."

"Me, either." She nuzzled against his neck.

"Well, that makes three of us, then," Natalie piped up from the couch. "Now don't you two look all cozy." She smirked.

"Yeah, something good came out of last night after all," Jex agreed, never letting Carly go.

Natalie rose from the couch. "I waited for you to come in."

"You were sound asleep when Carly and I got here, so we left you where you were."

"Too bad. I could've shared the good news with you earlier, had you come in at a respectable hour," she teased.

"What good news?" Jex released Carly and pulled another bottle of water from the fridge.

"Well." Natalie propped her elbows on the countertop. "I went back to the Tower to find you two after I finished at the McCormick, but I couldn't get in. And, of course, neither of you must believe in answering your phones."

"What's the news, Nat?" He opened the bottle and took a long drink.

"I wonder how painfully slow I could draw this out?" Natalie tapped her chin.

After draining half the bottle, Jex cut his eyes at her.

"Oh, alright." She blurted out, "When I went back to the venue to get your camera case last night, I ran into Mason Cartwright."

"Who's Mason Cartwright?" Carly asked.

Natalie wagged her eyebrows. "Only one of the top investors in photographic and optical equipment in the country. I found out last night that he's been a big supporter of Hughley Photographics. Turns out, he was hoping to talk with you. He and a few of his colleagues at the ceremony were turned off by Hughley's shenanigans. In fact, they were already prepping to meet Monday morning to pool their investment clout and shoot it toward a company with what he called a 'better consumer message.'" She added air quotes.

Jex stepped closer. "So, what's that got to do with me?"

Natalie grinned. "Have I told you lately what a genius sister you've got?"

"Natalie." Jex tucked his chin and looked at his sister through hooded eyes.

"Okay, okay. So, Cartwright's been eyeing a new company based out of Atlanta, a rather lightweight competitor of Hughley's, at least at the moment. They've had a lot of promise but not enough backing to pull off the same large-scale projects as Hughley. Anyway, Cartwright indicated an interest in your prototype—something to take to the table when he proposes his endorsement terms. I guess he likes to bet on sure things, and he thinks you happen to fit that bill."

Natalie scanned her French-manicured nails. "They said the montage and floor show last night—sans the molestation scene, of course—sold them on your camera." She blew on her nails. "And I just happened to secure an appointment in Atlanta with Cartwright's team next week."

Carly turned to Jex, her excitement already bubbling to the surface. "This is what you've been waiting for."

"Natalie Radcliffe, you *are* a genius." Jex rounded the bar and hip bumped his sister.

"Glad you realize that. And you know, Camden Grove *is* less than two hours from Atlanta." She cocked her head.

Carly's smile broadened. "Maybe you should come to Alabama and see me, then?"

"Maybe I should." He winked.

Epilogue

Carly and Jex

At the airport, Jex wheeled Carly's carry-on to the security checkpoint. When they stopped, he pulled her hands to his lips. "I don't know how ready I am to let you go now that I've found you."

"We'll see each other before long. With this new gig in Atlanta, it's just a hop and a skip to Camden Grove."

"I know, but *before* long is *too* long."

"I'll be waiting." She grinned.

Jex leaned in and kissed her forehead, then nuzzled against her cheek until they found each other's lips. They kissed long and slow, drinking in the comfort of one another.

When they parted for a breath, he traced the curve of her jaw with his thumb. "Tell me two lies and a truth."

His request for a round of the game had, in the last hours, become their new way to discover more about each other.

"Hmm. Let me think," she said. "Okay, one, I love to eat ice cream when it's half melted. Two, I used to take photos of hot, sweaty football players during summer conditioning, and three, I'm a beast at shooting pool."

"Oooh, I say the sweaty football players is true, and the other two are lies."

She laughed. "Maybe I'll make you sit on that and wonder about it for the next week."

He leaned his forehead against hers. "Will the South like a city slicker like me?"

"Of course," she answered.

"Then I can't wait." He gave her another heart-melting kiss, then turned the handle to her carry-on over to her.

On the other side of the ropes, he watched her zigzag through security and blow him a kiss before stepping out of sight toward her gate.

With a half hour left until boarding, Carly entered one of the terminal convenience shops, and thumbed through the book selections, wondering what Mr. Brinkmeyer would have chosen if he were there. She smiled as she settled on a romance and proceeded to the checkout.

With the book and a bottled water in hand, she found her gate and had barely turned a page when her phone rang. She half expected Jex, but instead it teas Ava.

Carly didn't waste time on hellos. "Hey, girl. I can't wait to tell you about my weekend. You won't believe—"

"I want to hear about it," Ava broke in with a sniffle. "But I can't talk for long. I've got to leave Nashville, Carly, and I don't need to wait. How soon can I come take a look at those properties your dad has available?"

"Are you okay?" Carly knew fear, and she could hear it in Ava's voice.

"I'm in trouble, Carly. Real trouble. And I'm scared."

Dear Reader,

Thank you so much for spending time inside the pages of *The Perfect Shot*! If you enjoyed Carly and Jex's story, your review would mean so much and would make all the difference. Also, be sure to turn the page for an excerpt from the next book in the Camden Grove Series, *Picture This,* featuring Ava and Logan's romance. (And you'll see more of Carly and Jex in the future too!) You can PRE-ORDER now at your favorite vendor!

Happy Page-turning!
Tessa

Chapter One

Ava

All Ava Fenn needed was a place to forget and be forgotten. She just wanted to start over. When she pulled into the drive of her newly purchased home, she hoped she'd made the right decision.

Is starting over just my version of running away?

That question had gripped her thoughts every day since before summer.

She put the car in park, rested her hands on the steering wheel, and peered up at the bungalow in front of her. The tapered columns framed a spacious porch, and she decided at a glance that the trellis, layered in a lush tapestry of pink climbing roses, offered just the kind of privacy she'd need when a break from the world while swaying on a porch swing called.

She also scanned the street and could see the knob of the cul-de-sac, where a couple of kids rode bikes in circles at the keyhole. With a deep breath, she stepped out of the car and yanked the SOLD sign from its perch in the front yard.

At least she had one friend here. That would be enough. Carly Kirkpatrick had been the one to convince Ava that Camden Grove would be a safe, quiet place to call home. She'd also been the glue holding Ava together through the whole fiasco that had been her life in the last few months—the disaster she still worried hadn't seen its end.

With key in hand, Ava opened her front door. Boxes stacked in every corner greeted her as she stepped into the entry. While packing back in Nashville, she'd bought color-coded stickers to go on each container and requested that the movers put them in specific rooms according to the color legend she handed them after signing the forms.

Color-blind movers.

After she set her purse on the floor, Ava peeled off her shoes and threw her jacket on top of a covered chair. They had put that in the right room at least.

The four-hour drive to Camden Grove had been tiresome, but she hoped the distance would be enough. When she looked at the boxes, the thought of unpacking exhausted her even more. She grabbed a water bottle from her purse and took a long, slow sip. Her phone jingled with the annoying ringtone she associated with the Nashville office. She made a mental note never to use that ringtone again.

Cradling the phone with her shoulder, she peeled back the tape on a packing box. "Hi, Paige, what's going on?"

"Some mail came for you. Should I forward it to your new address, or will you be back in town?"

"New address is good. I'm hoping I'll have no reason to come back. The sooner I can separate my name and reputation from Corbin Simmons's, the better." Ava paused. "Look, Paige, I didn't have a chance to talk to you before I left. I wanted to tell you how much I appreciated working with you. I just . . . well, this has all been such a mess."

"I'm really sorry," the secretary lowered her voice. "Things shouldn't be this way, Dr. Fenn." Before Ava responded, Paige whispered, "I knew from the beginning you weren't involved with Dr. Simmons. I-I mean with any kind of fraud. Well . . . I should probably go."

Ava straightened her posture and clutched the phone. The muscles in her shoulders tensed with the mention of his name. "Thanks, Paige." She ended the call and set the phone on the coffee table.

Short as it was, the conversation left her head swimming with the need for that porch swing. No doubt, her life in Nashville had taught her two valuable lessons: one, don't place faith in someone just because he shows personal interest; and two, she should steer her own ship if she wanted to stay out of troubled waters. She hoped that Camden Grove would be the best place to dock that ship. Either way, she had no other choice.

As she focused on unpacking, Ava regretted not taking time to cull her old stuff when she'd left Nashville. She'd promised herself that when she got settled, she'd simplify and reduce. Those words had become her mantra.

When the phone rang a second time that evening, the living room had turned into a heap of black lawn bags full of papers, trinkets, and keepsakes no longer worth keeping. Climbing over the mess, Ava located her phone and saw the tawny, attractive image of her wavy-haired best friend smiling back at her.

"Hey." The tension in her voice hadn't dissipated much since the earlier call.

"Why, hello, Dr. Fenn," Carly said, her tone a cross between bubbly and badgering. "Did you not see it was me calling? You sound so serious."

"Sorry. Guess I'm a little touchy." Ava could tell Carly was on the move. "Where you headed? I can hear you in the car."

"Just pulling onto your street. Put on some shoes. We're going out for ice cream."

Ava pushed a box out of her way and looked out the window. "How'd you know I needed some Rocky Road?"

"You're not only serious, but you're also predictable. I'm guessing you're unpacking, dredging up all the old stuff your psyche needs to purge. That's what my therapist says old stuff does to you."

"You don't have a therapist."

"I know, but it's fashionable to say such things nowadays. Open your door for me. I'm almost there."

Ava had been friends with Carly since college when the housing office assigned them as roommates. They'd come from similar working-class backgrounds but with different ambitions and vastly contrasting ideas about how to manage campus life.

Carly spent most of her academic time in the photojournalism department and the rest trying to find the perfect specimens to photograph. That often found her on the practice fields at the University of Tennessee, which later landed her the top spot for the school newspaper's sports department.

For Ava, undergrad was her first plunge into workaholism. After a car accident claimed her parents, she allowed her class load to consume her—a combination of morning labs, afternoon tutoring, and evening study groups all providing the escape she needed.

Carly wouldn't allow her to fall into the well of self-pity and overwork, though. They complemented each other well and became even closer friends.

Staying in touch through med school hadn't been as easy, but they always connected during downtime, catching up on Carly's latest news assignment or the grossest of Ava's current medical studies. Residency had been much the same. But after Ava started practicing with Corbin Simmons, Carly made no secret she didn't like her friend's new gig or love interest. Her goal had always been to get Ava to move to Alabama, and she insisted that something was off-center about Corbin.

When Ava called her last month at the point of a nervous breakdown in the middle of the scandal, Carly took charge and helped her focus on starting over. In the end, she kept her emotionally afloat.

From the living room window, Ava watched an SUV pull into the drive. The magnetic sign on the driver's side door read Then Comes Marriage Photography in a flowery script—Carly's new passion since her own personal life had tanked a year ago, and her photojournalism dreams hadn't panned out. The local newspaper she worked at and planned to purchase had gone belly-up before she could afford a takeover, and as relationships went, Carly wasn't without her own battle scars.

As her friend approached the front door, Ava could see her auburn waves bouncing in rhythm with her step. Something about having an ally to take you for ice cream at dinner time made life seem a little more tolerable.

Dawson's Creamery stood, a quaint staple along the more modern side of Camden Grove's colonial-style courthouse. It sat between a family-operated drug store and a chic Southern boutique, the windows of which were bursting with the newest styles in linen.

Carly ordered a confetti scoop in a cup and parked herself in a corner booth. When Ava scooted into the bench across from her, holding a generous serving of Mint Chocolate Chip in a waffle cone, Carly's eyes came alive. "What's with you and the minty-ness, and where's my best friend? I thought Rocky Road was your flavor for life."

Ava took a defiant round-the-cone lick of her ice cream. "You're looking at someone who's ready for change. My life's been a rocky road for a long time now. I need a new flavor. Did I tell you I'm scrapping a lot of my old stuff? Simplifying and reducing. My new buzz words. And besides, the Mint Chocolate Chip just sounded good."

"How existential of you. Here I got you a new place, you're setting up a new office, becoming one of those zealots who have an empty house with two shirts in the closet, and you're rockin' a new ice cream flavor? This, my friend, is a bit much, don't you think?"

"What? Are you paying for my house now?"

"Hardly." Carly sucked on her loaded spoon. "But I do claim a reasonable percentage of responsibility for getting you in that little beauty and at a steal." A smug grin appeared over the top of her ice cream cup. "It pays to have a friend whose dad is in foreclosure banking. Wouldn't you agree?"

"Mmm." Ava ignored her friend and stared at the cone. "This is delicious. Don't think I've ever tried mint before."

"Since you're all about the new, I have an idea. How about you help me with a little project to throw some business my way."

"Does this have anything to do with that Chicago trip last month and the guy you met with all the photography ideas? By the way, you've been a totally different person since you got back. I'm half afraid to ask what's up your sleeve."

"Different person, huh?"

"Yeah, it's like you got your old college-days sass back, times ten."

In the last month, Carly had hinted at some new developments in her personal life, but with all the chaos of her own, Ava hadn't taken much time to get the details. It was good to see her friend perked up.

"Hm." Carly shrugged. "Imagine that."

"So? Does it have something to do with Chicago and the new guy? You've still got to fill me in on him, you know. Jex was his name, right?" Ava prodded.

"I'll tell you more about him later. Right now, I need your help."

"Sorry, I'm far from hunting for a wedding photographer."

Carly waved her off. "That'll come eventually. But it's not a wedding shoot I want."

Ava continued to work on her cone.

"You remember Jessie, right?" Carly had partnered with Jessie Galloway to take on the role as an engagement photographer while Carly's specialty was capturing the big day.

"We met once."

"Yeah, well, she's just getting back on her feet from ACL surgery[CM1] . And, among other things, because the First Comes Love photographer has been out of commission, our Then Comes Marriage photoshoots are taking a loss." She waved her spoon in circles between them. "You know, people like to line up our services together. Anyway, to drum up business, I need to feed the engagement schedule, and to feed the engagement schedule, I learned in Chicago that I need to think outside the box. Knock a few fresh ideas around. Basically, I want to try a little experiment to see if a new concept I've been working on would be feasible to generate some ads. Carly cocked her head. "Make sense?"

"Sorry, no engagement on the horizon for me, either, but if I hear of anybody—"

"No, that's just it. Let me explain."

"Before you get started, I've never been a good godmother to your brainchildren, and honestly, despite the fact that I've been completely negligent of our friendship, I've got a lot on my hands right now getting back on my own feet."

"That's why this is perfect! It would only be for a day. A Saturday, maybe. We just want to do this test run and I think we can get some great results. You know how I like to have all my ducks in a row before I go full-scale with anything."

Ava cut her eyes at Carly.

"At least let me tell you about it."

"I'm sure you're going to anyway."

"Exactly!" Carly settled into her seat. "Okay, so I just need you for a couple of hours at most. You'd get rid of your lab coat and come dressed in some cute little jeans and maybe a camp shirt or one of those nice little peasant tops—those are adorable on you. Oh, and you could bring a dress. Something summery and feminine."

Ava swallowed a cold bite. "Now that we've got my wardrobe picked out. What am I supposed to be posing for?"

"Ready for this? You are going to be doing a 'Stranger Thing.'" Carly's eyes widened in anticipation.

"When it comes to hanging out with you, I've already done stranger things than most, but I'm not sure I catch your drift."

"No, it's not you doing something strange. You kind of go on a . . . blind-date photoshoot. You know, with a stranger." She took the last bite of ice cream and licked the edge of the cup.

"Wait, are you saying I get all dressed up to take photos with a blind date?" Ava dropped her hand. The bottom of the waffle cone crunched against the table. "That's beyond strange, Carly. That's dumb." Her forehead wrinkled in confusion. "And what do we do? Just stand there and look awkward while somebody snaps a picture? That's the most ridiculous thing I've ever heard. I think your brainchild just suffered an aneurysm."

"Come on, give me a minute. I think it could be fun. We'd vet potential partners, and . . . think of it, a spontaneous afternoon, then it's no strings attached. It's even better than a blind date because you have an excuse to bow out. You know, you were just helping out a friend, everybody has a fun afternoon, and then, you get to leave."

"No, you're really just trying to get me to go on a date. This isn't me helping you with your business. It's you trying to fix me up and calling it a favor."

"Seriously, you would be helping me with my business . . . aside from any other possibilities, and take it from me, potential exists." Before Ava could respond, Carly continued, "Don't shut me off yet. Just think about it. We would set up boundaries, but you'd be posed in different settings, holding hands, hugging, looking into each other's eyes. Just think of it as your being a model for an engagement shoot."

"But I'm not engaged. I'm not a model. And I'm not interested."

Carly sighed, her words dragging through a vocal sludge. "Honestly, Ava. Go with me on this."

"For what purpose?"

"To help a friend in need . . . and maybe to see if any sparks fly," she quickly added.

"I once thought there was such a thing, but the only honest, elemental sparks I've had in the last ten years have been trying to get through chem classes in med school. I'm sure you can find somebody else with a taste for the kind of chemistry you're talking about."

"That's exactly why you'd be perfect. No expectations. No practice. Total spontaneity. It makes for fantastic candids."

Exasperation set in. "I don't think so. I don't need this in my life right now, Carly. You should find another friend."

"Everybody else is married. Besides, that's not the draw for a shoot like this. It's to see if, when you're put in an intimate situation with somebody you don't know, you find the fireworks. And if those fireworks are caught on camera, then that's the bonus for me."

Ava finished her waffle cone. "The answer"—she crumpled a napkin into a tight ball— "is no."

Carly's tone became pointed. "You owe me, Ava. I got you a house for a fraction of what it's worth. If it hadn't been for that, you wouldn't have had the money to put toward the old newspaper office. I had to pull some strings to make all that happen. And need I remind you that I've been a faithful friend? You couldn't live without me." Carly scooted up on the bench. "The least you can do is come to a shoot. We can scrap it all if it doesn't turn out."

"And what will you do if it does turn out?"

"I'll get you on my calendar for some wedding shots in the near future?"

Ava's eyes widened. "That's not what I mean. If the photos were to look decent, I wouldn't be comfortable with your using them in ads. I came here to establish a reputable practice in Camden Grove. How would my patients respond if they've seen me in some cozy little picture with a guy I don't even know? That doesn't exactly scream professionalism."

"Already thought about that. We could shoot in the next town over—Hartley's booming with possibilities. In fact, I'm vying to get in the door with the Generations Bridal Boutique there. They have a sought-after wedding planner on staff, and she's in my sights. The only thing I'd possibly use your shoot for is to network with them at the next regional bridal fair. Show them some samples. This could be a big break for our business." Carly put on a droopy face. "I need this, Ava. Come on. Help your best friend."

Ava sat brooding in silence.

"Please?" Carly's voice rose an octave.

"I get all the veto power if this is a wash."

"All the power."

"And you can't pin me in a corner anymore about your helping me get the house or office."

"Never again."

"And my second scoop of ice cream is on you."

"Mint Chocolate Chip?"

"Blue Cotton Candy." Ava threw the wadded napkin on the table.

Carly rose from the bench. "You're getting more exotic every second."

Ava rolled her eyes. "Looks like."

Chapter Two

Logan

The construction office for Modern Design and Building sat on the dusty side of town along the last row of structures deemed the Industrial Park. Logan Carter had built his business, like most of the projects he'd completed, from the ground up. Holding his own in the ranks of builders for the Camden Grove and Hartley areas, he managed the workload much the way he handled life in general, from under the hard hat.

His workhorse approach served as the best replacement he could find for forging more personal things, like relationships. He'd wasted way too much time in that arena the second Eliza Montgomery stepped into his life eight years ago. But at least he had Toby. A six-year-old ray of sunshine was the only good thing that had come out of his train wreck of a marriage.

When the office door sprang open, he barely looked up. Pouring over the plans for a contract he'd been trying to win took priority over the visit from his twin brother.

"Hey man, you get much closer to those prints, and your nose'll be blue."

Logan eased back in his chair to face his mirror image, only in a suit and tie. "On lunch break?"

"Nope. Taking the afternoon off." Wyatt Carter plopped down in the chair across the desk from Logan, his jacket now unbuttoned and tie loosened.

"What brings you to the Grove? You land an account or something? Off early to celebrate?"

"Just wanted to come see my brother."

"You can look in the mirror and call me next time. Save you the drive."

"Nope. You seen yourself lately? I'm more handsome, so it wouldn't be the same."

Logan had long ago stopped rolling his eyes at the stupid things his brother said. Instead, he turned his attention back to his work. "Lydia okay?"

"Yeah, she's great. We've got a trip planned next week. Going to the mountains for a few days. I was wondering if you and Toby could come stay at the house and take care of Milo for me." Logan and Toby were the go-to sitters for their golden retriever with hypothyroid issues and a propensity for chewing socks.

"Guess we could do that. Just clear off a spot for me in your office. I've got a ton of work to do to get these plans ready. And you could also stock the fridge."

Wyatt nodded and pulled at his ear.

"So, what else are you doing here besides asking me to keep your chunky mutt alive?"

"He's sensitive about that, so don't go making fun of him." He cocked his head. "And what makes you think I want something else?"

"You just pulled at your ear. Mom always knew you were lying or stalling if you pulled at your ear."

Wyatt ignored Logan's question and ran a hand through his hair instead. "It'll do you some good to come to Hartley, watch Milo, and get out of Camden Grove for a while. Maybe get a breath of fresh air."

"Don't start in."

"On what?" Wyatt shrugged.

"On why I should be dating and getting my life back together. Who put you up to it? Lydia?"

"She's worried about you too. You're sitting in this office all hours. Toby always has a great time through the summer with Mom and Dad, but you need to take a break, man, have some fun with him. The work'll be here when you get back."

"Now you're trying to tell me how to raise my boy?"

"You know better, and don't get all uptight. You've got the best kid around, but I think he's been missing you lately."

"Because you're suddenly the authority on six-year-olds."

"Because that's what he told Lydia when Mom and Dad brought him over last weekend."

Logan bowed his head and pinched the bridge of his nose. "That's what he said?"

Wyatt nodded. "Yep."

"I've been working late hours this last week, trying to keep a business afloat so he can have a good future."

"And that's a great thing. Just don't forget that he needs a good present, too, and that happens to involve you."

The silence lasted until Wyatt stood and crossed to the coffee pot on a corner table. "You thought about going out lately?"

"You mean on a date? First, you tell me I'm not spending enough time with my son. Then, you tell me I should take time away from him to go on a date. Make up your mind, brother. It can't be both ways."

"That could be good for you and Toby if you had some fun with another adult." Wyatt poured a cup. "Just throwing out some thoughts. Your frame of mind is beginning to show."

Logan crossed his arms and frowned. "What's that supposed to mean?"

"Just saying"—Wyatt took a long sip— "you look like a lumberjack with that beard. And how long has it been since you bought a new pair of jeans?"

"Look, I've got work." Logan nodded toward the blueprints. "You can leave me your house key. We'll take care of Milo while you're gone. Let me know when you want us to be there."

"Are you trying to hustle me out of here?"

"I'm trying to get some work done so I'll have time to spend with Toby."

Wyatt scanned the spread of sheets on Logan's desk. "Is that the Brashear building you're working on?"

"For weeks now."

"I know. Big scale changes for them. Our office was hired to beef up their ad campaigns and social media presence. You know, I could probably get you the in with Mr. Brashear."

"Nope. Don't need your help."

"Of course, you do. All this business needs is one huge project, and you'd have more contracts than you can handle."

"I've got more contracts than I can handle right now. Most of them are just not paying." Logan rubbed his stubbled jaw.

"You've wanted to add employees, but it takes revenue. And revenue comes from people who have the money waiting. Like Brashear. More money would give you more time with Toby." Wyatt pulled out his phone. "Here, listen to this."

He dialed and put it on speaker.

"Brashear Technologies, Sandra speaking."

"Sandra. Wyatt Carter here. How ya doing?"

"I'm well, thanks." A voice with a deep Southern drawl replied.

"Say, Sandra. I had a meeting scheduled with Mr. Brashear for next Friday at 3 p.m. We were finishing up a few of the layouts for the new campaign. But I'm having to go out of town next week and was wondering if I could push that meeting up to Tuesday?"

"Let me see." She paused. "Yes, it looks like he has a brief opening Tuesday at 10 a.m."

"Perfect. Oh, and Sandra, could we keep the Friday appointment open for Logan Carter? He's developing some blueprints for Mr. Brashear's new facility. I happen to be here with him now and was hoping to lock in that appointment for him."

"Brothers watching out for each other, I see," Sandra's saccharin voice purred. "Why, yes. I think I could do that."

"You're an angel." Wyatt winked at Logan. "Tell that good husband of yours I'm jealous."

The phone call ended, and Logan sat shaking his head. "How do you pull off such things?"

"I know her birthday. I know her favorite chocolates. And I send her flowers every time we score a campaign. Charisma goes a long way, brother. You should try it sometime."

"I guess you're waiting for me to say thanks, then."

Wyatt began to pick at a fingernail. "You should."

"So, you show up and ask me to take care of the dog, schedule an appointment to share blueprints with this man I've been trying to meet with for a month, and make me feel like I owe you something else. What is it? What else do you want?"

"We may have too much of the twin vibe going. I can't have you in my head."

"I've been in your head for years. It's a scary place."

"Well, since you asked. You remember Lydia's sister, Jessie?"

"Stop while you're ahead."

"Just shut up. You don't have to comply with what I'm asking. Just listen." He started again. "Lydia wanted me to talk to you about Jessie."

"I'm not going on a date with Jessie."

Wyatt sighed. "That's not it. She's trying to fill up her photography calendar and needs some help. She and her business partner are searching for a couple of people to do a photoshoot for some advertising. She wants a rugged type." He eyed his brother up and down. "And you, man, fit the bill if I've ever seen a bill fitter."

"Rough around the edges, maybe. But photogenic? I don't think so."

"You look like me. You're definitely photogenic." Wyatt smiled a dimpled grin. "You just need to spiff up a little."

"I don't do suits, and I don't do shoots."

"No, a suit's not what she wants. All you've got to do is trim the beard and buy a good pair of jeans. Maybe throw on a button-up shirt that doesn't look like it's been dipped in concrete."

Logan sat still for a moment. "Why don't you find somebody else? I'm apparently on a tighter deadline now that you've got this appointment for me."

"Lydia asked if I could get you to do it for Jessie. She thinks you'd be perfect."

"Ah, the truth comes out. You're under pressure from home and hearth."

"Happy wife, happy life. And besides, now you owe me. Tell you what, I'll make you a deal. You get this contract? Then you do the shoot for Jessie. You're happy because you got the contract, and my wife's happy because Jessie's happy. We're all just one big ol' happy family. Right?"

"And if I don't get the contract?"

"I'm on the couch for a week because I didn't come through."

Logan smirked. "That's almost worth it."

"Just shake on it, man." Wyatt flashed another carbon copy of Logan's perfect smile and grabbed his brother's hand. "We'll be leaving for the mountains Tuesday evening. Milo'll be glad to see you and Toby."

"Yeah. Get outta here. I've got work to do."

"I'm going. I'm going." He opened the door to leave. "Oh hey, you might want to get those new jeans soon." Then, he ducked out in a hurry just before a paper wad bounced off the closing door.

Chapter Three

Ava

The small office building Ava purchased in the town's business district had been sitting empty for a while. Though Carly liked to remind her she'd gotten it at a good price, the cost of the renovations required to convert it to a doctor's office was racking up.

After her first walk-through in late spring, she'd discovered why the sale price had been within her spartan budget. The previous owners of the old newspaper office must have liked brown carpet, walls with smoke stains, and dingy windows. No wonder the bank jumped at the chance of letting it go, and Ava didn't have much choice except to buy something cheap. Once she closed on the property, she began making calls to contractors to arrange the needed updates.

Now, a week after arriving in Camden Grove, Ava entered the front door of the building, hoping for a near-magical transformation. Instead, she found two dust-covered contractors huddled against the floor installing tile in the far half of the small waiting room. They looked up as she came inside.

"G'morning, Miss. Something we can help you with?" The oldest of the two men stood.

Ava scanned the room. "I'm, uh, Dr. Fenn. I was just coming to see the progress." Her hopes that she could open within a month settled in a heap right along with all the old grout dust. She needed a solid grand opening before school started, with parents lining up vaccinations and sports physicals. It was the best time besides flu season she could put out a shingle. But, looking around, she didn't know how it could all come together. Making eye contact with the contractor, she asked, "Do you think this can be ready by my contract deadline?"

"There's a lot of work to do, yet. If you walk through, you'll see that may be a lofty goal. A lot more than floor work has to be done in the back."

Ava stepped past the reception area. From room to room, panic began to bubble up in her throat. They were nowhere near ready for an opening. The drywall wasn't even up in two of the rooms, and electrical wires hung out of the studs like drooping bouquets. Not to mention the flooring, cabinets, and exam tables needed installing. The office would never be ready in time.

When she came back to the entry, the men were back at work, stooped again in the far corner of the room.

"Excuse me. Are you supposed to be working on the drywall and electrical too?"

The older man on the floor pulled up the back of his pants as he stood again. "No, ma'am. That's not our crew."

"What do you mean?"

"We're the tile subcontractors. You'll need to contact the main man to find out when he's getting all that done."

She sighed. "When will you be finished with this room?"

The man shrugged his shoulders. "Probably in the next week or two. We've got another job to finish on the south side of town. We were just waiting on some materials, so we came here to work a few hours."

Ava put her hand to her head. "But I need this job done. I can't have the office half-finished on opening day."

"We'll do what we can. Shouldn't be a problem for us." He nodded toward the back rooms. "But past the lobby, you're looking at a lot of work in a little time. Don't know about that getting done by your deadline."

Ava stormed into the office space. That was the trouble with hiring people over the phone. Getting any kind of commitment was a rarity if you weren't face-to-face—sometimes even if you were—and chasing down contractors to finish their work was the last thing she needed.

As she scrolled through her phone to find the number of the man she'd hired, the screen lit up with Carly's face.

Ava huffed into the phone as she answered it.

"Hey, Doc, you sound mad."

"I've got a grand opening in a within month, and nothing is ready."

"Relax, it'll come together. In the meantime, let me brighten your day." Carly's voice rose to singsong. "I've got a surprise."

Ava manifested the enthusiasm of a slug. "What?"

"That photoshoot. I've got it all set up. Jessie's doing the pictures, and she's picked out a great match for you."

"Carly, I—"

"Don't you dare try to back out now. I've been counting on this, and so has Jessie. Besides, it'll be fun. Spontaneity, remember? Have you gotten your clothes yet?"

"When have I had the time? I'm playing construction manager these days."

"Go shopping. You have until Saturday. I'm sending you an address. It's at the Old Mill at Fordham Creek on the other side of Hartley. You should be there by four. Show up in the jeans outfit and take the summer dress with you. There's an old barn there you can change in."

"Seriously?"

Carly sounded offended. "Yes, I'm serious. Now, plan for some fun. I can't wait to see the pictures."

"Wait, you said something about a match."

"Yeah, Jessie picked him out. Sounds like you two are totally compatible. He's a workaholic—you're a workaholic. He's not interested in relationships—you're not interested in relationships."

Ava breathed a little easier. "Perfect. Just so he and you and everybody knows this is a favor and not a real date."

"Definitely. But I'll tell you this: Jessie says he's pretty hot."

"Don't. Just don't, Carly." She could almost hear her friend smiling on the other end.

"Okay. Okay. Just be there Saturday."

"And where will you be?"

"Doing some venue planning with a couple I've got on the calendar, so I can't be on-site with you. It's probably for the best, though. You might hold back if I'm there to witness."

"Lucky for me."

"I'll call you Saturday night, see what kind of fire I've set." The phone clicked as Ava stood looking at the drooping electrical wires.

After shoving Carly's photoshoot to the back burner, Ava scrolled through her phone again and called the contractor she'd hired weeks back. On the fifth ring, his voice mail picked up. When the tone sounded, Ava's words spewed like steam from a pressure cooker. "This is Dr. Fenn. I called you a few weeks back and hired you to do a remodel job at the old newspaper office, and I'm standing here right now in a heap of rubble. I'm supposed to open my door for business in less than a month. I have two men here putting down tile only because they're waiting on another job. Wires are springing out of the walls like fountains in a fishpond. I have no furniture or cabinets installed. And, I have naked studs everywhere. Are you planning to do something about it? Please call me as soon as possible."

When Ava ended the call, she rubbed the back of her neck and then realized the regrettable part of what she'd just spouted into some man's voice mail. "Naked studs?" she whispered as she covered her mouth.

*****Hope you enjoyed this sneak peek!*****
Go now to tessakinkade.com or your favorite vendor to
PRE-ORDER PICTURE THIS: Book Two of the Camden
Grove Series
Also, sign up for my newsletter and for a free Camden Grove short story while you're there.

Acknowledgments

Acknowledging all those who have in any way contributed to the words in this book seems insurmountable. As with most writers, the list would trail back to a time when my mother read to me nightly chapters of The Wizard of Oz and my dad taught me ways to push back fear. In a modest gesture by comparison, I simply put a few of your names here at the end. You truly have been a fundamental part of the journey.

Thank you to my parents—that reading mom and encouraging dad—whose belief in me continues to motivate me every day; to my sister, who still doesn't know how much she influences me by her example of quiet generosity and service; to my extended family, both by blood and adoption, who asked for progress reports even when the needle wouldn't seem to move; to KJ (Oh my goodness, what have we NOT been through to get our books into the world? You rock purple turtles, girl!); to my critique gals, Megan and Amanda, who helped me brainstorm, fine-tune, and revamp to the Nth degree; to my editor Jennia, for whom there are no adequate words to describe her wordsmithing talents; to my cover artist Aisling, who took on my project and produced a gorgeous cover down to the smallest detail; and to all my cheerleaders—Cass, you're at the top of that list, and others, you know who you are.

My most heartfelt thanks goes to my extraordinary kids, who have an uncanny ability to hug me at exactly the right moment. You've had patience beyond your years and are my reason to breathe. To my husband, who'd fly to Jupiter to see me happy, I love you sounds way too small when I'm with you, baby. And to my God, who put all these people in my life and who provided me with the will to put words on a page and to dream. For all my blessings, I am eternally grateful.

One last thought—the joy I get from writing is intrinsic, but when someone picks up something I've written and finds value in it, I'm motivated to do and to be better. So to you, my reader, thank you for your investment in me. The ripple effect of that gesture alone goes far beyond encouraging me to put a few written words in the pages of a few books.

About Author

As a child, Tessa Kinkade composed her first stories in chalk on her bedroom door. Editing was much more fun that way. Her workspace nowadays is still her bedroom, and she can often be found propped among favorite bed pillows, tapping away on a laptop with a water bottle by her side (though she continues to look for easy ways to edit). Tessa has spent much of her career in education, and in her spare time—when her children were old enough to get their own cereal bowls from the cabinet—she began writing her first novel, 15 minutes at a time.

In the past, she's worked in a rape crisis center, kept bees, organized large events, run half marathons, and traveled most of the contiguous United States, drawing upon all her career experiences and hobbies to enrich her writing. She loves to create characters who face life-altering challenges yet find a happily-ever-after through the struggle.

When she's not bingeing on research, outlining, or drafting her next novel, you'll find her dreaming about a beach vacation where she might also find a lighthouse to explore.

Connect with Tessa for information on new releases, exclusive extras, newsletter sign-up, and more at http://tessakinkade.com

Also, catch her on her on social media!

instagram.com/tessakinkade

facebook.com/tessakinkade